The Mastermind

Also From Dylan Allen

RIVERS WILDE SERIES OF STAND ALONE STORIES

Listed in suggested reading order

The Legacy
Book one of the Rivers Wilde Series. An opposites attract, enemies to lovers standalone that kicks off this brand new series.

The Legend
This is a second chance at love story. Remington Wilde has loved one woman in his life and even though timing and family manipulations keep pulling them apart, it's a love worth fighting for.

The Jezebel
Regan Wilde and Stone Rivers were born enemies. But love has other ideas. This sweeping, second chance romance spans nearly twenty years and will make you believe in soul mates.

The Daredevil: A Rivers Wilde/ 1001 Nights Novella
This story has all the hallmarks of Rivers Wilde—drama, sex, humor, heartwarming family interactions, and two amazingly driven, brilliant, bold characters who are also PERFECT for each other. A fake relationship, a weekend in Paris and all the feels.

SYMBOLS OF LOVE SERIES

Rise
Remember
Release

STANDALONE NOVELS

The Sun and Her Star
Thicker Than Water
The Sound of Temptation

The Mastermind

A Rivers Wilde Novella

By Dylan Allen

1001 DARK NIGHTS

PRESS

The Mastermind
A Rivers Wilde Novella
By Dylan Allen

1001 Dark Nights

Sign up for the 1001 Dark Nights Newsletter
and be entered to win a Tiffany Key necklace.

There's a contest every month!

Go to www.1001DarkNights.com to subscribe.

**As a bonus, all subscribers can download
FIVE FREE exclusive books!**

Dedication

To everyone who has danced in rain that should have washed you away.

Acknowledgments from the Author

It is humbling to have such a loving and constant village made up of people.

I wouldn't be writing and publishing this story without the dream weavers at 1001 Dark Nights/Blue Box Press—Liz Berry, Jillian Greenfield-Stein, and M.J. Rose. Being a part of the 1001 Dark Nights family is a dream come true, and I hope to always be worthy of the faith they showed when they took a chance on me and this series.

As with every story I write, *The Mastermind* was a collaborative effort. I'd like to thank the following people for their help brainstorming, alpha and beta reading—and putting up with the chaotic workings of my creative mind. Annette King, Kweku Aggrey Orleans, Kennedy Ryan, Astrid Abassith, Chelé Walker, Tijuana Turner, Christy Baldwin, Stacy Travis, and Susannah Nix—I couldn't have gotten the story to where it is without you.

A huge thank you to the general in my first line of defense—developmental edits—Lauren McKellar. You help everything make sense, help me find the heart of my stories. Your encouragement means more to me than I can properly express. Thank you so much.

Thank you to Kasi Alexander, whose copyedits made this book shine. It's a pleasure to work with you.

This writing job can feel like a lonely, hard slog, but it's made so much easier by my author colleagues who are the constant gardeners of my inspiration and motivation. You are all so dear to me. Thank you for making the journey so much fun.

To Melissa Panio-Petersen, who is the other half of Team Dylan, thank you for holding everything together and making my life so much easier. I am so grateful for all your hard work.

To my Dreamers all over the world who read my books, write me emails, hang out in my reader group—I write for you. And I always will.

To my amazing family—from whom all my blessings flow—I couldn't be without you. Thank you for loving me without restraint or condition.

Dream Big, Dreamers!
Love,
Dx.

One Thousand and One Dark Nights

Once upon a time, in the future…

*I was a student fascinated with stories and learning.
I studied philosophy, poetry, history, the occult, and
the art and science of love and magic. I had a vast
library at my father's home and collected thousands
of volumes of fantastic tales.*

*I learned all about ancient races and bygone
times. About myths and legends and dreams of all
people through the millennium. And the more I read
the stronger my imagination grew until I discovered
that I was able to travel into the stories… to actually
become part of them.*

*I wish I could say that I listened to my teacher
and respected my gift, as I ought to have. If I had, I
would not be telling you this tale now.
But I was foolhardy and confused, showing off
with bravery.*

*One afternoon, curious about the myth of the
Arabian Nights, I traveled back to ancient Persia to
see for myself if it was true that every day Shahryar
(Persian: شهریار, "king") married a new virgin, and then
sent yesterday's wife to be beheaded. It was written
and I had read that by the time he met Scheherazade,
the vizier's daughter, he'd killed one thousand
women.*

*Something went wrong with my efforts. I arrived
in the midst of the story and somehow exchanged
places with Scheherazade – a phenomena that had
never occurred before and that still to this day, I
cannot explain.*

*Now I am trapped in that ancient past. I have
taken on Scheherazade's life and the only way I can
protect myself and stay alive is to do what she did to
protect herself and stay alive.*

*Every night the King calls for me and listens as I spin tales.
And when the evening ends and dawn breaks, I stop at a
point that leaves him breathless and yearning for more.
And so the King spares my life for one more day, so that
he might hear the rest of my dark tale.*

*As soon as I finish a story... I begin a new
one... like the one that you, dear reader, have before
you now.*

Introduction

Dear Reader,

Welcome to Rivers Wilde! The master planned enclave's popularity has never been higher. The old guard still have the run of the place. But there are plenty of new arrivals—few as notorious as the Royales.

Led by their wayward but well-meaning matriarch, the Royale Family has come to Rivers Wilde for a new beginning.

The previous year saw their family go through a turbulent upheaval where impossible choices had to be made, fortunes were lost and won, and fates were sealed forever.

This book, *The Mastermind*, predates their arrival. Our heroine, known to the world as Juliana Quist, is a stranger to the Royales when the story starts. By the end of it, she'll be at the very center of the hurricane that rips this family apart.

If anything can heal them, it's a second chance in a place that gives you more than just a home—the heartbeat of Rivers Wilde is its inclusivity and warmth.

With the help of their new neighbors and friends, they might just find the happy ending they are looking for.

It won't be easy. They've got debts to pay…and collect. And more enemies than they know. Their unpredictable path toward happily-ever-afters will come with moments of doubt and plenty of drama.

But have heart, dear reader!

Because *this* is Rivers Wilde—and drama may rule, but love *always* wins.

November 2021
Rivers Wilde,
Houston, Texas

1

THE MASTERMIND
Omar

"Today we are toasting to the end of an era." My father lifts a sleek stemless champagne glass in a silent command to the two hundred and fifty people gathered in the large, chandelier lit ballroom. Like they're obeying a maestro, everyone lifts their flutes in near perfect unison.

Everyone except for me. After a lifetime of bending to his will, the final straw has landed, and I'm done.

"But we're also toasting the start of a new age—that The Balanced Scale Fund is proud to be the driving engine of. This Community Co-op is the country club reimagined as a space where *all* residents are welcome. The fees are minimal and on a sliding scale. And the amenities are state of the art and groundbreaking. This isn't a dressed-up YMCA." He gives a pointed look at the journalist who coined that phrase in an article he wrote right after we announced the project. The journalist, who is sitting at the front VIP table, has since changed his tune. Laughter ripples across the room at the roasting, and I begrudgingly acknowledge that my father is good at this.

"This is a place where you can play golf while your kids have soccer practice. Or take a class on coding or teach a class on budgeting. You can celebrate milestones here. Or just drop in for dinner when you don't feel like cooking but want a meal in a space that feels like home.

"The vision to build a space that fosters leisure *and* productivity is the result of our collaboration with Wilde World and The Rivers Family Foundation." He turns to face my table and smiles magnanimously at me. "But it is the brainchild of our board chairman and founder and my son, Omar. And today, he's given us two reasons to celebrate. Just this morning he was conferred his Bachelor of Arts with Honors. Very proud of you, son." He hoists his glass up, and the rest of the room joins him.

I accept the cheers, sip my drink, and smile despite the bitterness it leaves on my tongue.

When the cries of "speech, speech, speech," ring out, I acquiesce and stand to meet my father's eyes for the first time all afternoon. He's smiling for the benefit of the onlookers, but his eyes tell a different story. And the anger in them is a mirror image of what I've been feeling.

He's been my manager since I was scouted and has overseen every investment I've made over the years. In life and work, we've been perfectly in sync. Or so he thought, until this morning when he realized I'd broken his most sacred rule. And had been for years.

But it was my refusal to apologize when he commanded me to after our raging war of words that *really* got under his skin. The furrows of anger in his forehead are joined by grooves of worry on the side of his frowning mouth. The last thing he said to me before we walked into the room together in a false united front was, "Don't even think about going off script today."

His worry that I'm going to let our private argument spill into the public is in vain and insulting. My father, with his background in business operations, was instrumental in getting The Fund off the ground ten years ago. He runs the Fund with a mastery that's earned us both a lot of money and clout. But it was my vision that launched The Balanced Scales Fund. After a decade of investing in brands built on image, I wanted to invest in ideas. This isn't just a business to me, it's a passion.

Which is why, at the age of 32, I put my old ass through three and a half years of college while working by day as the chairman of our board and the unofficial director of joint ventures.

I break our silent war of wills and reach into the inside pocket of my suit for the piece of paper containing the short statement my publicist drafted for tonight. I hate public speaking with every fiber of my being, and nerves make my stomach tight.

I scan the room and find the table where my three best friends— Graham, David, and Reece—are sitting with their partners. They're my touchstones, and I'm so glad they're here. Also at their table is my one-night stand turned good friend, Reena. My eyes linger on the empty seat next to her where my mother was supposed to be sitting, and my ire returns anew.

While I read the meaningful but somewhat shallow platitudes of hope and gratitude, I'm careful not to look in my father's direction for fear that my anger will overpower my good sense.

I stand smiling until the polite applause dies down. When it's over, the attendees move en masse to the room where dinner will be served. After a round of congratulations and a group selfie with my friends, I excuse myself to use the bathroom.

I catch a glimpse of my father and my agent, Dean, with their heads pressed together in deep conversation. He laughs, and I'm angry that he can manage to when I'm still seething.

Everyone else is too busy posting their videos and pictures on Instagram or TikTok to notice me walking away from the restrooms and toward the balcony that runs along the back of the ballroom. I loosen my tie the second I step outside and expel the resentment-tinged breath I've been holding all night into the cool night air.

I pull my phone out of my pocket, and my stomach clenches painfully at the number of missed calls from my mother.

I have her saved in my phone as "Marley" because Bob Marley is her favorite musician and because I knew my father would *never* get the reference.

I open my texts to write to her and see the message she sent this morning. It's a picture of her dressed in a blue Chanel suit she bought specially for the day. The text reads "**Dressed to kill because I am so proud of my baby.**"

I write back. "**I'm sorry.**" Because that's all I feel besides guilt.

They call me the mastermind out on the pitch—I'm a strategic and nimble midfielder who can think three steps ahead in the middle of a match. But when it comes to just about everything else, including saying aloud what I'm feeling, I'm as agile and precise as a tractor.

I'm glad I didn't witness the confrontation when she arrived at the graduation ceremony this morning and took her seat in the same row as the rest of my family. I can imagine it, though. Their fights when they were married were epic.

But they happened privately. Today must have been humiliating for her.

My stomach tries to push its way into my intestines, or at least that's what it feels like. Anxiety is no joke. The physical ache that always accompanies mine is nothing new, but it's been a long time since I've felt it.

"Fuck me." I self soothe with a hand flat on my belly and close my eyes, this time focusing on the tickle of air on the edge of my nostril when I draw in a deep breath and exhale it out.

Houston's taken some getting used to—the summers are extremely hot and humid. Being outside is something that only happens if I absolutely need to. But I love the city's mild winters more than I hate the heat. It's early December, but a warm evening.

I let my head fall back and relax in the spotless headspace that being alone and outside always gives me.

My parents got divorced when I was ten. My mother is an alcoholic, and my father got sole custody of us in the split. She would come to stay with us for one weekend a month, and my father would vacate the house. And for a couple of days each month, I was happy. Until the summer before I turned fourteen when everything changed and she disappeared.

My father sat us down to explain, and I cried as he told us that she'd left LA, and he didn't know where she was. He consoled us by explaining that while she may be fun and loving on the weekends, she was selfish, weak, and unworthy of our forgiveness *all* of the time, and we were better off without her. He made us repeat and promise never to forget it.

I didn't have any contact with her for fifteen years. Then, on the day after it was announced that I was a free agent again, she called my office and told my secretary she was my Aunt Mimosa, her sister, to get through to me.

She began by begging me not to hang up. I hadn't even considered it. She went on to apologize for letting her addiction rule her life and apologized for almost letting it ruin mine.

I accepted her apology and gave her one of my own, which she refused to accept because she didn't blame me for what happened that summer. She said she was only calling because she watched the news conference and could see the sadness in my eyes even though I'd done a good job of pretending to be optimistic and somewhat relieved while I was on air. She said she was living in Houston, had been sober for five years, had a job, and really wanted to see me.

She was the only person who noticed or cared enough to comment on how much I'd been struggling since the knee injury that had kept me off the pitch for a year already.

And the nearly hour-long conversation we had that day was the first one I'd had in a long time where no one was demanding that I tell them what was next.

I was a hobbled one-trick pony. And the empathy and understanding she offered was just what I needed.

I flew down to see her a few days later for a weekend that turned into a week. We spent time doing all the things we'd done when I was boy. Listening to music, bingeing Anime, cooking together, and catching up. She didn't ask me for anything but a chance to get to know each other.

It was the most relaxed weekend I'd had in years.

On my last day, I felt comfortable enough to open up to her about how anxious I'd been about my uncertain future. At 30, I was older than most of my teammates in the LA Galaxy. But there were plenty of players older than me in the League who still played close to their peak levels of performance.

After six months of physical therapy and grueling workouts, I still found myself facing a limitation I couldn't overcome with the sheer force of my will. And after multiple injuries and surgeries on the same knee, it was weak, and my peak was behind me.

She floated a suggestion no one else on my team or in my personal life had: Was it time to retire? I rejected that suggestion. Who was I if not a football player? Being a midfielder for Chelsea Football Club and then the LA Galaxy wasn't a calling, but I was very good at it. I loved the rush of leading my team to victory and being at the top of my game. The money I made in my eight-figure contract with Chelsea has been put to very good use over the years, and I've built a brand with an impressive business portfolio that includes clothing lines, night clubs, restaurants, and part ownership of an MLS team.

Not that I knew anything about running my investment company, Pacific Partners. My role as chairman of the board was only held because I was the founder and the face of the brand.

I couldn't spend my life being a paid spokesperson and letting other people run my business. What the fuck would I do all day if I didn't have practice?

My mother listened to me pour all of my doubts out. Then she reminded me how much I'd loved school and that before I was drafted to the Premier League, I'd wanted to go to college and study economic development and marketing. She encouraged me to think about retiring before I was put out to pasture, pursue the degree I'd always wanted, and chart a new course for myself.

I liked what I'd seen of Houston. The slower, less celebrity-obsessed city was just the change of pace I needed. I applied to the University of Houston, and my father was actually glad I'd made the decision to pursue my degree. I didn't feel the need to tell him my mother was here and that I saw her on a regular basis.

"Mr. Solomon," a deep, baritone booms behind me. I want to be alone, but if it had to be somebody, I'm glad it's Noah Royale. He puts out one of his large hands and shakes mine vigorously, letting it go with a snap of his fingers. It's how he greets anyone he likes in lieu of hugs.

His father is the founder and head of a multi-billion-dollar business. Noah could have asked his father for the money to fund his project. Instead, he went out on his own—believing in it and wanting it to succeed or fail on its own merits. His was the very first business Balanced Scales funded.

"Eloise." I lift my glass to his wife, who is draped onto his side. Their fingers are laced, arms twined. Her free arm is latched around his waist, and her head is on his shoulder. She's got a look of complete bliss on her face, and he's smiling the way he *only* does when he's with her. They're a unit, and they hashtag all their sickeningly in-love pictures and posts with #Noel. It's a private account. Unlike his other siblings, he keeps a low profile and his relationship private.

"Look at you, doing mogul shit." He grins and turns to give the terrace an appreciative appraisal. "It's fucking great. And this neighborhood, I love it. I never thought I'd consider living outside the loop, but this is *nice*. Really smart move."

"Just trying to be like you."

He laughs but shakes his head. "If that were true, you'd have been on at least one second date in the last year," he jokes.

I *wish* I'd found any of the women I've been out with inspiring enough to want a second date.

"Why are you out here? You okay?" Eloise asks, her eyes concerned.

I smile and force myself to relax. "I just hate parties."

They flash twin smiles of sympathy. "Us too. We love you, man, and we came to show our support, but there's only so much socializing we can handle. Mind if we take off?"

"Only because I can't go with you. My dad would never let me hear the end of it."

He winces and groans. "Sorry, man. I was supposed to say as soon as I saw you that your dad is looking for you."

"Shit." I throw back the rest of my drink, and he pats me on the shoulder before they walk around the terrace toward the stairs. The last thing I want is a replay of our argument earlier.

When I decided to launch The Balanced Scale Fund in my third year at U of H, I used my personal funds as seed money. My father helped me organize and launch it. When it came time to find someone to administer it, I asked him to consider the position.

If he hadn't spent his life managing my career, he would have been a very successful executive somewhere. There was no one I trusted more to take care of the money and execute my vision.

The rest of the board agreed, and I was grateful for his leadership. But when his first decision as the Fund's managing partner was to relocate the headquarters of the Fund to Houston, I pushed back.

I didn't want my two perfectly separate worlds to collide. When he presented the numbers to the entire board and everything from the cost of office space to the cost of human capital was so much cheaper than our headquarters in LA, I couldn't continue to oppose the idea without appearing unreasonable and raising eyebrows. So I voted with the rest of the board in favor of the move.

My worry was in vain. My mother lives in North Houston, and my father bought a house a few blocks from mine in Rivers Wilde, which is in the southwest of the city's fifty-mile sprawl.

It doesn't take a lot of effort to keep him from knowing she is there. But I hate lying to my father. And I hate how isolated she is from the rest of the family. Her sister, our Aunt Mimosa, has effectively taken her place, and it's like she doesn't even exist to the rest of them. They have their reasons for doubting her. We all do. But if they could see how much she's changed, they might change their minds.

Inviting her to my graduation ceremony this morning was a passive-aggressive confession. And boy, it did not go at all how I hoped.

"There you are." This time, the voice behind me doesn't put a smile on my face. My sister, Layel, is older than me by two years, and we've always been close. When I reconnected with our mother, I told her. She made it clear she had no interest in a reunion herself, but she kept my secret.

She missed the fireworks between my father and me, but I know exactly where she stands on issues concerning my mother. I'm sure she's looking for me on his behalf, too.

I turn around with a frown in place, ready to preempt her. "I know, he's—" I stop short and turn my frown into a smile because my nine-year-old niece is with her, and she *only* gets smiles from me. "Hey, Hannah."

"Hey, Uncle 'Mar." She dashes ahead of her mom and hugs my waist. "Congratulations." She grins up at me.

I pat her head. "Thank you, half pint." I look up at my sister, and my expression cools. "I know Dad is looking for me, so save your breath."

"That's not why I'm here." Instead of rolling her eyes like she normally does, she gives me a too-friendly smile that usually proceeds a big ask.

"What do you want?"

"To talk to you. I've decided that the kids and I should move to Houston to be with Dad."

"Are you serious?" She swore she'd never leave Los Angeles, and when I left, said she'd be waiting for me when I finally came to my senses and moved back. "Why now?"

"I love it here. Ethan is starting high school, and Hannah's about to start middle school, so hopefully it will be a natural transition for both of them."

I nod. "Well, congrats. And it'll be nice to have you here." But I know she didn't seek me out to tell me that. "So what do you need from me?"

She clears her throat and smooths a hand down the skirt of her dress. "I found the perfect house." She grins.

"You did?" Hannah and I ask at the same time.

She beams and clasps her hands under her chin. "Yes, it's right next door to yours."

I frown. "I didn't know it was for sale."

"That's the *best* part." Her grin can't be contained. "I met your neighbor when I went out for a walk, and she told me they were moving to California for her husband's new job and were just about to put their house on the market. I asked if I could see it, and she let me. I made her an offer, and she called me just now to say they accept."

"Wow," I laugh in surprise and admiration. "You don't waste time, do you? Welcome to the neighborhood."

"Yeah, I'm excited. It's only a few blocks from Dad. And it's perfect for us."

"Did you at least get a good price?" I ask.

She grimaces. "That's what I wanted to talk about. I need some help with it."

"Sure, I know a good realtor."

"No, I mean, I made a cash offer. But I don't have the cash."

I do a quick calculation in my head. The house next door is a tad smaller than mine, but I only bought mine three years ago, and housing prices haven't risen much in that time.

"Once you sell the house in Calabasas, you'll have more than enough to pay whatever they're asking."

She clears her throat and gives me a tentative smile. "About the house—"

"What's the kitchen like?" Hannah asks her mom.

"Just like Uncle Omar's. Nice. Brand new."

"What about the house, Layel?" I give her a pointed look.

She shrugs. "I don't want to sell it. I was thinking I could rent it out and use the rent money to pay you back for the loan to buy the house next door."

I purse my lips. "I see you worked it all out without me. I suppose you've got the check all filled out and just need me to sign, right?"

Hannah's expression grows pained at the harsh tone, and I bite my tongue. I say a silent prayer for patience and remind myself that I created this monster.

Between my ten years of astronomical income when I played for Chelsea and eight years of smart investments and profitable business ventures, I've made enough money to last me several lifetimes. I've been supporting my family since I was a teenager, and I've always been proud that I can. I went straight to the pros and skipped college, not so I could drive a Bentley, but so my dad wouldn't have to sweat another mortgage payment again. I've never been good at saying no to the people I love. Sometimes, though, Layel makes me wish I'd been less generous. She acts like money grows on evergreen trees.

After her divorce three years ago, she took the lump sum settlement she received and decided that the time was ripe for dipping her toe in the world of crypto currency.

She lost every penny she invested. But she was fine because the annuity I created for her gives her a very healthy monthly income for life. The house in Calabasas is hers, free and clear.

"I'll give you a loan. Let's talk about it after the party, though."

I can afford to give her the money outright, and I feel a touch of guilt that I'm not. But as long as she thinks budgets are for other people, she'll always need me to bail her out. And I don't want Hannah and Ethan to think that's how life works.

"There you all are," my father calls from just inside the open terrace doors.

"Oh great," I mutter under my breath.

"Poppa!" Hannah mobs him, and I use the distraction to brace myself for this conversation.

I'm 6'2, but I still have to tip my head back to look at my father. He's a giant of a man, in more ways than one. But he's never used his size to intimidate me. He didn't need to. I've been in awe of him my whole life and respect him tremendously. But right now, he's the last person I want to see.

"Girls, excuse us, please. Omar and I need to talk alone." The please is only because he's unerringly polite, but it's not a request, and they know it. We say our goodbyes, and they hurry back inside.

As soon as the door closes behind them, his expression hardens. "How long have you been seeing her?"

He picks up the conversation exactly where we left it when I climbed out of the car at the Club's valet.

"Since I left the Galaxy."

His mouth falls open, his wide stare incredulous. "You've been in touch with her for *four* years?"

I nod. "Uh-huh."

His eyes narrow, and his nostrils flair, the same way mine do when I'm angry. "And you were going to what? *Surprise* me?"

"It had nothing to do with you. Sure, I hoped you'd live and let live. But I wanted her here because she was the catalyst for it all."

"*She* was the catalyst for your graduation?" His eyes bulge. "After everything I've done—*she* is the catalyst?"

"She encouraged me to go back in the first place. And before you ask, she hasn't asked me for a single penny. All she wants is to be in my life. And you had her removed from my graduation ceremony like she was a criminal."

"She *is* a criminal. And I didn't have her removed. I offered her money to leave, and she took it because that's all she's interested in. Like I've always said."

I shake my head in a vehement rebuke. "I don't believe you. She's never asked me for anything. Not once in the four years I've been—"

"Because *I've* been sending her money every month. And all it took was the threat of that ending for her to turn tail and abandon you. Again," he shouts.

"You've been sending her money?" My stomach clenches, and my lungs constrict. "How? I thought you didn't know where she was."

He closes his eyes briefly and lets out a sharp breath. "Look, son. I'm sorry. I did what was best at the time. I would do it again. I just wish she'd stuck to her end of our deal."

The implication of his words hits me square in the chest. Disoriented, I take a reflexive step away from him. "You knew where she was all these years?"

He doesn't flinch or look away. "Yes. I did. Of course, I did. It was the only way to keep you safe."

My heart feels like it's twisting around itself. "How could you look us in the eye and say she didn't want us to find her? To make us think she didn't want anything to do with us?"

"She didn't, son. I don't know what prompted her to get in touch with you. But all it took was the threat of ending my support to make her leave you again. I'm sorry you've had to find out this way. But I warned you. She's only interested in what you can do for her."

If his goal had been to wound me, he hit a bullseye with that poison-tipped revelation. His self-satisfied, pitying expression doesn't hold a hint of remorse, and that hurts nearly as much as his words do.

Years of pent-up resentment and frustration bubble to the surface, and all I want is to wipe that smug expression off his face.

I cross my arms over my chest and curl my lip in a disdainful sneer. "So she's just like the rest of my family, then."

He pales and then reddens. He leans toward me, his eyes slits of fury, his chin quivering. "*What* did you say?"

I've crossed a line, but I'm too angry to care. "I started paying your bills before I was old enough to vote, and you have *never* asked me how I feel about having to make every single decision with you all in mind because you're completely dependent on me." I stab the air with my finger, gesturing between us.

"Dependent?" His temper, which burns as hot as mine, snaps. His voice is nearly a snarl, and he points an accusing finger at me. "I have been your backbone when you couldn't stand. Your knees when you couldn't figure out how to bend. Your fucking brain when you didn't know what to do." He slaps his broad chest. "And *I'm* dependent?"

I scoff. "How do you make a living, Dad?"

He rears back like I slapped him. "You think I wouldn't trade that money for your respect? If I'd known you felt this way, I would have quit a long time ago."

"Well, now you know. Quit," I challenge with my eyes narrowed.

Instead of the hurt I was trying to inflict, his expression fills with a dark malice I knew he was capable of but have never seen directed at me. "You run around taking pictures, fighting with idiots, and dating one woman after the other. You would have been broke and a punchline years ago if it wasn't for me. I wish I could walk away, but no one else would be willing to clean up your messes. You owe me an apology."

"You lied to me for years. And now you want an apology? I'll starve before I ever apologize to you."

The phone in my hand rings, and *Marley* flashes on the screen. I hesitate for a beat before I answer, ready to give her a piece of my mind. I turn my back to my father and answer. "Mom?"

"Hello? I'm trying to reach next of kin for Matilda Solomon," a male voice responds.

"Who is this?" I demand.

"I'm sorry. I'm an attending physician at Ben Taub hospital. Ms. Solomon was brought here by ambulance after a multi car accident this afternoon. Her phone has you listed as her emergency contact. Are you a family member?"

"I'm her son," I say, but dread has lodged itself in my throat, and it's barely audible.

"Sir, can you speak up?"

I clear my throat. "I'm her son. Is she okay?"

"She's in surgery, but her condition is critical. I'm sorry to ask you this over the phone, but time is of the essence. Do you know if she has an advance directive or a do not resuscitate on file somewhere?"

My ears start ringing. "I don't know."

"Okay. That's okay." He sounds like he's trying to reassure himself. "The team will do their best. In the meantime, it would help if you were here so we can make decisions about next steps quickly. Are you local?"

"Yes. She's going to be okay, right?"

"I'm sorry to say her prognosis isn't good. She's got multiple fractures and internal bleeding. It would be best if you got here as quickly as possible."

I close my eyes and grab the railing of the balcony for support.

"Omar, what's going on?" my father demands from behind me. He doesn't sound angry anymore, but my blood is rushing so loudly in my ears I can't hear him well.

"Sir?" the doctor presses.

"I'm on my way."

"Son, what is happening?"

"She's been in an accident. She's at Ben Taub in surgery. I have to go."

"I'll come with you."

"No."

"You just try to stop me."

I don't have time to argue as I rush down the steps and give the valet attendant my claim card. My father is right behind me, and when the car pulls up, he climbs into the passenger's seat without a word. I don't say a word either, even though there are plenty on the tip of my tongue.

I focus on getting there as fast as I can. But it's not fast enough.

On the way home, I let loose the words I held back earlier. Words I can't take back. Words my father hurls back at me. We are broken, and nothing will ever be the same again.

2

THE CALL
Jules

Staying alive and living aren't the same thing, and I've only ever been able to do one at a time. Mostly staying alive. But today, that changes. I pull the worn scrap of paper from the pocket of my robe and unfold it.

"I am the mistress of my fate."

It was only a wish when I wrote it down on the night of my 18th birthday.

Since then, I've become an expert at reaching into the yawning maw of ruin and yanking my future out of its jaws.

Every step I've taken has brought me closer to making the fanciful words my truth.

Over the last year, I've walked across the ancient flagstones that meander between the cloisters and the glorious rose gardens that inspired Shakespeare and played host to some of the most important moments in human history dozens of times.

Today, as I navigate these time-locked lanes, the comforting weight of history's cloak settles on my shoulders. And I'm reminded that what's built to last, *lasts*.

The ceremony that brought us all into the Chapel of the Temple Church on the day of the Winter Solstice starts with the melodic gurgle of an organ calling us to attention.

Not that my attention is anywhere but here, anchored in this moment that I've been working my fanny off for. Eight years of intense focus, sacrifice, and fear.

Tonight, I turn the corner and move toward the light. The winding serpentine-like tunnel this portion of my life has been is almost over.

In just a few minutes, I'll be granted entry to the profession I've chosen to make my life's work. My eyes are drawn to the vaulted dome of the Temple Church, the earliest Gothic building in London. Built by the Order of The Knights Templar in 1160, it was designed to imitate the Holy Sepulcher in Jerusalem—the site of Christ's death, burial, and rising.

This building was the reason I chose The Inner Temple Inn where I'd complete my training to become a barrister.

This building's history feels like an echo of my own. It was nearly destroyed in the great fire of London in 1666, but it was restored to a glory far greater than its original.

I don't have delusions of grandeur, nor do I believe that this place could resurrect the part of me that's dead. The fire that took away everything I love also gave me the chance to live a life of wondering what else I might have been.

I wasn't born for a life spent in the sheer magnificence of the Inns of Court. Nor was I reared to dine with men and women whose quick and ready wit was as nourishing as the decadent meals we shared.

The sharp jab of a hard elbow into my side draws my unfocused gaze from the master of ceremonies to my friend, Reena. The sparkle in her eye that's been there since she came back from her weekend jaunt to California is undimmed, even in the low light of the hall where we've gathered. The man at the podium cedes his place to a woman garbed in the black silks and gleaming white starched bibs worn by all the Masters of the Inn.

It's time, Reena mouths just as the woman begins to speak. She mimes a scream of elation that I return with a grin that hides the turmoil I really feel. I grip her hand that rests on the seat of the wooden pew next to me and turn my attention back to the front of the room.

"Master Treasurer, the students here present are desirous of being called to the Bar of England and Wales. Student members of the Inner Temple, being called to the profession of barrister, you have declared that for as long as you remain a barrister, you will solemnly use your knowledge and skills in keeping with the principles of the profession's ethics, uphold the rule of law, and in doing so, comply with the code of conduct and court duties of the Bar of England and Wales."

The desire of which she speaks is a visceral, vibrating thrum on every nerve ending in my body.

"I confirm that the students here at this Michaelmas term Call Night 2021 have made the required declarations and have gained the qualifications necessary to be called to the Bar of England and Wales and therefore deserve to be called by the honorable society of the Inner Temple as follows."

The master of ceremony begins to call the inductees, in alphabetical order, and my heart lodges in my throat. My gut crests and crashes in a tumult of excitement, anticipation, and panic that sets my pulse racing.

The row in front of us rises, and Reena squeezes my hand. The tiny stone set in the ring on the third finger of my left hand bites my skin. The pain does more than ground me in the moment, it's a reminder of what I sacrificed to be here. And that every tear I have shed along the way has been proof that I survived what should have killed me.

"I wish she'd hurry. I'm ready for cake and champs." Reena's parents have come from Rome to witness their daughter fulfill her lifelong ambition. After the ceremony, I'll join in the celebration with her friends and family. She let it slip that her mother bought two cakes—one for both of us—and begged me to act surprised when she brought it out.

But I'm also beset by self-pity that I know is pointless and usually beat back. I've gotten used to being the only one of my peers whose head doesn't swivel about the room looking for friends and family. But tonight, I wish someone who knew me was here to see what I've made of myself.

An usher comes to stand by our row and places a hand on my shoulder.

My heart beats hard and slow as I stand and lead the queue to the aisle. I've dreamed of this for ten years. When I charted this course, the moment I would gain access to the tools I need to rewrite my history was a prize so far in the distance that I could barely fathom it. Yet I set my eyes on it and never looked away.

As the person in front of me steps forward, I take a deep centering breath and start counting. In our rehearsal, they said each presentation should only take twenty seconds.

One, two, three, four.

In accepting the call, I will gain access to the tools I need to rewrite my history. But I've decided that I'll never use them.

Nine, ten, eleven, twelve.

I don't want to look back to where I started and measure how far I've come.

The life I'd only meant to leave behind temporarily—the life I'd begun this journey to resurrect—is better off dead.

Seventeen, eighteen, nineteen, twenty.

This night is where *I* begin.

"Juliana Quist. Bachelor of Law, The London School of Economics and Political Science, CPE City Law School, Princess Royal Scholar, proposed by Master Bone." I move to stand before Master Hugo Bone. His shrewd eyes meet mine, and we exchange a smile.

"Master Treasurer, I move her call," he says in his deep, authoritative voice. He sticks his hand out. "Congratulations, Ms. Quist."

"Thank you, Mr. Bone." I shake his hand, and he gives mine a warm squeeze at the end. "And see you on Monday."

I smile, a million hopes fluttering inside me as I float back to my seat. He's a Kingmaker. Only in his early fifties, he's one of the youngest Masters of this Inn and the only Black one. A pupilage at his chambers, one of the best criminal practices in all the Inns of Court, is one of the most sought after. I'm one of the lucky four they've brought on. My hard-won future is here.

Instead of the triumph I anticipated as I return to my seat, I'm beset by disquiet and the distinct feeling that I'm being watched. I swivel my head to the left and right, but it's too dark in the church to see beyond a few rows. I sit and try to ignore the hairs standing up on the back of my neck.

* * * *

"Congratulations, Juliana," a hushed voice whispers in my ear, sending wafts of beer and cigarette smoke into my nostrils.

"Conrad?" I turn my head to look over my shoulder, smiling at him for the benefit of everyone else at the table where we're gathered to celebrate. But my palms grow so damp I don't dare lift my glass to quench my suddenly dry mouth.

I stand to face him, suddenly grateful for the heels I've been cursing all night when they make us nearly the same height. He's bulkier, grittier, harder than when I last saw him more than four years ago. The beard covering the lower half of his face is so full it obscures his mouth. But the mayhem in the eyes of this ghost from my past life is nothing new. I keep the smile in my voice and on my face, but my eyes are shooting daggers. "What are you doing here?"

He returns my smile with an excited and equally insincere one. "I was passing by and happened to look in the window and saw you and thought, that looks a lot like Juliana. I took a second look, and holy shit, it *is* you. After all these years, it felt like fate. I had to stop and say hello."

My stomach plummets to my toes, and I have to focus to keep my breaths from coming faster. "Of course you did."

He smiles at the table of people behind me, and I wish I could throw a cloak over them and make them disappear. "We're in the middle of a celebration." My voice is harsh, even to my own ears.

Beside me, Reena clears her throat. "Jules? Is everything okay?"

I glance at her and nod. "He's just a friend from home. Give me a minute."

I'm sure her parents will think me rude not to introduce them, but I don't care. I'd rather that than give him any more information than he might already have.

I grab his arm and lead him out of the restaurant and into the icy cold evening. I wrap my arms around myself instinctively, but the frigid temperatures barely register as I face the barnacle I can't seem to scrape loose.

"How did you find me?"

"Luck. Purely. Literally I was walking down from the Tube and saw you going into a gate, dressed in robes and all, so I followed."

"What do you want?" I snap.

He runs an assessing eye over me, pulls something from his pocket, and unfolds it. It's the program from this evening. Cream, trifold. That explains the sensation I felt during the ceremony. I thought he was in a prison two hundred miles from here. Clearly, I was wrong. Dread and resignation settle at the same time.

"I thought you still had a year left on your sentence."

"Good behavior pays off. Who knew?" He grins, flashing his teeth, the deeply pointed canines gleaming sinisterly under the harsh outdoor light.

"Juliana Quist, eh? Nice. I didn't know they let offenders become lawyers. But I guess that's why you changed your name? So you didn't have to tell 'em? Clever."

He's dressed impeccably in a pin stripe grey suit and black wool overcoat. His Chelsea boots gleam, and the gold signet ring on his pinky glints in the same harsh light.

I remember when he wore ragged, threadbare clothes. When his hair was stringy and disheveled, and dirt rimmed his fingernails. He's come a long way from the boy he'd once been, when no one wanted him around. I've come a long way from the girl who thought my neighbors were unkind and selfish to turn their backs on him.

I don't know how I didn't see the malignancy of his intent. That I thought he was my friend and trusted him with precious things that he's used against me ever since.

I thought I was finally free of him when he was arrested four years ago. But here he is, armed with everything he needs to destroy this fragile new beginning.

"How much will it cost me to get rid of you?"

He frowns and touches his chest. "Ouch. I thought we could catch up first. I'll come back to yours. We'll have tea—"

"I'll give you fifty thousand pounds right now. I will buy a plane ticket to anywhere you want to go, tonight, and you will never bother me again."

"I was going to ask for ten, but fifty sounds much better." He puts his hand out. "We have a deal."

I ignore his hand. "Wait here."

I go in and make my excuses. It's a lot of money. But I have it. I haven't touched the money my father left me since I graduated from uni.

I juggled two jobs along with my classes. I'd fall into bed every night, exhausted from a day of physical and mental labor, and unsure whether I could get up and do it all again.

But then I'd dream of my father. They were happy dreams of us in his shop, exploring a village in the countryside. And when we'd part ways, he'd hug me and whisper, "Hard work is never a waste of time."

Those early mornings in my kitchen pouring candles, late nights studying, and weekends spent behind a bar. Every time I saved instead of splurging. All of it brought me one step closer to where I was trying to go.

After six years of graduation, successful application, and commendation, the prize I couldn't fathom has become the hare and I the cheetah chasing it.

I don't remember the moment this world, hidden behind doors I had to lie to get through, started to feel like home.

But it does, and I'll do anything to stay here.

My father left me this money to secure my future. Fifty thousand is a lot, but only makes a dent in it. And with this career, I'll make it back quickly. It feels like a small price to pay to get rid of him.

Conrad is waiting on a bench outside the restaurant and grins when I walk back out.

I keep my expression neutral and sit down beside him.

"What happened to you, Conrad? How can you do this? After everything I did for you."

His chuckles, but his expression hardens. "You used me and then when you were all right, you didn't need me."

"We were friends," I protest.

"I don't have friends, *Jules*. I've only got myself. You're not a bad person. You got the shit end of the stick. And for what it's worth, I hope you're never desperate enough to understand how I could do this. Now, Ms. Money Bags, how are we doing this? I have a passport with pages to fill."

I wire the money to him right there outside the restaurant and then order us an Uber to Gatwick. On the way to the airport, he asks me to buy him a ticket to Ibiza. So I walk to the counter and buy him a one-way ticket. I stay with him as far as security will allow and then take a seat by the entrance to baggage claim where he'd have to pass to leave the airport.

I wait two hours after his flight time before I'm satisfied that he's really gone. On my way out of the airport, I toss the scrap of paper with the fanciful words into the trash.

When I get home and finally crawl into bed, my mind is racing, and sleep is elusive. I have no doubt Conrad will blow through that money sooner than he should. And when he does, he'll be back. He doesn't know where I live or work. And no one at Inner Temple would tell him. He'll have to get lucky to find me again. But I have no doubt that he'll try.

London England,
February 2022
(Three Months Later)

3

HIM
Jules

The delectable scent of centifolia roses and vanilla announces Reena's presence behind me before she speaks. "I've been looking for you everywhere," she shouts to be heard over the music. I turn, happy as hell to see her, and pull her into a hug. "I've been looking for *you*. I can't believe how many people are here."

When she told me she was renting out this entire restaurant at the top of the OXO tower, I imagined a few tables of good friends, having dinner and raising a toast.

The only seating is outside on the balconies that ring the entire floor of this building and the three stools in front the bar. Otherwise, it's standing room only. And despite the pretty uninspired music the DJ's got on, the dance floor is packed.

"I'm leaving for good this time. I had to go out in style." She places a kiss on each of my cheeks and nods at the glass of clear liquid on the bar in front of me. "That better be filled with gin or vodka *and* tonic and not *just* tonic…"

I raise my glass to her nose for inspection. She sniffs and smiles approvingly at the distinct effervescent aroma of vodka and tonic. "Good girl," she says and hops up on the barstool next to me. "God, my feet are killing me."

"Why do you think I'm sitting?" I glance down at my black stilettos with disdain. I've had them on all day because I came here straight from work. But my trainers are in my rucksack, and I'll put them on the second I walk out of here.

"You look amazing, babe." She gives me a once-over and nods in approval. "I will never understand how you are single."

I nudge her slim hip with my more ample one and tut in mock disapproval. "I've got two jobs, candle orders to fill, and zero interest in relationships."

She pulls away, her large brown eyes twinkling with mischief. "What's any of *that* got to do with finding someone who'll eat your ass with gusto before he busts your pussy wide open?"

Her explicit description draws a laugh that's born of humor but also shock and embarrassment.

She scrunches her face into one of speculative amusement and narrows her eyes at me. "Jules, if you didn't look the way you do, and I didn't know all the men *and* women who lust after you at the Inn, I'd swear you'd never been with anyone before."

My face heats with a blush she can't see, but that she clearly senses. She lets go of me and steps away as if my body has suddenly caught fire. "Are you a *virgin?*" She draws back and gawks, mouth wide open. Despite the noise in the room, I glance around to make sure no one heard her. "Shhh."

"Oh my God, you *are.*" She stares at me in amazed wonder.

"So what?" I shrug and try to keep the defensiveness out of my voice. I know it's rare, but so is my life.

"You're twenty-six, right? Love, it's *time,*" she declares.

"Says who?" I retort.

"I don't plan to be a virgin forever. When I meet someone who checks my boxes, I'll take the plunge," I say when she keeps staring at me.

She nods, but her expression is full of skepticism. "What are your boxes?"

"Attractive, patient, unavailable."

"Unavailable?" Confusion furrows her brow.

I flash a jaunty smile. "Unavailability is the modern thinking woman's catnip."

"So you say…" She scoffs and glances around the room. "Speaking of unavailable, I invited Omar and told him to bring some friends, but I'm sure he won't. He's as averse to making friends as you are."

I try to stifle my gasp at the mention of his name, and a chunk of ice slides down my throat. Reena pounds my back when I start coughing. "I'm okay." I hold a hand up to stop her when I can talk again. "You were saying?"

"That it's a shame Omar doesn't have any friends I can introduce you to." I don't know why I haven't told Reena that I, sort of, already know him and have had a crush the size of Australia on him for months now.

"So are you very good friends?"

"The *best* of friends," she says with a waggle of her brows. "And he comes with all the benefits. Stamina, a nice thick dick, and a really, *really* talented tongue."

"So you're...dating?" I keep the disappointment out of my voice.

She laughs and rolls her eyes. "Omar doesn't date. He fucks and forgets."

"Wow. And that's okay for you?"

"There was a time, when Apollo had just started dating Graham, when it wasn't." Apollo is her American best friend who just happens to be married to one of the most beautiful men I've ever seen. Her husband, Graham.

"I swore up and down *I* was going to be the one to tame Omar and marry him. And then I found out he's untamable and not at all interested in meeting the parents. Which was actually a relief because my parents have sworn to disown me if I bring home a man who is not Indian *and* doesn't have at least a master's degree. They could accept one without the other, but not without both."

I wrinkle my nose in disbelief. "That can't be true. I've *met* your parents. They are both so thoroughly modern."

"It's a mirage—they're strict traditionalists when it comes to things like blending family lines. It's antiquated. But Omar and I would never have worked anyway. He's allergic to commitment and very set in his ways."

I frown at her. "Is there *anything* you like about him besides his prowess in bed?"

"Oh, yes. He's a *fantastic* person," she answers without hesitation. "And when he calls you his friend, he means it. He may be a *romantic* relationship commitment-phobe, but he's the most loyal friend I've ever had. He'll tell you how it is, *especially* when it really matters. He's gone all the time but manages to show up whenever you need him. And once he knows what you need, want, and crave, if it's in his power to, he'll make sure you always have it. And unlike most men, you *never* have to tell him anything twice. I adore him, and I can't imagine anyone knowing him well and not feeling the same way."

"I'm jealous. I want a friend like that."

She leans away from me in affront. "Well, what the fuck am I? Chopped liver?"

"No, I didn't mean it like that. I meant who could be that and also be my lover."

She scoffs. "Omar's not a lover. He's a one-night stand."

"One night is all I need."

"Oh no, honey. Yes, he'll blow your mind. But the next day, you won't even be a memory, and it'll hurt. And I have a feeling you've had enough of that in your life." A small smile softens her expression before she turns to scan the room again.

I suck in a deep breath at her comment and feel like she's just seen me naked, something I haven't allowed anyone willingly. But clearly, I've let my guard down around her enough that she's seen glimpses of the shadows behind my smile. I love her even more for also knowing they weren't up for discussion.

We met on the first day of bar school. She's an American qualified lawyer who had taken her first degree in London and then moved to New York but came to be called to the Bar here, too. At work, the steady stream of customers saves me from conversations that threaten to linger or delve into the personal. I tried my usual tactic at the first dinner I attended at The Inner Temple. I kept my head down, speaking only when necessary and as politely as I could without encouraging further probing. But Reena was undeterred. And when we discovered our mutual love of Anime and Lynette Yiadom-Boakye's art, that dominated most of our conversation.

I've made quite a few good acquaintances, but she's a real *friend*.

"I'm going to miss you," I tell her and squeeze her hand.

"Come see me!" she demands and then cranes her neck and lifts up onto her toes to scan the room. "All this talk about his sexual prowess makes me want to find him and make my last night in London really special."

I force myself to smile through the sharp pang of jealousy at the thought of them together. It's silly.

Omar Solomon dates women who look like Victoria's Secret models and run billion dollar brands. And in the three months he's been coming into my pub, I've never earned more than a passing glance from him.

"Well then go find him and mingle a bit before you drag him off into one of your dark corners."

She laughs, but when her eyes come back to my face, whatever she sees there erases the humor in them. "Are you all right?"

I nod and take a long sip of my cold, bubbly drink to quench my dry throat.

Now that I know their history, I'm glad I didn't mention my very loose acquaintance with Omar. But I hate lying to her. I shake my head to say "no" and take a deep breath.

She leans away from me with worried, wide eyes. "What in the *world* are you about to tell me?"

"I don't know why I didn't say it sooner, but Omar comes into the pub where I work three times a week. I don't know him, but he's not a stranger to me."

She blinks rapidly, and her mouth falls open. "Holy shit. You *like* him."

I don't play coy or deny it. "From afar, yes. But he doesn't even know I'm alive."

"That *can't* be true. But he's so used to women throwing themselves at him, he's forgotten how to make the first move."

I force my smile wider and nod. "Yeah, maybe. But I'm not going to either. I mean, he's like, an actual famous person. I'm just me."

"Well, just you are *amazing*. The right person for you will see what I do."

I roll my eyes and feign boredom. "And what is that?"

"You light up the fucking room without even trying. You are terribly kind and absolutely beautiful. If I wasn't already in love with two people, I'm sure I would have fallen for you, too." She glances down at my stilettos. "I'm surprised you haven't chucked them already. You love to dance."

"When the DJ plays something decent, I will."

She scrunches her nose. "I know. It's *awful*. But he's a friend and offered. I couldn't say no." She presses a kiss to each of my cheeks and then glides away toward a crowd of people who cheer as she approaches.

We were each other's date to every single one of the mandatory twelve dinners we attended in the year before we were called to the Bar. She knows me better than anyone I've met since I moved to London.

Having an unconquerable optimism sometimes feels like a curse. And like my thoughts conjured him, he walks through the door. I knew he'd be here, but this first glimpse of him still makes my heart skip a surprised beat.

He's walked into the pub where I work countless times over the last three months, but I've never had a chance to *really* look at him. And I take full advantage as he crosses the room.

I can't take my eyes off him and can't understand why everyone else isn't watching him, too.

He's a walking wonder—tall, but not too tall, lean, but muscular enough that he fills out the bright bronze blazer he's wearing over a black turtleneck. His slim-cut black trousers are tailored to hit right below his ankle, and his polished to a spit shine black Chelsea boots make his muscular legs appear to go on forever.

My dad used to say about anyone who was exceptionally good at something, "Now, that's a *break*." I didn't know what it meant, but he said it was something one of his teachers used to say whenever any of the students did particularly well. When he called me a "break," I knew he was paying me the highest compliment.

Omar Solomon, in every way, is a break.

The first time he walked through the doors of the pub where I work on weekends, I'd stared at him until the beer I was pulling overflowed onto my hands and snapped me out of it. His body reminded me of the yew trees that are native to Stow-on-the-Wold, where I grew up. They're muscular, strong trees. Perfect for climbing— you never had to worry if their branches could hold your weight. There were a few ancient ones that soared so high they appeared topless. I knew they weren't, and when my father fell asleep after lunch, I'd climb and climb, even when I was afraid of how high it was—because I knew the view from up there would be worth the risk.

Some Sunday afternoons at the pub, he sports a stubble that's a shade darker than his dark brown hair. But tonight, he's clean shaven. His broad, sculpted face isn't what most would call handsome, but it's intensely compelling. He has high cheekbones I'd kill for and highlight the shit out of if they were mine. And he's got a strong jawline and chin that don't need a beard to make them look that way. He wears no jewelry but a bracelet—a surprisingly delicate and feminine string of small black and white pearls that looks like it was made to be worn on his warlord-sized wrist.

In general, he always looks like he's on the cusp of a growl. His mouth is set in a straight line that makes his upper lip appear less full than the bottom. But when he speaks, that misconception is cleared up. There's also no hint of the dimples, so deep I could fit the tip of my finger in them, that punctuate his rare and beautiful smile.

In the dark wood paneled cavern of the pub, the color of his eyes was hard to see. But the lining of thick and dark lashes accentuated the almond shape of them. Set deep on either side of his unapologetically prominent nose, they always remind me of the wolf I saw at a conservatory in Reading when I was ten.

The animal stared at everyone like it was trying to read minds or find weaknesses. Tonight, in the overbright light of the room, his gleaming hazel irises are impossible to mistake for the brown I'd thought they'd be.

The one time we made and held eye contact was on a Saturday night two or three months ago, in the badly lit pub. His eyes narrowed, and his lips parted, and I was sure he was going to speak. But he just kept walking, and I turned back to serve my waiting punters. As far as I know, he's never looked at me again.

And once my boss told me who he was, I understood why.

I stayed up after work that first Sunday reading everything I could about Omar Solomon—and there was a lot. He left his ten-year career as a brilliant midfielder at Chelsea Football Club in 2012 after a persistent knee injury benched him for an entire season. That same year, he joined the Los Angeles Galaxy and was more of an expensive hood ornament than an asset on the field. And off the field he modeled and starred in campaigns for colognes and watches. He started an investment company and owned nightclubs and restaurants.

At the age of 36, he graduated from the University of Houston with honors and a double major in marketing and economic development.

As if that wasn't enough, while he was a student, he created an investment fund that invested in entrepreneurs from traditionally marginalized communities.

His Instagram account has thousands of pictures.

Since he started his account, there isn't a week that has gone by that he hasn't posted pictures from the fabulous places he traveled, the amazing meals he enjoyed, and selfies with the beautiful people he is always surrounded by.

The last three pictures were posted on the same day three months ago.

The first is of him with a young woman and a toddler with hazel eyes and deep dimples on her lap.

The second is of him in a black cap and gown with accents of dark red, smiling broadly and flanked by his famous best friends.

The last one is of his bare, beautifully muscled back, his head bowed, and his fingers giving the middle finger to the camera. Its caption read, *I'm out.*

It was nearly impossible to reconcile the extroverted playboy demigod online persona with the polite but reserved man who came into the pub to eat and watch whatever was on the tele.

The only thing about him in person that reminded me of what I'd seen in my hours of reading about him was the way he walked through the crowded pub to grab the same table in the back.

He keeps his gaze fixed on his destination, earbuds in, the world shut out. His stride is purposeful and merciless when you don't have enough sense to move out of his way.

Just from looking, I couldn't be sure if he was an asshole, just an introvert, or a little of both. Either way, I found the broadcast of his barbed edges refreshing. It's nice not having to guess what people are thinking.

He cuts through the crowd of people in glamorous garb, crystal cut tumblers or fragile flutes in their wildly gesticulating hands. Yet they seem to move just as he wants them to so that he doesn't need to turn sideways to accommodate his broad shoulders or taper his remarkably long strides.

Long strides that are bringing him straight toward me.

I barely have time to spin around before he's right behind me.

"Scotch on the rocks," he tells the bartender when he slides onto the empty barstool next to me. I disguise my gasp as a cough, place a hand on the bar to steady myself, and stare straight ahead.

The young man nods and grabs a glass. "We've got Macallan 18 for the masses, but I've got a bottle of *Craigelachhie* that might be more to your taste."

"I don't really care, whichever," he responds in a voice that's not rude but doesn't match the adoration in the server's. Undeterred, the young man leans forward across the bar and lowers his voice to a loud whisper. "I know you've been gone a while, but I'm still a huge fan, Mastermind. Can I snap a selfie?"

To my surprise, Omar doesn't rebuff the bartender. "Only if you promise you won't post it for a bit. No one knows I'm in London yet, and I'd like to keep it that way for just a few more weeks."

I watched an interview from very early on in his career when he was asked about his dislike of public availabilities.

He explained that he understood it was part of the job. So he did it. "I play for the love of the game, and if I had my way, I wouldn't do any interviews at all. I don't even know why you want to interview me. I say everything I need to out on that pitch. I get it. I had sports heroes, too. But when they fall off the pedestals you put them on, you swoop in and eat them alive."

That interview would prove prescient when he left Chelsea years later. The press tore him to shreds for sitting out an entire season, leaving as soon as he became a free agent and basically abandoning London, his fans, and his team.

He still doesn't talk to the press regularly, but he doesn't leave their accusations unanswered. He became his own press secretary and posted videos on social media pushing back on false headlines. And when they lost interest, he started sharing his private pictures. And sued newspapers that used his images without his permission.

I watch the exchange between him and the bartender out of the corner of my eye and am giddy that the wickedly sweet dimple *is* as deep as I'd imagined. And God, I want to lick it. *One day, my pretty.*

This *has* to be a sign. He's so far out of my league, I shouldn't be able to see him. And at the pub, I wouldn't dare approach him.

But here I am, close enough to see *and* touch. And I look good tonight. I'm glad I took special care to send my most fashionable friend off.

The bustier I invested in makes my otherwise unimpressively small breasts look their very best in the very low neckline of my scarlet red minidress. It's hugging every inch of a body that even CrossFit and a vegan diet couldn't kill the curves on.

The lighting in this ballroom sets off the healthy glow of my bare legs, shoulders, décolletage, and back that is courtesy of my homemade sugar scrub. It leaves me smelling like a tropical garden at midnight.

Liquid courage and my heels give me height and confidence that override my nerves, and I shoot my shot.

"Do you want to dance?" I ask loudly so there's no way he won't hear me.

Those wolf eyes slant down to look at me, unblinking, the smile he'd given the bartender long gone. There's no flicker of recognition, but there's no mistaking the interest as he stares at me. He's never done more than look past me at the pub, so I don't know why I'm disappointed that he doesn't recognize me.

"Excuse me? I didn't hear you," he says when he finally speaks. His *voice*. It's deep, smooth—no gravel but a lot of bass. And is there anything sexier than an American accent? I smile as widely as I can manage, the punters at the Effra call it my traffic stopping smile. Then I break my golden rule and repeat myself. "Would you like to dance?"

He doesn't return my smile, and when he turns to look at the dance floor, that scowl reappears. "I don't dance," he comments without looking back at me.

I follow his gaze. "Childhood trauma on the dance floor?" I ask with a teasing grin.

His lips tug up a little, but he doesn't smile. "No. General observation. People look ridiculous when they dance."

I can't deny that. But I shake my head in disagreement. "They're having fun, not putting on a show."

He shrugs. "That's not my idea of fun. Like I said, I don't dance." He reaches into his jacket pocket, pulls out his phone, and glances at it. He gives me a quick, stiff smile. "I'm sorry, but I have to take this call." He doesn't sound sorry at all and doesn't wait for me to respond before he walks off.

"Ouch," the bartender drawls, and I want to glare at him and tell him I didn't ask for his feedback. But he's so right I can't be mad.

"I know," I groan.

"For what it's worth, if I wasn't working I wouldn't have said no." He grins, and I wish I was attracted to him instead of Omar.

I smile gratefully and take the refill he hands me. But a few sips of it while swaying by myself to a song I've never heard before only makes me feel worse.

I put my glass on the tray of a passing server and head to the coat check to collect my things.

4

OLIVE BRANCH
Omar

Layel's text had simply read, "Call me."

Three months ago, I would have bristled at the entitlement of her demand and ignored her until I was ready to call. I love her, she loves me, and we agreed to live and let live when it came to my mother. But that became impossible for me when she died. And now my sister and I are as far apart as we've ever been on anything.

This is the first time she's texted me since I left Houston, and I know her well enough to know that it's an olive branch. After months of not hearing her voice, I miss her. And my issue isn't really with her, but my father.

She was as upset by my leaving as he was. We had a loud and bitter argument about my decision to take a leave of absence. But I couldn't stay. I didn't know how to handle the resentment I felt toward my father.

He and I have to communicate about matters to do with the Fund. But outside of that, we don't speak at all.

I duck out onto a deserted balcony, as far away from the noise of the party as I can.

It's a cool summer night, the air is still damp from the burst of rain we had a few minutes ago. The view of St. Paul's Cathedral nestled against the inky light speckled skyline is spectacular. I sink into one of the seats that faces it so I can at least have something nice to look at during what, I'm sure, is going to be a contentious conversation.

The phone only rings once before the call connects.

"Uncle 'Mar? Hiiii! It's Hannah. I'm eating Rocky Road. What are you doing?" A smile unbidden but welcome spreads across my face at the sound of my niece's sweet voice. I glance at my watch and do a quick mental calculation. "And why are you eating Rocky Road at home and at 1 p.m. on Friday instead of whatever perfectly balanced meal they serve in your overpriced school's cafeteria?"

"I lost a tooth and had to stay home."

"They allow sick days for that now?"

"They do when your brother knocks it out with his baseball," she chimes in a voice that's reminiscent of my sister's when she knows she's got you beat on logic. But unlike my sister, it doesn't irritate me to hear it out of her mouth.

"And how mad is your mama?"

She giggles. "She's super mad. We were throwing it in the house when she said not to. But she said my busted lip was punishment enough and gave me ice cream. And Papa said the tooth fairy pays more for knocked-out teeth, and he wasn't making it up like he normally does. I had thirty-two dollars under my pillow this morning. So I'm pretty happy. Even though I have a fat lip and have to go to the dentist appointment later. How are you?"

"Wait, you know the tooth fairy isn't real?"

"Of course. I'm not six years old anymore."

She certainly isn't. She's grown so much in the four years since I left LA for Houston.

I laugh, amused by her commentary. "I'm doing okay. And I'm glad to hear everything is normal over there. I miss you guys."

"Then come home."

Ah, to be a child and have everything be so simple. "I will. Soon. Is your mom around? She texted me."

"She's on the house phone with Mimosa, and she told me not to interrupt her unless I was dying."

"No, don't worry, I'll call her later." Mimosa is our mother's sister, who plays house with my father and tries to mother us. Just the sound of her name sets my teeth on edge.

"Do you want me to tell her *you're* dying? They've been on the phone for a while, and she really wants to talk to you."

I shake my head. "No, don't get into the habit of lying to your mother." *That's my job.*

"She'll be mad that I didn't interrupt her because she's been trying to reach you. She says you're avoiding her because you don't want to hear what she has to say."

I stifle my surprised, impressed, amused chuckle because this is a kid who doesn't know the difference between laughing with or at her. My sister says I was the same way as a kid. I hope she grows out of it faster than I did.

"I'm not avoiding her. I've just been busy this week."

"With what?"

"Stuff, kid. *Adult* stuff that you wouldn't understand."

"I understand a lot. And she's done now, anyway."

"Thank God. Go back to your ice cream, and leave me in peace, you little hellion," I tease. But she doesn't laugh.

"I love you, Uncle 'Mar. I just want you to be happy."

"I love you too, baby." This kid is the only person on the planet who says she loves me so freely and so frequently. I've missed hearing it, and I've forgotten how utterly comforting and reinforcing it is.

"Well, hello, stranger." My sister's exasperated relief is melodramatic, but I'm too happy to hear her voice to be annoyed.

"I've been busy."

"So you say, but I don't see how overseeing the renovation of your house can take up so much of your free time. Life-changing shit is happening, and you're not talking to anyone about it."

"Moving to London to renovate my house is hardly life-changing."

She groans. "I'm not talking about your house. I'm talking about *you* and Dad. You need to talk before you drive me nuts. He's turned into an unbearable grump. And the way you left. How can you treat him like he's disposable?"

"How could he treat our mother like she was nothing?"

"He loved her once. She treated *that* and us like we were nothing. And by the time she died, that's exactly what she was to him."

"She was the mother of his children."

"She may have given birth to us, but if being a mother has taught me anything, it's that blood doesn't give you the right to be called that."

"She was our mother," I reiterate. "And you two can act like she never existed, but don't expect me to." My voice is much quieter than the anger this conversation is whipping up inside me.

"She abandoned us."

"She was an *addict*," I shout.

"She made a choice, Omar. She doesn't deserve your loyalty or grief."

"I loved her." The ache in my chest hasn't dulled one bit since she passed away.

"She abandoned you," she repeats. "And yet it's the parent who stayed, who loves you back, you're treating like the enemy."

Layel has always been good at throwing a punch and stroking at the same time. But she doesn't know what happened, and what I owe our mother.

"You should call him. Talk this out. He won't admit it, but he's distraught that you left."

"Well, I was too distraught to stay."

She sighs as if in exasperation. "Omar, please. I know he hurt you. And he's sorry."

I scoff. "Right. So sorry he hasn't called me in months."

"You said some terrible things to each other, and he's a proud man. But he's also your father. And you owe him respect." That is the traditional upbringing of ours showing itself. Where respect is deserved simply because someone is older than you. I never believed in that, and I'm not a kid anymore.

"Please call him," she pleads.

"I will. As soon as I can."

She doesn't respond. But I know that's not good enough without her telling me.

I cough to clear the lump of guilt out of my throat. "I love you. Bye."

I hang up and put my phone on silent.

I sit there, my eyes glued to the scenery but not seeing any of it. "Shit." I drop my head into my hands, sadder than I am angry.

I left. And now I can't fix it without eating humble pie I have zero appetite for.

"The best revenge is forgiveness." The words, whispered by a voice so close to my ear that the speaker's lips brush them, startles me out of my seat.

It happens so quickly that I hear a telltale crunch of bone and her howl of pain before I realize the back of my head has connected with the soft cartilage of a nose. I turn around, full of apologies, and freeze.

It's Jules, the girl behind the bar at my local that makes my tongue tied and clumsy.

Her sob of pain and the blood running from her nose and down her chin onto the floor shake me out of my stupor.

I pull my handkerchief from my pocket. "I'm so sorry. Here, use this, I'll get help."

"What in the world is going on out here?" Reena asks as she approaches from inside the open terrace door. She stops mid-stride when she sees her friend doubled over and crying with my dark yellow handkerchief pressed to her bloody nose.

"Christ on a cracker, what did you do?"

"He broke my nose. Cause he's a break," Jules says in a nasally but garrulous voice. She laughs and then moans in pain.

"What does that mean?" Reena asks.

"I don't know, maybe I knocked her senseless. Who cares? She needs the A&E." I slip the backpack now dangling from her elbows off and sling it over my shoulder. I can't believe I hurt her. I put a hand on her shoulder and try to pat it soothingly.

Reena pulls out her phone. "I'll order the Uber."

"No, I have my car, I'll drive."

"Perfect. Let me grab my purse."

"You can't leave your party."

"I can't leave my friend," she pushes back.

Beside me, Jules moans softly. "We're wasting time. I'll call you and let you know where we are. I promise."

"You better. I'll come as soon as I say goodbye to everyone."

I put an arm around her shoulders, and she lets her body relax against mine as we walk to the lift. I was a deer in the headlights at the bar earlier and totally fucked up. But she went from cute bartender with a killer smile to a sex pot with zero warning. I blanked. I hoped I'd think of a way to rectify myself by Sunday.

"It hurts so much," Jules says in a small voice that tugs at my guilt and worry.

"I know, but we'll get you fixed right up."

I'm sure her nose will be fine. But after this, I'll be lucky if she ever graces me with one of those put the sun to shame smiles again.

5

BREAK
Omar

I scowl at my reflection in the mirrored glass window of the waiting room at the Accident and Emergency. I'm waiting for Jules.

A text from Reena pops up on my phone.

"I'm so sorry I didn't respond sooner. My phone died. I'm home. Tell me where you are and I'll come over and see her home."

"It's fine. I'll wait with her and see her home," I text back.

My phone rings a second later with Reena calling on a video call.

"Hey."

She narrows her eyes at me. "You'll do *what?*"

I furrow my brow in confusion. "I said I'll take her home."

She cocks her head to the side as if she thought I'd just told a boldfaced lie. "What were you two doing outside on the balcony?"

"I was on the phone with my sister…her I have no clue." Even though after the way I behaved at the bar, I'd put money on her coming to tell me to fuck off.

"Omar, she's one of my best friends, and she's nice as hell."

I return her disapproving smile. "All I did was offer to take her home from the hospital *after* I broke her nose. I know I play one on TV, but you know I'm not *really* an asshole."

"You're not a bleeding heart either," she snaps and then crosses her arms and raises her eyebrow. "I *know* you. If you're still there and offering to take her home, you like her. And if you like her, you know her." She taps her fingers together as if she's wracking her brain.

"Why are you so pushy?"

"Just tell me, and I wouldn't have to be."

"Fine. She works at my local, but we've never spoken before tonight. And I have a small crush on her."

She punches the air in victory. "My ship-dar is *never* wrong."

"Ship-dar? What the hell is that?"

"My radar on people I think would be good together."

"You're getting ahead of yourself."

"I *talked* about you," she says and bites her lip. "She's very private. But sweet."

"So am I."

"No, you're a walking scaffold of heartbreak."

I scoff. "Thanks, friend."

"Although, if you weren't, *and* if you were a little bit younger, this could be something." She presses her hands together excitedly and then frowns. "But she's *not* a fuck it and forget it girl, Omar."

"I've never thought of anyone like that. And I've never had any complaints." Not that I've stuck around long enough to hear them.

"Omar, I'm serious. She's a virgin." She slaps a hand over her mouth and winces.

I'm speechless. How in the world has a woman that sexy never had sex?

If she's a virgin at this age, she's either saving it for marriage or one of those "born again" innocents—and those are both red flags. It makes blowing the chance she dropped into my lap much easier to stomach.

"I shouldn't have said that," Reena says after a few seconds.

"No. I'm glad you did." *Very.*

She narrows her eyes, and her frown grows stern. "You better not hurt her, Omar. She's not as tough as she acts. Tread carefully."

* * * *

The first time I saw Jules, she was having a heated, but good-natured, argument with a group of men who were congregated at the bar where she was serving drinks. Even in the poorly lit pub, her deep brown skin glowed like it was filtered through pearlescent light.

Her husky and unbridled laugh drew and held my attention the way a glass of whiskey perched on a round ass used to.

Long wisps of hair dark chaotic curls escaped from the huge bun at the top of her head. They danced around her oval face and brushed the nape of her long, slender neck as she gestured with her hands.

But it was her smile, bright and warm as the noonday sun, that made me nearly swallow my tongue and walk into a wall.

I asked the owner of the bar, Dominic, about her as casually and randomly as I could. She was a law student, had worked at The Effra for five years. She was from somewhere in the Midlands and wasn't a football fan at all.

Beautiful, hard-working, and didn't seem to know who I was? She was a unicorn.

I came in every day for two weeks until I figured out her schedule and then made sure I was there every time she was working. It was full-on creepy, but that smile made me forget it was raining outside.

But my head was still all over the place after the fallout with my family. I wasn't really in the mood for company, and the smile she gave me when I walked in, she'd never indicated any interest in me at all.

And I know unicorns don't exist. I was good enjoying my fantasy from a safe distance. But after months of watching everyone else bask in the rays of her sunshine, it was getting harder to stay in the shade. And I'd started to reconsider my position.

I noticed her as I approached the bar. I admired her shapely legs, the curve of her hip, and the promise of a spectacular ass spilling over both sides of the bar stool.

But as nice as it all looked, it wasn't enough to compel me to take a closer look when I sat down next to her.

Because I had no clue it was her. Her hair is different—it's straight, and the loose, blunt ends of it skim her shoulders. The body-hugging red dress she's wearing reveals a curvy figure that the loose-fitting black T-shirt she wears at work concealed. But there is no mistaking that smile—and it is even more riveting up close.

I was just starting to reconcile this sex pot with the cute bartender I'd been crushing on for months when she asked me to dance. My brain short-circuited. When Layel's text came, I bolted and figured I'd never be able to show my face in The Effra during one of her shifts again.

We're halfway home when she moans. It's a low, dry noise that's barely loud enough to be heard over the road noise from my tires and the incessant rain drumming on the roof of my car.

I was relieved when she fell asleep as soon as the nurse and I settled her in the passenger's seat.

If she hadn't been coming outside to tell me to fuck off, she most certainly will now that I've broken her nose.

"Ouch," she groans and reaches up to turn on the overhead light and pulls down the mirror in front of her. She leans in and turns her face from side to side. The bruises under her eyes are a deeper purple than they were when we left the hospital, and the dressing on her nose makes it look like a beak.

I stop at a red light and glance at her. She's still staring at her face and hasn't said a word.

"Jules?"

She turns her head to look at me, and then she blinks. "Hi, Break." She tries to smile, but then winces. "Oh"—and touches her nose—"I thought it was a dream."

The doctor warned me she'd be loopy, but clearly she's totally out of it. And I don't know who Break is, but I hate him already.

"You should sleep, we'll be at your place soon." The light starts to flash yellow, and I pull away, relieved to be able to turn my eyes toward the road and away from hers.

"You're taking me home?" Her voice is rough and low, but her surprise is unmistakable.

"Of course." My throat is dry, and I sip from a water bottle in my cupholder. Then I hold it out to her. "Are you thirsty?"

She sits up a little. "Oh God. Where's Reena? Did I ruin her party?"

"No. It was still going strong when we left. I told her I'd take you home."

"Did you eat her ass?"

I bark out a surprised laugh that turns into a cough. She watches me expectantly, and I know it's the meds talking, so I humor her. "I can't say I've ever had the occasion to do that, no."

"Oh good." She sounds genuinely relieved and slouches in her seat a little. "No offense to Reena. I'm sure her ass is as clean as anyone's could be. But I don't think I'd ever be able to kiss you if you had."

I stifle my laugh. "Well, then I'm *very* thankful I didn't."

She blows a raspberry with her lips and waves a hand in dismissal. "You don't want to kiss me. You don't even like me."

I sputter a laugh. "Of course I like you. How could I not?"

"That's what *I've* been wondering." She sits up again. "I'm *wonderful.* And I *always* smile at you."

If she didn't sound so put-out, I would laugh again. "You smile at *everyone.*"

"Not the way I smile at *you.*" She sings the last word. "*That* smile is all yours. But you never smile back. And you never come to the bar."

The car in front of me brakes suddenly, and I slam on my brakes to keep from rear-ending him.

She groans, and my daydream is shattered. "Shit, I'm so sorry." I've already broken her nose. If I harm one more hair on her head, I'll save Reena the trouble and kick my own ass.

When I stop at the next red light, she's prodding her forehead with the pads of her long, slim fingers. Her fingernails are painted in an alternating pattern of silver, white, and gold. The ring on the third finger of her right hand is in the shape of a tiny crown with a small diamond in the center of it.

"The crown jewel?"

"What?" Her head whips up, and her bruised eyes are wide with what looks less like pain and more like panic. My heart slams against my ribs at the amber-flecked molasses-colored irises that I have a feeling I'll be seeing every time I close my eyes from now on. God, they're beautiful.

Trying to be casual, I relax in my seat, pick up my coffee cup, and lift it to my lips. "Your…" To my horror, I croak and feign a cough, then take a sip of my coffee before I finish my sentence. "Your ring, it's a crown with a jewel in it."

"Oh," she says and closes her eyes, relaxing in her seat again. "Yeah, that's right."

"Are you okay? Does your head hurt?"

She sighs in deep discontent and pouts, her bare lips compressing into a pout that's nearly as disarming as the smile it replaces. "Not as much as my pride, but yeah."

"Your pride?"

"I asked you to dance. And you said no."

I grimace. "I'm sorry. I don't dance. Ever." *But. I would have done anything else you asked.*

She looks at me knowingly. "You'd think I would have learned my lesson. I was coming out to get some air. I saw you sitting there, looking so angry. I thought…this was my chance."

"To have your nose broken and end up in A&E?"

Her sudden laugh appears, and then she winces again.

"Shit, here, I forgot." I reach into the back seat and pull out a small white bag that they gave me on discharge. "There's a gel ice pack in there. It's probably melted a little, but the cold will help."

"Thank you." She pulls it out and lays it across her forehead and settles in her seat with a sigh. "So what happened to make you look like that? So sad?"

"I thought you said I looked angry." I inject teasing humor in my voice to defuse the way her question makes my heart skip a beat.

"I saw both, but mostly sadness."

My heart skips another beat.

My body, my fame, the car I drive, the company I keep—tell a very particular story of who I am. I've cultivated a public persona that says I'm strong, controlled, decisive, unapologetic, successful. But there is a cost that comes with allowing people to believe that it's all there is to me. I live with the consequences of it—isolation, insecurity, imposter syndrome, and deep skepticism. And I never let anyone see me sweat.

So how can she see what I've only acknowledged to myself? The light turns green, and I'm grateful for a reason to turn back to face the road.

"Maybe I'm just projecting because that's how I imagine I look when I think about my dad. I miss him every day. But I'm so mad at him for dying and leaving me alone, too."

Maybe it's because she saw the sadness I didn't think anyone else could. Or maybe it's because we're alone. Whatever the reason, I feel able to speak aloud words I've only recently found the courage to acknowledge.

"My mother died three months ago. It was sudden. And there is so much I wish I'd had the chance to say to her."

She doesn't say anything, but she puts a hand on my arm and squeezes it as if to let me know she's only quiet because she's listening. I blow out the breath I was holding. "And I hate this friction between my father and me. Everything else can be grand, but if we're not, nothing feels right."

She doesn't say anything, and I could kick myself. I've put her through enough already. I don't want to add triggering painful memories to my list of transgressions.

"I didn't mean to dump on you like that. You should relax."

She draws away and back into her seat. "You didn't dump on me. I know what it's like to feel that way."

"I can't even imagine that. You're Miss Walking on Sunshine."

Her eyes flash with something that disappears before I can decipher it. "Don't let the filter fool you. I'm as human as anyone else." She closes the mirror, and the car falls into darkness again.

We ride in a companionable silence, and I'm lost in my thoughts until we pass the neon-lit Tube sign of Brixton Station. We're close to her house, but I'm nowhere near ready to say goodnight. I could talk to her all night.

"I've imagined what it would be like to have a conversation with you so many times."

My heart thuds in my chest. "With *me*? Really?"

She laughs at the slack-jawed surprise in my voice. "*Yes*. With you. I have so many questions to ask you."

"You do? Like what?"

"What do you miss most about your life in America?"

I'm so surprised by the question that I forget whatever I'm about to say and pause to think about that. When I left, I couldn't wait for the change in scenery and haven't really looked back. "I miss the sun. Being close to the ocean. My family. Even though they get on my fucking nerves, think money grows on trees, and only call me when they need something."

She leans back in her seat, her eyes lose their humor, and she bites her lower lip. "Do you have a big family?"

"My older sister Layel, her daughter Hannah, and her son Ethan. My dad has five siblings, so I have a slew of aunts and uncles and cousins. It's someone's birthday every damn week."

"And your parents are from Tonga?"

I smile, impressed and flattered that she knows that. It's one of the least mentioned aspects of my background. "Yeah, my dad is a native, but my mother's parents were Australian transplants whose roots wind themselves all the way back to this very city."

"Wow, it's so cool that you can trace your roots so precisely."

"What about you?"

She squints at me with a teasing smile on her lips. "If you had to guess where I'm from, what would you say?"

I frown and scrunch my nose as if I've never pondered that question before. "Well…" I draw out the word and give her an exaggerated head-to-toe assessment. "I'd say I had a friend from Ethiopia in high school, and you could be her sister. And when you wear your hair straight like this tonight, you look like a young Iman."

She laughs. "A young Iman who's too short and thick for sample sizes, but I'll accept that. My dad was from Ghana. My mom was American, according to him. But I don't know anything else about her."

"They split up?"

"No, she died giving birth to me." She swallows audibly. She's lost both of her parents. And here I am ignoring my father.

A crack of thunder rattles the glass-paned windows of the car, and she breaks eye contact. "God, it's about to pour. And I've got an early morning. Thank you for bringing me home."

She leans down and grabs her green and red Puma trainers off the floorboard. She rests her heel on the seat. Her toenails are painted bright red and as pretty as everything else about her.

She looks up, and I can't look away fast enough this time. Or maybe it's that I don't have to now that we're completely alone, and I know she has a thing for me, too.

Her amber eyes trap me as if they were sap and I the proverbial dragonfly, and I couldn't look away to save my life. "You're so beautiful." Even with that packing on her nose, she's riveting.

"When you look at me that way, I believe you mean it."

"I mean everything I say."

"We'll see." She tips her head ever so slightly to the right, a lock of hair falls over her forehead, and I reach over to tuck it behind her ear.

She exhales a long breath when my fingers skim the petal-soft shell of her ear.

"I'm a sucker for a chance to prove myself right."

Her heavy-lidded gaze drops to my mouth. And mine moves to hers just as her voluptuous, gloss-slick lips part and the tip of her tongue wets her lower lip before she bites it.

The pull of attraction turns into a tug of want that has a life of its own. I skim my fingers down her silk-smooth throat and cup her neck.

I lean in and brush a kiss across her lips. It's light as a feather, but it dances across every nerve ending of my body like the shocks I used to get when I dragged my feet over the carpet and then touched the door handle.

She leans away, her eyes wide with surprise that appears as acute as mine.

Her fingers skim her lips, and she closes her eyes as if she's in pain. "Are you okay?"

She shakes her head, and my throat closes.

"I'm sorry." My voice is just above a whisper, and my heart is beating wildly in my chest. "I don't know what I was thinking."

"Whatever it was, I want you to keep thinking it." A smile tilts one corner of her mouth, and she places a hand on my shoulder, leans over, and presses another damp, lingering kiss to my cheek.

She reaches into her bag and rifles for her keys, pulling out books, scarves, a tablet, and a small bag before she finds them.

"Thank you again for bringing me home."

"Let me see you up." I unbuckle my seatbelt and run around to open her door before she can say no.

She hands me my jacket, which I draped over her when we left the event. "No, it's okay. I'm really tired, and it's late. But thank you so much. I'll see you on Sunday."

She walks with a speed that belies her injuries and disappears down the path that leads to the back of the pub.

I wait until I see a light come on in the upstairs window before I drive off. I haven't had a crush since I was in high school and fell for my chemistry teacher. But somewhere between seeing her for the first time and tonight, I've managed it again.

6

KEEN VIRTUE
Jules

It's well after supper time when I turn onto the top of my road. I'm still tired. The aspirin I took this afternoon is wearing off, and my nose is starting to throb. And after walking all the way home, I'm starving. But the prospect of eating alone only makes me slow my steps.

I left my iPad in his car and hoped that he'd see it and run after me and we'd kiss in the rain but not feel a single dreary drop while we got lost in each other's lips.

When that didn't happen, I spent the entire day at work and the Tube ride home imagining that he would be waiting outside the flat for me. He'd have my iPad tucked under one of his anatomically perfect arms and pull me into his lap for a kiss. And as soon as our lips touched, it would start raining and we'd sit kissing and getting soaked.

He wasn't there. It didn't rain.

But three days later, I've accepted he's not going to come seek me out. I just hope he brings it to the pub with him on Sunday when he comes in for his regular afternoon meal.

But as I approach the small gate that leads to the residents' entrance, I see someone leaning against the gate, and I quicken my steps, only to have my foolish romantic heart sag when I get closer and can make out that it's Dominic.

"Evening, Dom."

"Good evening. You hungry?" he calls and waves me over.

"Yeah, I guess."

He frowns. "Why d'long face, child? Your nose bothering you?"

I shake my head and attempt a smile. "Long day."

"I'll have one of the boys run dinner up to you, okay?"

My heart lifts for the first time today. I press a kiss to his weathered cheek and thank whatever good luck brought him into my life. He and his wife, Jodi, own the Effra. He runs the back office, she runs the kitchen. They're not quite old enough to be my parents, but they seem to like taking care of me. So I let them.

When I first arrived in London in 2011 to complete my A-levels, I rented a student house in Kensington Church Street, close to my college. The small savings account that my father set up and deposited into every month until the week he died had more money in it than it should, and I didn't know how he'd managed to save it all. But there was enough in the account to pay the exorbitant fees that came with admission and board at what my research said was the best A levels program in London a thousand times over.

I'd never seen so much money in one place, and I was afraid to spend it. He told me the account was to pay for university, and if there was any left, a down payment on a house when I got married. What I found in that account was enough to buy a few houses if I wanted.

I didn't think I'd ever marry the way he hoped. So I planned to use it for the other things he wanted me to. I paid for the best education money could buy and prepaid my rent for the year. And then determined I wouldn't touch another cent unless I had to.

One of my classmates was a barkeep at a place in Kensington and got me a job there, too.

I'd never even opened a bottle of wine at that point, so I spent a few days practicing pulling corks and watched YouTube videos on pulling the perfect pint and mixing the staple cocktails served at pubs. I worked there until Conrad and I crossed paths again.

When he disappeared with what he thought were my lifesavings, I decided that a neighborhood off the beaten path where I could blend in was a better fit for me than the high-traffic tourist trap of Kensington.

I knew just the place. Brixton—where my father had lived as a student before he abandoned London for the bucolic setting of Stow-on-the-Wold.

My tutor in the law department had warned me of the rampant crime and drug dealers that plagued every corner and suggested I take a weekend and get to know the area, see it at night, first thing in the morning, and in the middle of the afternoon before I decided.

So I did.

What I found was a bustling, vibrant neighborhood that was exactly as my father described it. My father, who'd never had a chance to formally study anything, had been a self-taught historian, and he'd regale me with stories he'd read about the famous Windrush years and the way they shaped the area. But the memories that brought more smiles to his face than any other were from The Effra, a pub where he and his friends, newly arrived from Ghana in the 1980s, found hearty welcomes and each other.

When I arrived here nearly six years ago, The Effra was still there and run by the son of the former landlord. It was nestled on a residential road away from the busy Coldharbour Lane, where the majority of night clubs, pubs, and restaurants in Brixton were crammed together.

The Sunday I walked into The Effra, they said they were hiring a barkeep and that the job came with a small flat upstairs. It was kismet. Dominic hired me on the spot, and I accepted before I even saw the place I'd call home.

It's tiny, dated, and the noise from downstairs only relents when the pub closes at midnight. But it's all mine and has allowed me to save up all the money Conrad stole and then some while I went to school full-time.

Six years later, I love living here as much as I love working downstairs.

But tonight, I'm dreading the quiet that's waiting for me. As if being lonely wasn't bad enough, I'm also bored because my one source of entertainment is with a man who probably forgot my name before he woke up the next morning.

* * * *

The buzzer at my door wakes me up with a start. I blink at my watch and groan. How is it already nine o'clock? Last time I looked at the clock, I'd just finished drowning my sorrows in vanilla ice cream topped with an indulgent amount of chocolate sauce and had closed my eyes for what was supposed to be just a few minutes. My buzzer goes again, and I come fully awake and push myself off the sofa.

"Coming," I call as I approach the door. This late, it's either the lady from next door bumming alcohol off me or my best mate from college, Kyle, who never calls before he shows up.

I don't bother looking in the mirror as I pass it. They've both seen me in a lot less than my pajamas.

I can't recall the last time I've felt such an acute regret about a decision as I do about that when I open the door and see Omar Solomon on the other side of it.

I stand there rumpled and pray that I don't have drool dried on my face or crust in the corners of my bugged-out eyes. I give him a once-over and swallow hard. He doesn't look like he's spent the night eating his feelings. His black shirt is open at the top and frames his golden, clean-shaven, exquisitely formed throat like the work of art it is. It fits his broad chest and trim torso like it was cut *just* for him. The cuffs are linked with a small gold "S." And it's tucked into his black trousers. They cling to his slim hips and long legs and give just a hint of the muscle that cords them. His dark hair is wet and slicked back like he just showered, and his rugged jaw is shaved clean. He smells like a sultry summer night and looks like a dream. I want to run my hands all over him.

"Is this a bad time?" he asks. I clasp them in front of me and refocus my eyes on his.

"No, I just... I wasn't expecting you," I say, amazed that I can speak through the buzz of frantic butterflies that are flying around inside me, knocking against my heart, fighting their way up my throat as if they've had enough and want out.

He bites that sensual top lip of his, and his dark hazel eyes, the color of the golden syrup the restaurant uses for their famous sticky toffee puddings, narrow on me, and I recognize that expression from hours of watching video of him on the pitch. He looks just like that right before he makes one of the moves that earned him his nickname of Mastermind, and I hold my breath to see what he's going to do next.

"You left your iPad in my car." His voice is as gruff as it is when he's barking at someone for a misstep in a play.

"Oh, I *wondered* where that got to," I lie through my teeth. "It was good of you to bring it all this way. Sunday would have been fine." I flash a sheepish grin.

"I wanted to bring it sooner, but a pipe burst in the kitchen, and the week got away from me." His gaze narrows on my face, and he winces. "And I don't think I had a chance to say how fucking sorry I am about your nose, Jules."

I forgot I'm sporting a pair of black eyes and still have the bandage across my nose. God, I wish I'd looked in the mirror. "I'm pretty sure you apologized, and it was an accident," I admonish him.

The facsimile of a smile touches his lips, but his eyes remain focused on my face.

"I broke my nose like that a few times. I know how painful it is in the moment, and that it looks worse than it feels for a bit…but of all the breaks and tears I've had, it was the easiest to live with and healed fast. Is it feeling better today?"

"It's a little sore, but the pain meds help." I touch the side of it gingerly. He's right. The worst of it was the impact, and all that blood.

His smile seems forced, and he shuffles his feet. "Okay, good." He pats the pocket of his slacks. "I really like the painting you use for your screen background."

I'm thrown by the change of subject and have to look at the tablet in my hand before I fully understand what he's saying. "Oh, yes, it's by Lynette Yiadom-Boakye, I love all her work, but this painting is my absolute favorite." I run a reverent fingertip over the picture of the dark-skinned, dreadlocked man sitting with a black cat perched on his shoulder. I was drawn to it because the firm set of his jaw reminds me of my father.

He nods in agreement. "Yeah, I looked her up. All her paintings have titles that are as evocative as the actual images."

"I know." I groan in half pleasure, half pain and clutch my iPad to my chest. "This one is titled *In Lieu of Keen Virtue*. She's had a series of private audience events at the Tate Modern running since January. It ends this week."

"I saw. Have you been?"

"I *wish*. The tickets sold out in less than a day. I was on the waitlist in case any came available, but I'm number six hundred and something, and I can't imagine anyone returning those. So I've just resigned myself to wait until she does it again." I sigh heavily.

"Or you can see her on Thursday." He slides his hand into his pocket and pulls out a small envelope that he holds out to me.

"No way," I gasp. I put my iPad down on the console table and grab the envelope. I slide my finger under the flap and pull it open to peer inside, holding my breath until I see what's there with my own eyes.

I let the breath out with a whispered, "Oh my God, I can't believe it." I look up at him, my eyes wide with wonder and a kaleidoscope of butterflies in my stomach. "How did you get these?"

The flush that was already on his cheeks deepens even as he shrugs off my amazement. "I called my agent to ask if he could get his hands on some, and it turned out the Tate comped him these last year. They were just sitting there."

"Wow, that's amazing. In my next life, I want to be a talent agent who gets comped tickets," I quip with a grin.

He nods and smiles, but it doesn't quite reach his eyes.

"Is something wrong?"

"No." He clears his throat. "No, it's just...there are two tickets. I was hoping we could go together and maybe have dinner after. It's Thursday night, and I know you have your shift—"

"I'll get Jodi to cover it for me. It's fine," I interject loudly.

"Perfect." He rocks back on his heels with a nod.

"Thank you so much. This might be the most thoughtful thing anyone's ever done for me," I confess and stare down at the treasure in my hands.

"You're very welcome, Jules." That rare smile of his is fully present, dimples and all, and I feel a surge of pride at putting that hard-won rarity on his face. "I'm glad I could get them. It starts at six. I can pick you up from work and drive us over."

I tap my chin and think about what my day looks like on Thursday. "I'll be in chambers that afternoon. If you don't mind, we could meet at Blackfriars Underground Station at five-thirty. It's only a fifteen-minute walk, so we can take our time."

"It's a date," he says easily. Probably because he's said it countless times before. But I haven't. And it's not just a date. I have a date with *Omar Solomon*. I'm squealing like a maniac on the inside, but I keep my exterior as cool as it can be and smile. "Sounds great."

"Let's exchange phone numbers so we can touch base if anything comes up before."

"Absolutely. I'll give you mine and you can text me so I'll have yours," I effuse, my voice pitched higher than normal. I rattle off my number as he types it into his phone. That maniacal squeal is close to turning itself inside out by the time he looks up and says, "Text sent."

He glances at his watch and winces. "I'm meeting a friend for drinks in Mayfair. I've got to dash, but I'll see you Thursday at Blackfriars at five-thirty?"

"Great," I croak and lift a hand to wave.

"Enjoy the rest of your evening." He doesn't move, though, and his eyes drop to my T-shirt. His lashes beat against each other softly as he blinks in surprise and looks back up at my face. "There's, uh... something on your shirt," he explains and points to it.

I look down at the dark brown dollop of chocolate hanging off the tip of my left nipple.

"It's... Shit," I grumble, annoyed and then mortified. "No. It's not *shit*. It's chocolate sauce," I explain and wish I had a rewind button on this whole encounter. I swipe it off with the tip of my finger and gasp at the jolt of pleasure the friction creates.

"I fucking love chocolate sauce," he says in a low, quiet voice. I look up and find his eyes fixed on the tip of my finger.

My heart is beating a wild timpani that's too fast to be healthy, but I attempt a breezy smile and casual tone when I catch enough breath to speak. "Oh, well, next time you're here, I'll have you in to try some. It's Tesco's brand but really—"

"Can I try it right now?" he asks.

"You mean..." I look at my finger. "You want this?"

"Yes. Please."

I hold my finger out to him, and he leans forward, grabs my wrist, and sucks my finger into his mouth.

I gasp at the hot rasp of his tongue as he twirls it around my finger, and his eyes flick up to meet mine. And if the naked heat in them hadn't nearly given me an arrhythmia, the sensation of his lips closing over it and sucking would certainly have.

My nipples, already primed by my touch and his desire, furl and stiffen with a sharp shot of pleasure I feel all the way to my core.

He releases my finger and lets my go of my wrist.

I instinctively cross my arms over my chest at the same time that he takes a step back and off my welcome mat. "That was delicious. Thank you."

"Okay. Sure." I manage to speak even though I'm sure my lungs have collapsed.

A barely perceptible smile tugs the corners of his lips. "See you Thursday."

I close the door and walk to my kitchen. I pull out the food Dominic sent and heat it up in the microwave.

While I wait, I pick up my phone. It takes me a second to register that the text from a number I don't know is from Omar. "Eeek," I squeal, and open it.

Thursday 5:30, Blackfriars.

I save his number as Break in my phone and put it down. "I'm going on a date with Omar Solomon." And then the words sink in, and my excitement surges and bursts through the dam of stupor. I run back out to the hallway, repeating myself the whole way.

"Oh Jesus," I gasp at my reflection. It's worse than I thought. My eyes are red, my hair is a disaster, and the bandages on my nose make it look twice as big as it is. But my smile says it all. "Omar Solomon asked me on a date." I walk back to my couch, flop onto it, and replay his entire visit. But this time, I let that maniacal squeal loose, and it's so loud that my upstairs neighbor pounds her floor in protest.

"Sorry," I shout, but not even her complaining can dampen my excitement. "My fucking finger was in his *mouth*. And he put it there himself. And we have a date on Thursday." I kick my legs and scream again but this time into one of the throw pillows on my couch.

When I'm finished with my solo celebration, I send Jodi a text and ask if we can switch shifts this week and offer to take her Saturday night one. I know she'll say yes, but I can't wait to see the look on her face when I tell her why I need the night off.

7

PENALTY AND PEACE
Omar

She was twenty minutes late meeting me at Blackfriars. She sat talking to the artist so long past the end of the show that we missed our reservation time by almost two hours and couldn't be seated. And then, we spent the next hour retracing our steps to search for her phone, only to find it at the bottom of her overly large purse.

All of that happened, and it's still been a perfect night. We're walking back to Brixton, all the way from Trafalgar Square where we sat eating kebabs we bought from a hole in the wall place in Leicester Square where they knew her by name and gave her double portions. We stumbled in, tipsy after the two rounds of shots we did at Zoo Bar to congratulate ourselves for finding the phone she never lost.

"Friends from my uni days," she explained as we walked out of the kebab shop and onto St. Martin's Lane with our hands full of food, and I made a note to ask more about that after we ate and were on our way home.

We sat on the steps of the National Gallery, eating and talking about the exhibit and the artist who brought it all to life and missed the last train to Brixton.

I wanted to order an Uber, but she wanted to walk until we could catch one of the night buses. I put my phone away, took her hand, and followed her lead.

It was obvious, as soon as we started down The Millbank, that as well as being an art lover, a bartender, a lawyer, and a ray of sunshine, she's also a history buff. Every few blocks, she'd stop and point out a building or a statue and tell me why it was important.

By the time we reach the Lambeth Bridge, we've already missed two buses that could have taken us home because we've been so deep in conversation. We agreed that we wouldn't talk until we were on a bus unless it was urgent. We've been walking in companionable silence for ten minutes when she puts a hand on my arm and slows her pace.

"This was a prison once."

"Hmm?" I look down at her, and she's looking to our left at a building with a Pantheon-like façade set back from the road.

"That's the Tate Britain," she informs me, and we come to a complete stop.

"Ah, I've always wondered where it was."

"I'm surprised you've heard of it at all. It lives in the Modern's shadow."

"I've heard of it because I used to write donation checks to them."

"A patron of the arts, are you?"

"Hardly. I just did whatever the team's PR company said we should."

"It's got a narrower focus, but the painting of Ophelia by Millais alone is worth a visit. I sat and looked at it for two whole hours before I'd had my fill."

"I'll make a point to visit it before I leave."

"I come here a lot," she says, and her hand slips out of mine as she moves toward the building. "It was built to punish people, but now it's a place of peace."

It's a warm summer night, but she stands with her arms wrapped around herself like she's cold as she gazes at the building.

"What are you thinking?" I wonder aloud.

"About forgiveness. About my dad."

I'm struck by the similarity of our thoughts. I've been thinking a lot about my father, too. I haven't spoken to him in three months. He's stopped calling and only communicates through email and only about work.

"I'd give anything to have him back. But I'm afraid he wouldn't want me even if he was here. I was a terrible daughter most of the time. And when he needed me the most, I was too weak to help him. I didn't set the fire that killed him, but it's my fault he's dead."

I'm struck by several things at once: Her normally animated voice is completely colorless. And she's telling me about her family.

She knows so much about me already, and I barely know anything about her. Unlike me, whose whole adult life is chronicled online, the only place she appears online is her chambers and Inn Websites and her Instagram account.

"It can't be your fault." Before I can add anything else, there's a telltale squeaking of brakes and a gust of wind as the bus blows by us toward the stop at the end of the road. She turns and starts to run for it. "Come on, we can catch it," she shouts over her shoulder. She's running fast and reaches the bus a few steps ahead of me just as its doors are closing. "Wait!" She leaps from the sidewalk and onto the bus and uses her arms to stop the doors. When I catch up, she's panting and grinning. "Slow poke," she teases and dashes up the stairs.

My Gucci loafers are hardly made for walking and definitely not made for running, and when I drop into the seat next to her, I wince and stretch my slightly sore knee.

"And that's why I always have trainers in my bag. Gotta be ready to run at any moment." She turns in her seat and looks out of the window as the bus rambles off the bridge and swings onto Kennington Road. "Have you been to Vauxhall? If not, you should. It's—"

The light on the bus is harshly bright in contrast to the dark night lit only by the moon and an occasional streetlamp, and it takes me a minute to adjust. When I do, the redness in her eyes says what her lighthearted voice doesn't. I put a hand on her arm to interrupt her. "You were saying something before the bus came, about your dad? What did you do that you feel guilty for?"

8

PERSUASION
Jules

I've been staring at my hands since he asked about my dad, and he's been sitting waiting patiently for several minutes before I can pull my thoughts together.

I don't know what I was thinking when I started talking about my dad in front of that museum. I'd had too much to drink, too much to eat, and was happier than I could remember being when we approached the Tate. I wasn't going to say anything, but there was a tug of something as I walked by that made me stop. I didn't realize it was guilt, and I answered Omar's question.

I know if my father were here, he'd be standing by my side. I know he wouldn't blame me for leaving him the way I did. And as soon as I said it, I heard his voice in my head saying, "Don't be silly." And wished I could take it back.

I started my tourist guide routine as soon as Omar sat down, hoping he wouldn't press me on it. I should have known better than to rely on a fair-weather friend like hope.

I don't know him well enough to tell him the whole truth. But I don't want to lie to him, either. So I tell him the truth as I know it.

"The night my father died, there was a fire, and I woke up in time to get out of my room. I ran to his and tried to wake him up. But when I couldn't, I ran out of the house to get help. The roof over our bedrooms collapsed minutes after I got outside. While I was still calling for help. I left him to die alone in that house. I have nightmares that he woke up when the ceiling caved in on him and was scared and wondering where I was and that he died terrified and heartbroken while I was outside, safe. And tonight, I was so happy. And I didn't think about him once this whole evening. But that museum always reminds me of him, and I felt ashamed that I was so happy when I should be dead, too." I brush at a tickle on my cheek and am surprised when my hand comes away wet. "I didn't think I had any tears left."

He takes my hand in his and squeezes it. "I'm so sorry. How old were you?"

"Twelve," I say and have to swallow a sob and turn my face toward the window to brush away more tears.

"Jesus. I'm so sorry. You were a baby."

"It's more than half my life, you'd think I could make it through a date without crying, right?" I try to effect a laugh, but it sounds like a strangled cough. He lets go of my hand and drapes his arm over my shoulder, pulling me into the curve of his side. It's been ages since anyone has held me like this, but my body remembers, and I find a comfortable crook to nestle against. I bury my face in his shirt and sit up. "You wear neroli oil."

"Yeah, I do. Is that on Google, too?" he asks with a chuckle.

"No, my dad was a chandler—a candlemaker. And he grew most of the plants he used to scent them. But his favorite was the oil from his hothouse bitter orange trees—which is where neroli comes from—and he put it in everything: soaps, cremes, lotions. He even tried making cocktails from it. It smells much better than it tastes." I laugh at the memory of him spitting it out after one sip.

I let my eyes drift shut as the bus sways down Brixton Lane toward home and let the orgy of citrus, green grass, and air with a whisper of honey take me back to the last time I remember being truly happy.

Until tonight.

I'm sure my tears and melodrama have ruined any hope of this turning into a night of lost virtue and orgasms. The bus is one light away from the stop outside the station, and I sit up and unglue myself from his side to take a deep breath and compose myself. "I'm so sorry, Omar. I didn't mean to spoil the mood."

"Don't apologize for your honest emotions. I'm honored that you feel like you can share them with me. And you're not alone. I used to think I was all cried out, too. But I wasn't. Unfortunately, I don't think we ever are. No matter how long ago the hurt happened."

I remember what he shared with me in the car on the way home from the hospital. "I'm sorry about your mom."

He sighs deeply, lifts his arm off my shoulder, and presses his palms to his thighs, staring unseeingly at them. "Me, too. She and my dad split when I was thirteen. And it was my fault."

"Oh, come on. How can that be?" I ask, taken aback to hear him say it with so much certainty. "You were thirteen."

"One weekend, she took me to soccer practice and got drunk while she waited for me in the car. She was an alcoholic. It had been a problem for as long as I could remember. But that was the first time she'd been clearly too drunk to drive. So she asked me to."

"Is that legal?"

"No. But I'd driven a few golf carts, and it was either that or call my dad. So I did. And about a mile from home, I side-swiped someone on their bike. Knocked him clean off. When I got out to check on him, his eyes were closed. I thought he was dead. I've never been so scared before or since. I forced myself to stick my finger under his nose to feel for air." He closes his eyes and shudders.

I cover my mouth to muffle my gasp of shock and put a gentle hand on his back. "When I looked back at the car, she'd moved herself into the driver's seat and yelled for me to get in the other side. Then she called the police. She took responsibility. Told them she'd hit him. She was arrested for driving under the influence. The biker broke an arm and had a concussion but otherwise was fine."

"Was your mother charged?"

"Yes, with a felony DUI." He stops and takes a deep breath, his eyes closed. His hand grips the seat in front of us so tightly that his knuckles are white. "My dad hired her a good lawyer. She plead guilty, didn't get jail time, but was ordered to rehab and was slapped with a pretty hefty fine. While she was gone, my father filed for divorce. It was the final straw for him. I went to visit her once and told her I wanted to tell my dad. She shouldn't have to pay for something I did. She said she'd talk to him herself. But when she came to the house, he wouldn't even let her in. He threatened to call the police if she didn't leave. So she did. I just stood there. Watching. And didn't say a word."

"Why? I mean, do you think it would have made a difference?"

"I don't know. I won't ever know. I was too scared to tell him then. The day their divorce was final, my father told us she'd left the state and didn't want to be contacted by us again. And I knew it was because of me."

"Oh no." I can't hold back that reaction. I'm traumatized just listening to it. I can't imagine how he felt living through that. I know what it's like to pay for something that wasn't of your doing. But his mother was no victim.

He lets out a big breath, and his head falls forward so he's looking at the floor of the bus. "I didn't know where she was for almost fifteen years. But when I found her again, I did everything in my power to make it up to her. She died before I really could. I don't know what's worse, my guilt or my grief. But I had to get away. So I took a year-long leave of absence from my company. I came here to renovate this house I bought before I left. But the distance hasn't done what I hoped."

I don't know what to say. But I don't think he's looking for advice or platitudes. So I wrap my arms around him awkwardly from the side and hug him as hard as I can.

He hugs me back. "I've never told anyone that story."

"Thank you for telling me. I promise it won't go any further."

The bus hisses to a stop, and he lifts his head to look out of the window. "This is your stop. Let me walk you home."

We get off the bus and walk in silence all the way to Rattray Road. He follows me through the gate and up the stairs to my front door. I put the key in the lock, and he covers my hand with his.

"Can we have dinner tomorrow?"

"Yes. Absolutely." I smile, relieved that he wants to despite the chaos of this evening.

"Do you have any dietary restrictions?"

"Uh, yeah—I'm vegan." I say it with the trepidation all people who eat a less than conventional diet feel when asking for an accommodation to be made. "But I can eat anywhere as long as they have a salad."

He shakes his head. "No, I'll find a vegan place."

"I can recommend some places if you'd like," I offer and relax into a smile.

"I'm good. Unless you have an absolute favorite or a place you've been wanting to try." He raises an eyebrow in question.

"Surprise me," I quip. But my grin dies when our eyes meet, and his burn with indecision. "What's wrong?"

"Nothing. I think I'm going to say good night here."

"Oh, okay. Of course you must be completely knackered. Thank you for walking me home." I turn to open my door and hide my disappointment.

Despite the maneuvering I've done to get him here, I don't want to manipulate this moment. The decisiveness and commitment to his choices that he displays on the field is one of the things I find most attractive about him. If he came all this way and can't find the inspiration to step inside, then I don't want him to. The fantasy I have about the day I lose my virginity doesn't include me having to coerce my partner.

I push the door open and turn to face him with a smile. He doesn't return my smile. He doesn't move in for a kiss. He just stands there, looking torn.

So I say goodnight and force myself to close the door.

9

SHOW AND TELL
Omar

I should leave, I really should.

But I can't. She's on the other side of that door thinking I'm an idiot, and I don't blame her.

I was planning on going in with her until I saw her door and had a vision of her in a white T-shirt with a fat dollop of chocolate clinging to her unrestrained and jutting nipple. The memory of the sweet and salty flavors on her finger in my mouth made my dick so hard it hurts. And then licking off whatever traces of it are left on her lips, on her tongue.

She's sweet, and open, and easy while I'm...an acquired taste. Who I am in person pales in comparison to the fantasy people have based on whatever they've read about me. And I don't want to get involved and find out she's a stage five clinger who falls in love as easily as she breathes. Been there, done that, and once was enough to last me a lifetime.

But I knock on her door anyway, because I simply can't do anything else.

She's changed and is wearing a bathrobe that's gaping open.

Yes?" she asks, cocking her head to the side and watching me, her expression more serious than I've ever seen it.

"Ask me in, please." My voice is tense, tight with the effort it's taking me not to say more.

Her smile is slow and sexy, and a bolt of lust shoots through me. Fuck, I'm asking for trouble. "I did that when I left my iPad in your car."

She walks backward into the house, her eyes on me alight with the invitation.

"I'm fucking relieved to hear that," I admit, my voice finding its legs with every step I take toward her. My chest expands with confidence now that I've made up my mind.

She walks until her back is pressed to the door that leads to the sitting room, and I stop mere inches from her.

I glance down at her and smile at her pretty red toes. "You've got nice feet."

She looks down at them. "The things you notice," she says with a smile before she loosens the belt around her waist so the robe gapes open and slides off her shoulders.

My chest constricts, and my balls ache. She stands before me, naked from the waist up. Her body is beautiful. Her narrow waist is draped in two strings of tiny glass beads. Her skin glows and looks so smooth that I imagine it feels like silk. Her unbound breasts are small, barely a handful, with large dusky brown nipples that are puckered already and begging to be sucked.

I take a step toward her, putting me just an arm's length away. "You are so beautiful. I want to touch you. Can I?"

"I want you to, so much," she says and wraps her small hand around my wrist lifting it to her breast. Her nipple, already hard, swells against my hand.

I roll the plump bud in my palm, and she gives a short little moan. "What do you like? You like them sucked?" I lean down and pull her left nipple into my mouth for a quick hard tug. I take the other one in my hand and squeeze.

"Oh," she cries out, and I lift my head to watch her face. Her eyes are closed, her lip caught between her teeth. I squeeze it again, and she whimpers. Her breath comes in shallow pants, and she rolls her hips.

"Pinched, then?" I ask the obvious.

"I don't...I don't know. I've never done anything like this before," she whispers.

My libido clatters over that speed bump and comes to a screeching halt.

"Shit. And I knew that. I didn't mean to... I just saw you like that and forgot myself," I croak and then wince at the look of horror and humiliation on her face.

"You knew that? Am I that bad at this?" She crosses her arms over her chest and steps away at the same time I do. "Oh my God, Reena."

"No, Reena told me," I say at the same time.

"God, that woman and her mouth," she mutters.

"It slipped out. And honestly, I'm glad I know."

I try to meet her eye, but she turns her back to me and tugs her robe back up. Her smooth, shapely back disappears before I've had anything close to enough of it.

"Jules—"

She covers her face with her hands. "Oh God, I don't think I've ever been so embarrassed in my life. You can just go if you want. Forget this ever happened."

I put a hand on each of her shoulders and give her a quick but firm shake. "No. I don't want to go. Or forget this. I said it all wrong. Please turn around."

She shakes her head no, but her spine loses some of its rigidity.

"Come on," I coax and squeeze her shoulders gently. "I promise I'll make it worth the effort."

Her whole body sags in resignation, and she spins around to face me. Her eyes focus on a spot on my shoulder, and she blows out a breath. "I'm listening."

I don't know what it is about her that has me spilling my guts and being fucking vulnerable. Maybe it's because she's so vulnerable and open, too. And I've already told her my deep dark secret, this is nothing. "I spent my twenties having sex with women who I found attractive but had nothing in common with. I did it because it suited my lifestyle, and after my parents' clusterfuck of a marriage, a committed relationship was the last thing on my radar. At the same time, I'm not someone who forms shallow connections. But that's all I got when I jumped into bed with someone before I found out they were an asshole, or hated animals, or one of my friends, or traveling, or some other deal breaker."

"Okay... I'm not an asshole, I love cats. I love the one friend of yours I know, and even though I haven't done much of it, I love to travel."

I laugh at the expectant look on her face. "I was just using those as examples. But what I'm trying to say is no matter how many nights that chocolate on your nipple haunts my dreams, I don't want to rush this."

She blinks rapidly at her chest where her nipples press against the thin fabric, crosses her arms, and runs her narrowed, assessing eyes over me. "Are you serious? Or is this...a nice way of letting me down?"

I laugh. "I'm serious. Is that so strange?"

"It's just... Reena told me you were a complete commitment-phobe. I'm not looking for a relationship, either. I thought this would be perfect for you."

"So in other words, you want to use me for sex."

Her eyes widen in horror. "That's not what I meant. God—I just—"

"I'm joking." I laugh, but she doesn't. "Jules, I've had a crush on you for months."

"You have? On me?" She points at herself like there's someone else here.

"Yes. At first, just because your smile lit up the room. But then, because of the way you treat your coworkers and regulars like family. You're kind and funny and really, really forgiving. And did I mention your smile?"

She chuckles quietly. "You did. Thank you for saying all of that. I'm glad you like me for me."

I take her hand. "I do. I'm not looking for a relationship either. I'm going home. My first time was such a disaster, and it took me a long time to find my confidence as a lover after it. I wish I'd been with someone who knew what they were doing. And someone who cared about me. I don't want you to have any regrets I was your first."

She frowns. "Okay."

I turn her hand over in mine and inspect it while I try to find the right words to answer that. "I know the package I present. But I also know the way we see people changes once we know how they think. I come with a few warning labels that you need to be aware of."

"Okay, tell me," she demands.

"I'd rather show you."

She tugs her hands free and snatches a notepad off the small console table in her entryway and hands it to me.

"So write them down and show me now."

I snicker and take the notepad from her and put it back on the table. "I mean by spending time together."

Her smile peeks back out, and she bites her lip. "I like the sound of that."

"Great." I step back before I do something crazy like suck her neck until I leave a mark.

Fuck me.

Please let her be real.

Her eyes dart away from me and down the hall, and I discover a new shade of Jules—shy and uncertain. "Do you want to come in?"

"Yeah, I'd love to see your place."

"Okay." She walks through the thin swinging door that separates the kitchen from the rest of the living area. "Sorry for the mess, I've got a shipment of candles going out."

"You make candles, too?" I call as I walk into her sparsely decorated sitting room.

"My dad taught me. It's a side hustle. But my kitchen is too small to make more than a couple dozen at a time."

She waves her arm toward the small sitting room. "This is where I do everything but sleep and cook."

I glance around her living room. She has one wall entirely covered with photos. Mainly of a much younger her. Some of her with a man I assume is her dad. And interspersed with those are pictures of Aretha Franklin, Chaka Khan, Tina Turner, Madonna, Janet Jackson, Beyonce, and several of Alison Hinds. "You like music?" I ask when she comes out of the kitchen and joins me in front of the pictures.

"I *love* music. And concerts and these women, man—I could watch them perform and never get tired."

"You sing?"

"I wish," she sighs and then grins. "But if I could the way I do in my head? Darling, the world would be like Beyonce *who?*"

"You're funny."

"I'm not trying to be."

Which only makes it better. We plop onto the couch, and she tucks her legs under her and leans forward to touch the chain of pearls I wear around my wrist. "These are beautiful."

They were my mother's, but I don't want to bring that up again. "So are you. Broken nose and all." I brush a lock of hair off her shoulder, and her lips part. I want to slip my tongue in there and see if her mouth is as sweet as her finger was. But if I do that, I won't be able to stop. She leans closer, her eyes dropping to half-mast.

I stand so suddenly she yelps and leans back. "Sorry, I just realized how late it is. I've got the flooring people coming at eight in the morning."

"Oh, okay. Cool. So I'll see you tomorrow for dinner?"

"Yeah. I'll text you in the afternoon after I make the reservation. And I'm driving this time." I lean down to kiss her cheek and then get the hell out of there.

10

HALF FULL GLASSES
Jules

"It's been an entire month. We've been to dinners, art shows, to the cinema, to fucking Bayswater to shop for curtains. He holds my hand, he opens the door for me, he texts to say good morning. But he hasn't even tried to kiss me again, and I don't know what I'm doing wrong." I drop onto my bed with a frustrated grunt, and my phone flies out of my hands and clatters onto the floor. "Hold on," I shout and then snag it and hold it back up so Reena can see my face.

But all I see is the top of her dark head bent over her laptop. "Look at me when I'm freaking out."

She holds up one finger and then goes back to whatever she's typing. I glare at the screen. "What are you working on that's more important than this?"

She stops typing and moves her mouse around, finally looking at me. "I've got a brief due on Monday. And I told you already, he's a commitment-phobe." She widens her eyes as if to say, "What part of that didn't you understand?"

I shake my head in disagreement, but my stomach sinks at the reminder. "We've been on dates, he comes over several times a week. But he's never invited me over to his place."

"Really?" She frowns. "Not once?"

"No. He's doing renovations, but he's still living there, so it can't be that bad." I groan.

A month ago, I thought we'd spend a couple of dates talking a bit and then he'd fall all over me because he couldn't stand not touching me the way I couldn't stand not touching him. At first, I thought he was waiting for my nose to heal. The last of the dressing has been gone for a week. I invited him over when I got the all-clear from my doctor to resume all physical activity. "He came over and gave me a scalp massage that I was sure was foreplay. But then he kissed me on the cheek and left like he always does."

"That doesn't sound like him," she says with a frown.

"Could he be sleeping with someone else?" I ask Reena. My stomach bottoms out at the thought of him spending time with me but sleeping with someone else. "How would I even know?"

"You wouldn't. And I doubt it."

I squeeze my eyes shut to banish the visual of him naked, kissing someone else. It turns my insides to mush. "Oh God. Am I being an idiot?"

"Jules, you're normally so optimistic."

"Well, I'm not my normal self. I feel so…exposed." I draw my knees up and rest my cheek on them. "I'm falling for a rich, sexy, famous man who's only passing through. I'm stupid, aren't I?"

She slams her computer closed and picks up her phone so that her face is finally fully in frame. "Honestly, babe? I'm surprised. Last week you said, 'His commitment phobia and transiency is this thinking woman's catnip.'"

I narrow my eyes at her terrible impersonation. "I do not sound like that."

She smiles. "In my head you do. And I'm glad you've had the opportunity to prove yourself wrong."

"I'm not a thinking woman after all?" I say with more than just a little self-pity.

"That you're a feeling woman. And maybe I'm judging him based on outdated information. The fact that you've spent so much time together means something. And I could see that night that he likes you."

"If that's true, then why hasn't he kissed me again?"

"I don't know. But I also don't know why, when it comes to him, your usual glass half full approach doesn't apply."

"That's not true. If it was I wouldn't have approached him in the first place. I'm just not sure what I have to show for it. What if he is having sex with someone else while he grooms me for my defloweing or whatever?"

"Why don't you ask him?"

"I have some pride."

She sighs heavily and shakes her head. "Well, I hope that pride will be comforting when your vagina finally grows cobwebs. If you want to know, ask him. And if you don't feel like you can, then maybe he's not right for you."

I groan and then wiggle my shoulder to shake it off. "You're right. I'm going to put on my big girl knickers and just find out." I stand and rush into the bathroom. I'm covering Jodi's shift tonight. I glance at the clock on my wall. "I have just enough time."

"Time for what?"

"To fill this glass the rest of the way up."

11

AMBUSH
Omar

"Dad asked Mimosa to marry him."
Layel's text comes on a day where everything has gone wrong.

"Good for him?" I text back. They've been playing house for years.

"Glad they're making it official."

"I'll let you know when they set a date. You should call him."

I ignore that last text.

"I can't believe Mimosa's leaving LA."

"She's not. He's moving back to LA, to be with her."

That makes me sit up straight.

"What about his job at the fund?"

"He'll stay as long as it takes you to find a replacement, but I'm pretty sure he's decided."

I'm stunned silent and knocked nearly breathless by her bombshell.

I open my phone app to my favorites and call the first name on the list.

My dad picks up on the first ring. "Omar?"

"Hi, Dad." I don't know why I expected his voice to sound different after all this time, but it doesn't. And the months we haven't talked melt away.

"I guess you've heard the news."

"All of it. Yes. You're leaving the Fund?"

"Yes. I was only there because we were doing it together."

"We were hardly doing it together. You ran it. I was the face of it."

"You were the energy behind it. At least for me. And with you gone, it's not worth the sacrifices I made to take it."

"I'm not gone, Dad, and we're still doing it together. I just needed a break. And I've been addressing the items you send my way."

He sighs. "Listen, everyone knows we're not on speaking terms, and this tantrum you've thrown has undermined my authority."

"Tantrum? My mother died, and I found out you'd been lying to me for more than a decade. I haven't taken a break from work since I was fifteen. And if your email wasn't effective, you could have picked up the phone anytime and called me."

"Frankly, I'm not ready to speak with you either, son. Until you can apologize to me, I'm not sure when I'll be ready to. I know you're grieving, and I understand that you need a break. But I'm not going to put my life on hold for you. I'll give you until the end of the year."

My disappointment in his attempt to make himself the aggrieved party is only outweighed by my anger. "You know, this might actually be for the best."

"What?" He sounds shocked.

"You've done an incredible job, but maybe it's time for me to have a CEO who understands who he works for."

"I've given up everything for you."

"No, but you forced my mother to. And then you turned your back on her."

"I didn't force her to do anything. She made her choices."

"I don't want to rehash this, Dad."

"Fine," he snaps. "You know...you've made me so proud your entire life. I used to think it wasn't possible for you to disappoint me. How wrong I was." He hangs up.

Fuck. This has gone from bad to worse. My gut twisted when Layel said he was leaving. But after that conversation, I really do think it's for the best. He doesn't respect me, and I'm too angry still.

I rub my temples to try and ease the pounding between them. I don't want to think about any of that shit. I came here so I didn't have to.

I pick up the phone again to text Jules and then put it back down. I'm in a weird mood, and I'm not sure even her bright smile is enough to lift it. And I don't want to take it out on her.

But damn. I miss her.

She's a fireball of mystery and magic and is as complicated and clever as she is beautiful. She enchants and terrifies me. I've dated women who've made me feel both of those things, but never all at once.

I've also never spent this much time getting to know someone I wanted to sleep with. We've even established a routine. We eat dinner out unless it's Monday or Thursday when she's behind the bar. Those nights I walk down to the pub and wait for her to get off. We go up to her place and watch TV. Or just talk—about everything from politics to prose. And we laugh. A lot.

She hasn't complained about me being a homebody. She hasn't asked me to buy her anything. I haven't read any of the personal things I've told her about me in the gossip sheets. She's always game when I ask her out. She texts just to say hello. She's perfect.

And damn, I miss her. It's Saturday night. We didn't have plans, but we never really do. And I haven't heard from her since this morning.

I send her a text: **"Where are you?"**

A text comes right back.

"Outside."

"Outside, what?"

"Your house. Come to the window."

I lean over my sofa and pull the curtain back to look down at the street. Her head is tilted up, her eyes scanning the row of windows for my face. I tap on the glass, and she waves.

I am not keen on unannounced visitors. And the lower level of the house is still a construction site. But the instant I see her, I know I was wrong. Her smile is a cure for everything. And right now, I'm happier to see her than I think I've been to see anyone in my whole life.

"One second." I text her and take a quick inventory of my place. It looks the way it always does, which is barely lived in. There's a loud rumble of thunder, and I stop dawdling, sniff my armpits, and press the button that unlocks the front door. I walk out onto the landing and am halfway down the stairs just as the door signals that it's open.

When I get to the bottom, Jules is standing in my foyer as fresh as a daisy and prettier than anyone has a right to be on a gloomy Saturday night.

She's wearing a T-shirt that reads "Not Your Princess" gathered and tied in a knot at her midriff. And any irony created by her silver leggings and her sparkly pink trainers is quashed by the fire in her eyes.

"What're you doing here?" I call as I descend the narrow staircase.

"I made some candles. With neroli oil." She holds up a small brown bag. I take it from her.

"Wow, for me?"

She nods. "A housewarming gift."

I'm touched by her thoughtfulness and open the bag to have a peek at the two glass jars inside. "Thank you. As you can see, this level isn't ready for visitors, but they'll do great upstairs."

"Is that why you haven't asked me over?" she asks but doesn't quite meet my eyes before she turns to survey the first floor of my house.

"Yeah, but you're welcome any time. Seriously."

Her smile is sheepish when she looks at me again. "Thank you. I'd love to see it during the day. Those stained-glass windows must be glorious."

I'm thrilled she noticed. "They really are. Come by any time, and I'll show you around. Maybe even get your opinion."

"I'd love that. Thank you." She looks past me and up the stairs. "I didn't interrupt anything?"

Just my father pulling the floor out from beneath me. But I don't want to ruin my budding good mood by bringing that up, so I shake my head. "I was just flipping through my mail and texting my sister when you got here. Do you want to come up? It's only got barebones furniture and the curtains you helped me pick out."

She nods. "I'd love that. But I can't stay long. Jodi called in her favor, and I'm covering for her tonight. I have to be behind the bar in less than thirty minutes."

"Plenty of time." I hold my hand out to her. There's a beat of hesitation before she takes it. But when our palms connect, my mind clears of everything but how good and natural it feels to touch her. I've kept my hands to myself for the whole month, but only because I don't trust myself to stop with just a touch. But it gets harder to resist every time I see her. I can't wait to know what the rest of her feels like. Tastes like. I wonder what she'd do if I asked her to spread her legs for me.

"How was your day?" she asks, and I flush at the turn my thoughts just took and refocus on the present.

"Long, lots of issues with my contractor and a lot of paperwork to sign for work. But things are looking up now."

She laces our fingers together and tugs me to a stop. She's looking at the floor, and her shoulders are visibly tense.

I put my finger under her chin and tip her head up. "What's wrong?"

"Omar..." Her eyes are clouded by whatever is causing the furrow between her raven brows. "I didn't come over to bring you candles. I mean, I made them for you. But that's not why I came. This is an ambush."

"It is?" I frown. She nods but cringes as if she's embarrassed. "And what were you hoping to accomplish with the nicest ambush in human history?"

She bites her lip and fiddles with our intertwined fingers. "I wanted to make sure you weren't throwing wild orgies in here."

A laugh bursts from my gut, and I throw my head back.

"Did you get to know me and not like me as much as you thought?" she asks in a quiet voice.

My humor fizzles instantly. "Why would you think that?"

She lets go of my hand and squares her shoulders. Her eyes narrow, and her mouth thins to a straight, displeased frown. "Well? Yes or no?" she demands, one hand on her hip as she waits for me to answer.

"No. If I had, I would have told you and not spent nearly every day of the last month with you," I say in complete surprise.

She crosses her arms over her chest. "When you said we should spend time together before things got physical, I didn't know you meant you weren't going to touch me at all."

"I didn't mean that. We were touching just now."

She firms her jaw. "Omar, we've been on countless dates. We've shared dozens of meals. We hang out all night, say goodbye, and then talk on the phone until one of us falls asleep."

"Why do you make it sound like that's a bad thing?"

"Because we haven't even gotten to first base. And I don't understand why not. Did my tears turn you off?"

"Of course not. Nothing has turned me off."

Her frown deepens, and she continues as if she didn't hear me. "Did I fart when I fell asleep? Do I smell bad in general? Talk too much? What is it?" She throws her hands up with an exasperated frown on her face.

God, I'm an idiot. I put a hand on each of her shoulders and lower my head so we're eye to eye. "You didn't do anything. I was just trying to give you time to get to know *me*. I'm—"

"Yes, I know. You're an acquired taste." She puts air quotes around the words and rolls her eyes.

"What does *that* mean?"

"It means, who isn't?"

"You get along with everyone you meet."

"I do not get along with everyone I meet."

"Yes, you do," I insist.

She purses her lips. "No, I *don't*. It's my job to be friendly to the punters, Omar. Or to leave them be if that's what they want. And I've read your warning labels. You can be rigid and judgmental and not particularly forgiving. You can be overbearing and a bit of a know-it-all. And you're an introvert."

She reads me like a book, but her honesty is refreshing. "And I'm not going to change."

"I didn't ask you to."

"Not yet."

She scowls at me. "Not *ever*. If I wanted you to change, I wouldn't be here."

"You're saying that now, but wait until l annoy you."

She groans. "You've already annoyed me, Omar. And I haven't been shy about telling you."

I nod in agreement. "Touché."

She looks down at the floor and draws a pattern with the toe of her shoe. "Listen, the worst thing you can do besides ghosting me is to lead me on. So if you aren't interested, I want you to tell me."

God, her vulnerability makes me weak. But to be the source of her insecurity is unacceptable. I've been so focused on doing this right that I've let that override our natural progression.

"Jules, come here, let's talk." I sit down on my pale blue couch and wave her over.

She shakes her head and crosses her arms. "I came here tonight because I wanted to see if maybe you had some secret sex den or a bit on the side. And you're just… *here.*" She splays her hands and waves them around the room. "Alone. Doing *nothing.*"

I chuckle at the consternation on her face. "Come on," I coax with a hand outstretched.

"I'm serious." She stamps her foot.

It's fucking cute, but I don't dare say so. I stand and walk to meet her where she's planted herself. "So am I."

She takes a deep breath and meets my eyes again. Her amaretto gaze is clear and resolute. "I appreciate you giving me time to make an informed decision. But even someone as brilliant and determined as you can't see the future. Who knows? Maybe in another month, I'll hate your guts. But *right now,* in this dimension of time and space we're sharing, your hard-earned smile makes me as happy as a sunny day in the middle of winter. And after a month of getting to know you, I'm insanely hot for you. I want you to be my first. But only if you want—oh!" She gasps just as my mouth comes down on her sweet lips, and the contact sends little prickles of heat down my spine and blood rushing down to my rapidly rising erection.

She's stiff for half a second and then she melts.

Her fingers clutch at the sides of my shirt, and I cup her face in my hands, letting my lips sink into her so very soft ones. I didn't even know lips could be so soft. Her mouth is minty sweet and hot when she opens for me, and my tongue slips inside. I wrap an arm around her waist, cup her ass with my other one, and pull her flush against me so she can feel how badly I want exactly what she does. She's six inches shorter than me, so my dick nestles in her belly instead of where I want it. I lift her with one arm around her waist, and her legs wrap around my hips like she's done it a thousand times. The plush heat between her thighs envelops my throbbing dick. I cup her ass with my free hand and thrust up. She breaks the kiss on a loud gasp, and her eyes pop open a second after mine. I walk us back until my shins hit the couch and I turn so I'm seated and she's straddling me. I grasp her hips and roll them over my dick, and she whimpers, "More of that please." I oblige her.

Even through the layers of fabric that separate us, the friction we make is electric. When her kiss-swollen lips part on a silent moan, I lean forward to nip the bottom one and trail kisses over her chin and down the soft, sweet-smelling column of her throat. "I want to pull your panties to the side and bury myself inside of you," I tell her in between long sucks of her neck.

She's breathing hard, and her hips are writhing. "Do it, please."

I slip a hand under her skirt and trail up her silken thigh until I reach the holy grail.

Somewhere in the distance there's a shrill ringing, but I'm senseless and blind to anything but giving in to the need I've denied for weeks. My fingers are breaching the lace edge of her panties when suddenly the only thing I feel is cool air.

My eyes snap open, and I have to blink twice to clear the fog of lust from them. She's standing in front of me, holding her phone.

"Thank the stars I set this alarm. I have fifteen minutes to be at work."

I run a hand through my hair and nod. "I know. I didn't expect that kiss to escalate. It was supposed to be a deposit on later. But I touched you and—"

"We caught fire," she finishes for me, and we share a smile that tugs at my heart and my cock.

"That was so hot. I'm sorry I made us wait. But I can promise you…this will be the last time you'll have to ask me for something twice."

Her smile seems to double. "If you don't stop looking at me like that, I'll fall in love with you, and then we'll be in real trouble."

My heart flings itself against my sternum, and my mouth takes the leap it can't. "Sounds like a good kind of trouble to me. And this between us feels like the start of something special."

"Omar." She breathes my name in a heady sigh that I wish I was close enough to inhale. She stares at me through wide, wet eyes and presses a hand to her chest.

Thunder rolls and cracks the quiet dusk, and she drops my hand and rushes over to the window where she pulls the curtain back and peers outside. "It's really about to pour."

"I'll drive you."

Her eyes bulge. "No way. The only thing sexier than you is your car and the way you drive it." She tilts her head back and mimes fanning herself. "It's too hot for me to handle on a normal day. If we get in there now, that's where we'll stay."

I think my blacked-out Aston Martin Vantage is sexy as fuck too, but I raise a skeptical eyebrow. "You'll have to tell me more about how I drive later."

"I can tell you now if you'll walk me down."

"Sure." I take the hand she holds out to me and reluctantly let her lead me to the stairs. But only because I like the words coming out of her mouth. I'd rather walk her to my bedroom.

"You drive it like you own it *and* the road you're on in equal measure. And when you change gears, your shoulders bunch up, it's so fucking sexy. I love watching you."

I flush at the compliment and lift our joined hands to my mouth to press a kiss to hers "Then at least allow me to pick you up. What time do you get off?"

"Ten, but it's Calypso night. Jodi said she and Dom will be back to catch the last couple of hours. Dom hates to dance, and I told her I'd stay after the shift. You could join us."

"I'll be there. But I'm not dancing," I promise.

She grins, wraps a hand around my neck, and presses a too fleeting, too chaste kiss on my lips. "That was just a down payment on later."

"That's not even a deposit on a down payment. Come back here," I growl and wrap my arms around her waist to drag her back. I nip her lower lip.

She squeals and squeezes herself out of my grasp. When I reach for her again, she jumps away with a bubbling laugh that I'm instantly addicted to.

"I've got to go. It's about to pour, and I don't have an umbrella." She hurries to the door and flings it open.

"What kind of Londoner doesn't carry an umbrella?"

She stops to look over her shoulder with a smile that I decide is my favorite one of hers so far. "An optimistic one. Thank you for being worth the effort." And with a wave of her fingers, she's gone.

"Fuck me." I lean against the closed door and chuckle. She's worried about falling in love with me, but I've been falling for weeks. It's been a month of blue balls, cold showers, and marathon masturbation sessions when I get back from her place. But tonight, it feels worth it.

Over the last month, the beauty that first caught my notice has become the secondary driver of my attraction and respect for her. My dick gets hard for her work ethic and her empathy, too. If I'm completely honest, part of the reason I've been taking my time is because being with her feels so good, and I want to savor it. But my dad's call tonight did more than widen the rift between us. It's killed any fantasy I might have had about staying here indefinitely. I was worried about hurting her when the time came for me to leave. Now I'm more worried about how much it's going to hurt me to say goodbye.

* * * *

At ten o'clock, I head down the stairs showered, groomed, and ready for whatever the night brings. I stop at the mirror hanging at the foot of them and do a doubletake at the goofy smile on my face. Life may give me a lot of shit, but the last month has been one of the most contented in recent memory. I grab my keys and my wallet and whistle the whole way.

12

MELTING
Jules

I've always loved to dance. I wasn't kidding when I told Omar if I could, that's what I'd be doing with my life. The closest I got to having lessons was dancing in the mirror with my childhood best friend until we were sweaty and exhausted. But give me a crowded dance floor with a good DJ, and I'll give you my best impression of the dancing queen I've always wanted to be.

Tonight, the Calypso music has been just right. Jodi and I haven't been dancing long when Omar walks in. But my T-shirt is already sticking to my sweat-slicked back.

I wave at him, and he nods in response and heads to the bar where Dom is sitting. I'm about to go say hello when "Dolla Wine" by Colin Lucas comes on. It's one of those songs that, no matter how tired you are, will bring you to the dance floor. Jodi grabs my hands and draws me back to the center of the throng of people.

Nights like this draw in a crowd that's made up of first-timers and occasional patrons. And it's obvious who they are because they surround Jodi and me, grinding and touching in a way that no one who comes here regularly would.

Dominic appears behind her suddenly and whispers something in her ear. She waggles a finger at me to say goodbye and lets him pull her into one of the dark corners. As soon as she's gone, a hand slides across my abdomen and pulls me back into a hard chest. "Hey," I cry and push him away. He starts to come back for more, but something over my shoulder makes his eyes go wide. He doesn't look at me again as he dances away and sways his hips into the woman directly behind him.

I turn around to see what caused his retreat and throw my head back and laugh when I see Omar leaning against a table watching me with a terrible scowl on his face. I motion for him to join me, and he shakes his head.

If the mountain won't come to me...I'll make sure he knows what he's missing.

Winding my waist and moving my body to the music, I turn around and swing my hips even faster.

"You're playing with fire." His voice floats into my ear, his lips touching the skin behind it. "And you smell so good." His hands encircle me and pull me back until there's no space between our bodies. He moves his hips with mine. I drape my hands around the back of his neck, and he drops his head until his warm, soft lips are nibbling at the side of my throat.

Heat races over my entire body. "You taste even better," he whispers.

"I'm melting, Omar."

"Well, you've been dancing like crazy. I'm not surprised."

"I mean on the inside...when you touch me like this, everything turns to liquid."

He groans softly and grabs me by the hand and spins me out. I gasp with unadulterated delight and he twirls me back, dips me low, and holds me there.

His face is just inches from mine, and his eyes are so dark they reflect the lights over the dance floor like the sky does the stars. I'm breathless when he lifts me back up and pulls me into his chest.

"I thought you didn't dance," I tease.

"I guess I found the right beat, because here I am."

"You like the beat of Calypso?"

"I like the beat of *you*."

My heart is beating so hard I think it might explode. His lips are *so* close, but not close enough. "Kiss me."

I've barely finished speaking and his lips are on mine, coaxing but unrelenting and so soft that mine meld themselves to them. His cold tongue tickles them, and they part for him. Then, I'm completely lost.

He tastes like Guinness and salt and a *chance*. He's kissing me so hard, his tongue is so deep, it's like he's trying to steal the breath from my lungs. His hands slide down my waist, cupping my ass through my skirt, and he squeezes at the same time his body grinds into mine.

He's hungry. But I've been waiting for this my whole life, and I'm *starving.*

I grasp his head, trying to get deeper, closer, *more.*

He sucks, licks, bites, soothes, plunders, and possesses, and I pray this claiming kiss is a blueprint for what he's going to do to me later.

The dance floor is a sea, and we are an island erupting from a volcano in the middle of it—with parts unknown waiting to be discovered. But what burns between us is as ancient as time itself, and my body knows what it needs.

His lips blaze a trail down my chin to my neck, and I run my hands over his body, the muscles of his back and waist and ass only heightening my frenzy. "Can we go?"

"Where's Jodi?" Instead of being annoyed by the delay, my heart marks his question as proof of its good judgment.

"With Dominic."

"Get your things," he growls in my ear.

I pat my pocket. "It's all here."

He takes my hand and leads me through the crowd and out the door. It's raining hard, and he tugs me to a stop under the tiny awning. "Let's wait it out here. My car is at the end of the street."

He drapes his arm over my shoulder, and I wrap mine around his waist and snuggle against his chest. "Where's your umbrella?"

"At home," he mutters.

I lean back and clutch my imaginary pearls. "What in the world has gotten into you?"

He cuts me a side eye. "The forecast called for a 10 percent chance of rain."

"You were being optimistic," I say with exaggerated pride.

"I wasn't. I read the forecast and was stupid enough to believe it."

"Aww, come on. Admit it. You believed it because you were being optimistic." I tickle his side.

"I wasn't." He makes a grab for my hand, but I move it before he can. "Jules, stop it," he demands and tries in vain to catch it again.

"Admit it, and I'll stop." He stops struggling and stands still like he's completely unaffected, but when I tickle his other side, I find his funny bone. His stoic resistance disappears, and he bursts into a wild laugh. "Fine, fine. I was being optimistic," he shouts, and I stop.

"I've brought you over to the bright side." I wiggle my eyebrows and rub my palms together in relish.

"You sadist," he grumbles, then peers out at the rain and scowls.

"Fat lot of good it did me."

"Indeed. Because one of the greatest desires of my heart is to kiss in the rain. The universe knows and timed it all perfectly."

I step out from under our shelter and into the rapidly falling rain. The soft, tiny droplets cool my hot skin. My father loved the rain. I know he'd want me to be happy tonight. I know it as surely as I know my own name. I fling my arms wide, splay my fingers, and tip my head up to the heavens.

"It feels so good," I shout with my eyes closed and spin slowly, reveling in the downpour. The light touch of his fingertips to mine startles my eyes open.

He steps out from under the awning and slides his hand up until our wet fingers are linked. The rain soaks his hair and runs down his beautiful face as he walks me back until I'm pressed against the brick wall of the building.

He cups my face with one hand and slides the other into my wet hair, making a fist and tugging my head back.

He lowers his head so close that the falling rain drips from his lips and onto mine. "I had my mind set on being the only thing that gets you wet tonight."

The sharp shot of lust takes me by surprise, and I clench my thighs hard. I wrap my arms around his back to pull him as close as I can. "But if a kiss in the rain is what you want, then I'm going to give it to you." His lips cover mine, and the wet cool of the rain is no match for the heat his touch ignites.

If our kiss on the dance floor was an island erupting, this one is its first flower bud blooming: sweet, tender, and perfect.

But far too short. I try to drag his mouth down to mine when he breaks the kiss. He grabs both of my wrists in one hand and lifts them over my head. He cups my bottom and tilts his hips so the hard length of his dick presses against my stomach.

Then he presses his lips to my ear. "I'd love to keep kissing you. But once I start, I'm not sure I'll be able to stop. So unless you want me to take you right here, we need to go now."

"Oh," I gasp at the scrape of his teeth on the sensitive skin behind my ear.

He steps away but holds out his hand. "Are you ready?"

I slip my hand into his. "Absolutely."

13

HONESTY
Omar

It's still raining hard when we park in front of the house and make a mad dash to the door.

"Oh my God, it's so cold." She shivers when we're in the foyer. Water drips off her in a steady stream onto the tile floor. "Let's take everything off down here so we don't get the stairs wet."

"No fucking way," I retort. I kick my sneakers off and lift her by the knees, throwing her over my shoulder. "The rain stole my thunder once already tonight. I'll be damned if I don't get to strip you naked myself."

Her scream turns into a laugh as I take the stairs two at a time until we're on the third floor. I kick my bedroom door open and set her on her feet. She pushes wet hair out of her face and turns to look around the room. It's the only room in my house that I've decorated.

"Mm-hmm." She kicks off her shoes and saunters her sweet ass over to my bed to run her fingertips over the black paint that covers the wall behind it and crawls onto the mattress to get a closer look at the map of the Polynesian South Pacific, where the islands Fiji, Tonga, and American Samoa sit in a nearly perfect scalene triangle formation.

"Did you commission this?" she asks and turns eyes wide with awe and appreciation my way.

"Yes. I know it's really specific to me, and whoever buys this place will probably cover it up. I move so much that honestly, nowhere has really felt like home. But the first time I went to Tonga—I was eight or nine—I felt it. And so I've had this painted on a wall in every house I've ever lived in to ground me, you know?"

"Yes and no. For me, people represent home more than any place ever could. And this is exactly what I imagined your bedroom would be—virile, lux, dark, vibrant."

I pull my soaked T-shirt over my head. "What else did you imagine?"

She looks up from her perusal of the bed, and the smile on her face falters. "I imagined your body would be perfect, but I don't think I expected to think it was beautiful."

"It's not. It's definitely not what it used to be. I've got scars galore, a chronicle of all my injuries. Getting old is a bitch."

"I hear the alternative is even worse," she quips. "That's what makes it beautiful. And strong. I can't wait to touch you."

"Touché." I unbutton my jeans. "I want to know more about what you imagined. You've waited a long time. I want to make sure I give you a night you'll always remember."

"You already have." She shivers.

"I'm sorry. Let me get you a towel." I turn for the bathroom.

"I'm not cold, I'm excited. I don't want a towel."

"What *do* you want, Jules?"

"Thank you for asking." She smiles, and I melt. "More than anything? I want it to be honest, and I want it to feel as good as everything else between us."

That's not what I expected her to say, but I think I understand what she means.

I give the voice command so that all the lights in the bedroom come on in the dimly lit room.

"Come here." I crook my finger at her.

"Okay. Are we going to keep these lights on the whole time?" She walks toward me slowly.

I nod. "The whole time. No hiding. No shadows. Just us. Now lift your arms."

She does it without asking why, and I grab the small hem of her T-shirt and pull it over her head, and she lets her arms fall back to her side.

She's got on a strapless black lace bra. Her skin is as luminescent as I remember from that night more than a month ago in her flat. I run my palms down her damp shoulders and skim them down her back to find the clasp of her lingerie. I unsnap it, and she brings her arms up to catch it.

"Are we going to be completely naked?"

"Yes. All night." I tug at the elastic back strap of her bra, and she moves her hands to let it fall away. I loosen her skirt at the waist, and it slides over her hips and down her long legs to land in a pool of lace and tulle at her feet.

I stand then and pull off my jeans, kicking them aside so we're on equal footing.

Her eyes drop to my waistband where the head of my dick is peeking out.

She's silent, her gaze riveted and following my hands as I pull my boxers down and kick them aside. I cup my heavy, aching balls and squeeze.

"Oh, my." She places a hand in the center of her rapidly rising and falling chest, and her tongue darts out. "That is...a lot."

I grin, pleased as fuck that she looks excited and not scared. "Wait until you feel it inside of you." I nod at the bed. "Sit down on the edge."

She backs up until she reaches the bed and perches her sweet ass on the edge. Her wide, curious eyes are everywhere—my chest, my abs, my dick, my thighs.

"What are you thinking?"

"I'm not. I can't. I'm just...excited," she admits with a smile that's growing wider by the second.

I kneel in front of her, and she gasps, her knees press together, and she scoots back. "What are you doing?"

"I'm going to take your panties off and feast my eyes on your pussy before I eat it." I put a hand on each of her thighs and blow out a sharp breath. "Your skin is incredible." I slide my hands down to her knees, pull them apart, and stare at what I've earned.

"You're going to take them off...like, completely?"

"Completely." I nod and meet her eyes.

They're bright with all the right things: curiosity, lust, excitement, trust.

"I've never—"

"Take your time." I lean away, giving her space to maneuver, and she puts a hand on my shoulders to stop me from going too far.

"Are you sure you want to look?"

"Very."

"Okay." She tugs them down to her thighs, and I pull them the rest of the way. Her pussy is thatched with dark hair. I spread her thighs again and marvel that I'm the first man to do so. The knowledge kills my cool. I surge up, press her back on the bed, and cover her body with mine.

Her arms loop around my neck as I claim her mouth in a kiss that's been building since the first time I laid eyes on her.

I'm lost to the world the instant my tongue breaches her lips and tastes the intoxicating spice of ginger beer and sweetness that's all her.

I could kiss her all night, and I promise myself that one day, I will. But I'm too aroused to even consider taking more time than absolutely necessary tonight. I pull my mouth from hers and move to her neck.

"Oh, I love that." She arches her throat and spears her fingers into my hair, keeping them there as my lips discover the delicate symmetry of her collarbones and shoulders. I pay attention to what her hands do, lingering in the places where they grip my head, moving on when she relaxes them.

"Omar, oh God," she pants when my mouth moves to the small swell of her right breast. I kiss my way to the center of each one, savoring the new flavors and textures on my way to her hard, plump nipples.

"So damn perfect," I mutter before I pull one into my mouth. Her whole body bows beneath me. The soft hair between her legs tickles my waist. I brace my body on one arm and use the other to part her thighs while I kiss my way down her body until I'm kneeling between them.

Her lithe body undulates, she rocks her hips up, and I get my first peek at paradise. I settle onto my stomach and grip her hips to pull her down to my face. I part her pussy with my fingers and drag them through the moisture that's already there. "You're wet."

"In the only way that matters," she answers, and I look up.

Our eyes meet, and something more than lust pulses between us.

I've never been here before—where my feelings are leading the way, and not my libido. I'm not worried about my performance, because this isn't a show. This is us finding a new way to communicate. When my hands slide over her skin, it's not just my fingers that get to feel the warmth of her affirming energy—it travels over the network of emotions we've been building for the last month that connects my heart and my brain to my cock.

I'm the fucking Mastermind all right. Somehow, I convinced this goddess to trust me with the things she's never trusted to anyone before.

She's spread out on my voluminous white duvet, as wide open as I am. And bare as the day the world was blessed by her arrival. Her head is thrown back, her eyes closed. Her lips are puffy from my kisses. I lean down to run my tongue over them, and her eyes flutter open.

"Hi, you." Her smile wrinkles the corners of her eyes, and she strokes a hand over the back of my head.

"Hey." My grin is stupidly big, too. I don't want to have my face buried between her thighs and not be able to see what she looks like when she's unraveling.

I flop down on the bed beside her, turn on my back, and hold up my palm. "Lick it."

She inhales sharply at the command but doesn't hesitate to lean forward and drag her tongue up my hand. "Good girl." I wrap it around my dick and make a fist. It's hot, so fucking hard and ready. "Now, come straddle my face and sit on my mouth."

"Hell, yeah I will." She grins and clamors into position. I start pumping my cock as soon as she opens over my face. I stick my tongue out to flick at the lips. She moans, "Yes." And then she braces her arms on my headboard and settles onto my waiting mouth. I don't take my eyes off her exquisite face as she discovers how much pleasure she can stand. She goes from smiling, to moaning, to a greedy grimace in less than five minutes.

"Stay there, right there, please." She grunts and palms her breast, tweaking her mouthwatering nipples hard as she starts to come. Her mouth opens on a silent scream, and I lift her off my mouth and down to my hips. Her entire body is trembling, and she rests her palms flat on my chest, moans, gasps, and makes the most mind-blowingly sexy faces while she comes. I fist my aching cock, gliding the head of it back and forth across her slick skin and reach to the bedside table for a condom. I tear it open and slip it on before I lift her and set her down over me. "Rest on your knees, baby."

"Okay." She does, and I line myself up with her entrance and press up with a small nudge.

Her eyes open, and our gazes lock.

"You ready?"

She licks her lips. "Very."

I press up, and she's so soft, so wet that I breach her with my entire head before I meet resistance. She closes her eyes, and her hands curl into fists on my chest. The sting of her nails into my skin is fucking heaven, and my entire body is a long circuit of pleasure.

"Now slide down onto me. I'll press up, but I want you to take it as slowly as you need. I don't want to hurt you."

She nods, bites her lip, and closes her eyes as she rotates her hips until I'm balls deep inside the tightest, sweetest grip I've ever felt. It's too good. I'm not going to last.

I was going to let her ride tonight, but only because I thought it would be easier for her. But she's so wet and ready, and I'm desperate to fuck.

I sit up and wrap my arms around her. "Hook your legs around my waist."

"Okay," she pants in my ear. I roll us, sliding out a little but keeping us connected. I brace on my forearms on either side of her face. "I'm close, it's going to be fast this time. But I promise, we've got all night."

"We do?"

"Absolutely."

I press a kiss on her lips and push the hair that sweat has slicked to her skin away and nod. "Thank you for letting me be your first."

"You're welcome. Thank you for outdoing my imagination," she returns. I wink.

"Hold on tight and tell me if it's too much, okay?" She nods rapidly. "Okay, baby." I press my face into her neck and let my hips loose. She's so tight but slippery wet. I thrust up and up, and my orgasm is breathing down my neck. I fuck her as slowly as I can until I can't hold it anymore.

"Break, Break, Break..." she chants.

"Break what?" I lift up so I can see her face.

"Everything. Me," she begs. "Then put it all back together."

I nod, then groan as pleasure shoots a lightning trail through me straight to my balls. "Jules, fuck, I'm...ughhh, fuck."

Her eyes pop open, and I explode. The force of my release snaps my head back. I close my eyes and see a thousand colors at once. I hear myself shouting, but my mind is blown, and all I can truly do is feel. When I open my eyes again, she's sprawled out, her arms thrown to the sides, her eyes wide and staring at the ceiling, chest heaving and mouth open. I sit up and look down at her. Her lips are moving a little. "Jules, are you okay?"

She blinks hard, and her eyes focus on me. "Holy shit. I—That felt amazing."

"I know." I flop back down, relieved and exhausted and so damn happy.

"Is it always like that?"

"No. No, it's not."

Not ever. I'm fucked.

* * * *

I'm glad I followed my instincts and pulled the brakes on a physical relationship. That wasn't just the hottest sex I've ever had, I've never smiled so much during sex that my face hurt.

Reena might have been right. This could be...*something*. Neither of us are looking for it, but we're both mature adults, and we'll figure it out.

I know there are layers to this woman I can't even see yet. I want to pull each one back slowly, so that when I finally find that warm center of her, we'll both be ready for whatever comes next.

Three Months Later

14

LABELS
Jules

"We're so close." He points at the countertop where the two slabs of sample stone quartz we've narrowed it down to sit. *Finally*. We've spent almost two hours in the countertop showroom. "They're both beautiful."

"They are. You can't go wrong with either."

"I want you to choose," he says.

I balk. "That's too much pressure. This is your kitchen countertops. And you have a lot of countertop to cover. Are you sure?"

"I love both of these, and I trust your eye. So yes. I'm sure."

"Fine, but if you hate it, you don't get to blame me."

"I won't hate it. Now, please hurry so we can get the fuck out of here." He puts his hands together as if in prayer.

I laugh at his melodrama and run my hand over the cool smooth surface of the first stone. It's white with light gold marbling. The other one is white too but with prominent threads of silver and cool gray running through it. "I like this one." I drum my fingers on the white and gold.

"It's too plain. I think this one's better." He taps the other one and grabs a piece of paper from a stack on the table and writes down the number of the one I didn't choose.

I glare at him. "I don't know why you even asked me. You always know what you want."

He flashes a sly grins and tucks the paper into his pocket. "I couldn't know for sure until I faced the prospect of losing one of them. Thanks for your help."

"You're weird." I bump his hip.

"So are you." He drapes his right arm around my waist. "Let's go place this order and go home."

"Gladly." We've been out all day, and I'm exhausted. But I'm not complaining. Work is busy but going very well. I'm almost certain I'm in the running for a tenancy at the end of my pupilage. And at night, I'm at the mercy of a sex god. I can't get enough of him. But I show restraint when we're in public. Omar, not so much.

We haven't taken two steps when his hand starts to travel down my hip. I dance away from him. "No way, baby. I don't know the laws in America, but here you get arrested for public sex. We got lucky we didn't get caught earlier."

"I was just fingering you, which doesn't count as sex. And I was trying to finish what you started before we left."

I blush. "You heard me?" I shove at his chest. I was in the bathroom with my favorite vibrator when he announced himself.

He presses his ear to my lips. "Didn't you want me to? Isn't that why you were moaning my name so loud?"

I bite my lip and flush that he heard me. But not from embarrassment. "Why didn't you come join me?"

"I did join you. On the other side of the door. It was hot as hell, but I was just getting started when your phone rang and interrupted us both."

The visual that conjures up of him stroking himself while he listened to me get off makes my mouth water.

We join the queue at the order desk, and he maneuvers me to stand right in front of him. I anticipate the press of his body into mine, but it still makes my heart skip a beat when that warm, muscular chest touches my back. It's been three months since our first time, we've had sex every day.

On the day Aunt Flo makes her appearance, he fucks the valley between my breasts, and two weeks ago he introduced me to the mind-blowing pleasure of anal sex. He runs his hands down my arms, and they erupt in gooseflesh. He leans down to nuzzle my neck with his nose. I reach between us and cup my hand over his growing erection and give it a discreet stroke. "Is that a rocket in your pants or are you happy to see me?"

He hisses. "You're asking for trouble."

"Only the good kind, I promise."

It's our turn at the counter, and I step to the side so he can focus on paying.

"Mr. Solomon. Nice to see you again," the man behind the counter says, his glasses sitting on the edge of his nose as he scans the screen of his computer. "Ah, yes. Here are your measurements. This is for your kitchen, correct?"

"Correct, and here's the stone I've chosen." He slides the paper he wrote it on across the counter. The man types the number into the computer and smiles in approval. "Very nice. And does Mrs. Solomon approve?" he asks me with an expectant smile.

"I do like it. But I'm not his wife," I correct him.

"She's my girlfriend," Omar says and bumps my hip. I smile at him and the man, but I'm taken aback.

I like the way that label sounds, but we've never talked about it. I know he's not sleeping with anyone else, and I know he cares about me, but I'm not holding my breath. And I don't want to read more into it than he means.

We walk out to the car and are back on the road toward home when I finally ask.

"So I'm your girlfriend?"

"Sorry, would you prefer partner?"

"Either would be fine, but I didn't think we were labeling this."

He glances at me, and the corner of his mouth turns down. "Okay, how would you define us then?"

I return his sideways look. "As lovers. And friends."

"Who don't spend a single night apart. Who are inseparable. Who are exclusive?" he retorts.

"So there's no one else you're even interested in?"

"Fuck no." He turns his head to glare at me for a second before he looks back to the road. "You?"

"Absolutely not."

"Better fucking not. You're my girl, Jules. I didn't say it because I didn't think I had to."

His possessiveness is such a turn-on. But I want to be clear before we move on. So I keep my knees together and press him. "Well, I don't take hints and never get innuendo. It's just not how my brain works. So if you're saying all of those things add up to mean I'm your girlfriend, then that's cool. I've never been anyone's girlfriend. But I know people who have something like this with multiple people."

He scoffs, and his lips quirk in a dismissive smirk. "Then they're not doing the same things we do. Because if they did, they wouldn't be with multiple people because they wouldn't even see anyone but each other, right?"

"Right." My heart expands in my chest. I don't expect him to be here forever, but while he is, I want him all to myself. "So girlfriend?"

"I'll call you whatever you want as long as, to you, it means we're together."

"I like that." A little *too* much for comfort.

"I like *you*." He puts his hand on my thigh and squeezes.

My smile has a life of its own. It's not what I planned, but after years of planning and strategizing every decision, I'm happy to go with the flow. Especially when the flow feels so good. *And* has an expiration date.

His kitchen is the last major space that we'll need contractors for. The rest is just decorating, and he's let me help him with all of it. He's supposed to be on a leave of absence from work, but his time is almost up.

Despite the marvels of modern technology, he can't run his business from here. Time zone differences, poor connections, and all the other issues that come with trying to work remotely have been hampers on his productivity.

No, when it's done, he'll put the house on the market and go back home.

I have this fantasy that he'll come back from time to time. But the prospect of him staying and finding out who I am and what I've done is unthinkable. His leaving is the best ending I can hope for.

"Oh, speaking of, *Architectural Digest* has been in touch about the house."

"About what? They want to buy it?"

He casts me a sidelong glance. "No, babe, they want to photograph it."

"How do they know about the house?"

"They've been following my renovation account. Apparently this house has a history as interesting as its appearance. They want to write a feature on it and me."

"Wow, how great."

"There'll be a photoshoot, and I'd love for you to join us."

"Uh, me? Why?"

"Are you kidding? You've decorated the entire house. I only had the bones of it together when we met."

"I don't want to be in a magazine. Especially not one highlighting where I live. The house isn't behind a gate, anyone can walk up to it. I work in criminal law. It could be dangerous." My voice grows more vehement with every sentence.

He holds his hands up. "I hadn't even thought of that. Forget *that* idea. I'll just give you credit."

I shake my head. "No. I don't want to be mentioned by name. The public eye isn't for me."

"Understood. You don't need to say another word. Thank you for being so up front about it. I'm glad you know you can be with me."

I sag with relief and smile at him. "I'm so glad you understand. So thank *you*, Break."

He scoffs. "What does that mean?"

"It was what my dad used to call anything that was exceptional. I don't know why, but it stuck and I use it, too."

His expression is dubious, but he smiles. "Exceptional, huh? I guess I can deal with that."

"It's a great nickname."

He cuts me a sidelong look. "You're *really* going to call me that?"

"Yes. *Forever.*" I rub my hands together in wicked glee.

He smirks. "Then I'm going call you Beat."

"What does that mean?"

"That you're the only music I want to dance to."

"Break and Beat." I test the names out.

"I think they're perfect together," he says.

"Me too."

One Month Later

15

CHANGE OF PLANS
Jules

"Deeper, Omar, please," I beg.

"Fuck, woman, I'm halfway to Timbuktu," he grunts, his face contorted by effort and pleasure as he drills deeper and harder and faster.

The top of this table was cold when he lifted me onto it, folded me in half, and started fucking me. Now it's warm and slick with my sweat, and I slide backward with every thrust. He lifts my legs so they lie flat on his chest and holds them there with one of his corded arms and holds my shoulder with the other so I can't move.

"I love being inside your pussy so much, I could do this forever," he groans with his eyes closed and his teeth gritted.

Those words work in conjunction with his body to break the dam holding the rush of pleasure that's been raging for release. My orgasm is blistering and fast. My body bucks so violently that he has to fight to keep his grip on me.

I have no basis for comparison, but I can't imagine *anything* can feel as good as sex with Omar does.

He grips my hips and slows down his thrusts, leans over me, and takes my mouth in a wet, deep kiss that's as hungry as it is tender. I wrap my arms around him, holding him as he groans into my mouth. I feel the spurts of his cum inside me even through the condom, and I wonder if it's possible to die from happiness.

He collapses on top of me, his chest heaving against mine, his weight delicious and comforting.

"Let's stay here forever," I sigh into his throat.

"My thoughts exactly." He presses a kiss to my neck and lifts off me.

The slide of his softened penis out of my body is my least favorite thing in the world, but Omar is as careful about birth control as he is about everything else. As he walks to a small bathroom to dispose of the condom, I hop off the table and look around the cottage while I straighten my clothes.

It's changed dramatically since the last time I saw it. The south-facing large bay window is the only thing that remains of the original structure. The rest of the light pours in through stained glass that's replaced the clear glass in the small windows that line either side of the cottage. The walls that divided it into several rooms are all gone, and it's one huge space. Long dark wood shelves line the freshly painted white walls. And the worktable in the center of the room where I'd just been perched is bigger than my entire kitchen.

I could swear the surface of it is topped with the gold-flecked white quartz I picked out at the store. But it's been a minute, so my memory may be playing tricks on me. I walk back to get a closer look when the bathroom door opens behind me. "Did you go back and order this?"

He comes to stand beside me, hands on his hips and a very pleased smile on his face as he surveys the space. "Nope. Ordered it on the same day."

"You did?"

"Yup. For this cottage."

"And what are you going to do with it?"

"I thought you'd never ask."

"How could I? You pounced on me as soon as I got here. Not that I'm complaining." I nudge his hip.

His smile turns sheepish. "Yeah, I've missed you."

I melt at that boyish smile of his and wrap my arm around his waist, pressing a kiss to his chest. "I missed you, too. Work has been crazy busy. This is the first night all week I left there before seven." I cast an approving glance over the room. "But I see *you've* been busy. It looks great."

"Yeah, put those up myself." He nods at the three rows of wooden shelving running along two walls.

"And you still haven't told me what you're doing with it."

"Well, I was thinking it could be a workshop."

"For what?"

"Oh, I don't know. Say…a candlemaker who needs more space."

My eyes go wide with surprise, but my heart spreads even wider. I put my hand over my chest. "This is for me?"

"Yes. It's for you if you want it."

I smile at him, wagging a finger. "Were you being sneaky?"

His pleased smile is back, and he gives a small shrug. "I wanted to surprise you."

I turn a circle around the room while he's talking, nodding in agreement until he gets to the end. I stop and turn to face him. "This is amazing. Thank you."

"You're welcome. I wanted you to have more space so you don't have to wait to ship one batch before you have room to make another. And you'll have a quiet place to work, too."

I don't know what to say. I'm overwhelmed by so many emotions at once. I don't know what I've done to deserve so much good, but I've been soaking up every drop of it.

"Only if you want it, no pressure," he adds.

I run to him and leap up into his arms with enough force to send him stumbling. He wraps his arms around me in a bear hug, and we stand there, suspended in a moment I know I'll never forget. I press my face into his neck and take a long, deep inhale of my favorite scent in the whole world.

"I love it," I whisper before he sets me down. And I love *him.* So much. But I'm afraid saying it aloud will remind the universe that it is so good at shitting on me in moments when I'm defying the odds.

"Good. And it has a separate street entrance. I'm going to have a gate put up so it will feel like two separate properties. So no matter who's living in the main house, you'll have free rein here for as long as you want it."

The reminder that one day, someone other than him will be living here dampens the happiness I felt a minute ago. The renovations are almost complete. After the kitchen, he decided to knock out a back wall and put in a second set of French doors that open out into the huge garden from a room he uses as his office. The work on that has just started, but it won't take more than a month. "Do you have an idea of when you're going to put it on the market?"

He shakes his head and lets out a harsh sigh. "No. But some of it depends on you."

"Me?"

"Yeah. You have what? Three months left on this internship—"

"It's a pupilage," I correct. "Even though I'm sure there are internships that pay more than it does."

"Okay, when your pupilage is done, what's next?"

"Well, if I'm successful, I'll be offered a tenancy and go from glorified intern to a member of chambers."

"And how long do you have to do that?"

"The tenancy is at its core a partnership agreement. I'll share the carrying costs of the offices and staff, but in return I'll be able to leverage the prestige of the chambers to find high-quality, well-paying work. That said and to answer your question, I don't *have* to do it for any period of time."

"But…" he prods.

"But…this is what I've scraped and fought for. Fifteen Queen's Bench Walk is one of the best family law practices in the country. And I want to make the most of it. A successful start there will mean I can write my own ticket in the future."

He nods, but his gaze is unfocused.

"What's this got to do with you listing the house for sale?"

"Well, I have six months left before my dad steps down officially, and once that happens, I'll need to be in Houston to develop my relationship with whoever replaces him."

The disappointment I feel listening to him is crushing, even though I knew this was coming. "Okay. So six months?"

"Yeah, but I want to find a way to make the distance work until one of us can make a permanent move."

"You do?"

"Jules, I'm fucking head over heels in love with you, and I don't want this to end. Not when I leave, and not at any point in the future that I can anticipate. I'm not a religious man, but you have made a believer out of me. I worship the ground you walk on. You've become my best friend, and I don't want to be apart from you."

My vision blurs. It's too much information and emotion at once, and for a second my mind is blank. I can't think or speak or breathe.

My heart is racing a million miles a minute. This wasn't supposed to happen. If he stays, I won't be able to keep my past where it belongs without being dishonest. Could I tell him the truth? No. But I *want* this.

I want him.

The weight of a hand rests on my shoulder and shakes me out of my spiraling panic. I blink, and a tear rolls down my cheek. He swipes it away with his thumb and then cups my face and gazes down at me with so much tenderness and love that it hurts. "You don't have to say anything or decide right now. I know I'm throwing you for a loop. But I wanted you to know where I am. And what you mean to me."

I look up into the face of the man who has turned my world right side up. He's so much more than I ever dreamed of, and I know I don't deserve him. I should encourage him to leave. I should tell him this won't work. But when I open my mouth, I can't say anything but the truth my heart has known for months. "I love you, too. And yes, of course, I want to live with you."

His lips curl into a satisfied smile. "Glad to see you've finally caught up." He drops a kiss on my lips and pulls me into a warm embrace. "Come on, let's go inside. I've got a bottle of champagne chilled and ready to celebrate."

"You've always got a bottle of champagne chilled." He has a full-sized wine fridge that's fully stocked.

"But I don't always have a reason to pop one open."

I grab my bag, take his outstretched hand, and follow him out of the door and onto the hedgerow-lined path that leads to the main house. My phone starts to ring just as we step inside.

"Hold on, let me just check it's not work." I drop my bag on the counter and unzip it.

I chuckle as I fish it out. "If it is, tell them you're busy." He points a finger at me and walks over to the wine fridge.

"If it's them, I'm not answering until I've had a glass of champagne." I've worked almost eighty hours this week, and unless it's an emergency, I'm not calling them back until tomorrow.

I miss the call, but it's not work or any other number I recognize. The double zeroes at the front of it tell me that it's from outside the UK. "Hey, do you know which country has calling code 34?"

Omar is busy pulling down champagne flutes, but he answers right away. "Spain."

"Hmmm, I don't know anyone in Spain. How odd."

He tosses the gold foil he pulled off the champagne into the trash and starts pulling out the cork. "It's probably one of those time share companies trying to convince you to buy a place in Tenerife or Ibiza."

My stomach drops all the way to my toes just as the bottle relinquishes the cork with a loud pop and the bubbly liquid overflows. He busies himself filling the glasses, and we toast to the something special we took a chance on.

Omar starts to poke around his fridge to figure out what he's going to cook us for dinner and tell me about an endorsement offer he received from a watchmaker I've heard of.

But I can't focus fully because my mind has raced back in time to the night I took Conrad to the airport and bought him a one-way ticket.

To Ibiza.

If he's calling me, he must be out of money. Eight months is longer than I expected him to last, but it's not long enough.

"You should keep things here," he says suddenly, his eyes on me as his deft hands slice and dice tomatoes and onions.

"I already do."

"I mean, like everything. For good."

The glass nearly slips from my suddenly slack fingers. I place it carefully on the counter and climb down. "You mean…move in? But I thought you were going to sell it once the renovation was done."

"I've changed my mind. I love this house. Your touch is everywhere, and I want you to live here with me. You're here practically every night. I'd love for you to call it home."

I'm excited but surprised. "You want that?" I pause, bite my lip, and look at him closely. "Are you sure?"

"Absolutely. I'm head over heart and heels for you. I want us to start thinking about a future where we're together."

My poor heart doesn't know what hit it, and it flails. "You do?"

"Don't you?"

"Is Oprah rich? Of course I do. But what about your business in Houston? Your family?"

He puts the knife down and meets my gaze. "What about them?"

"You were only here until your house was sorted."

"Things have changed. There's you."

"You can't just upend your life, leave your businesses and everything you know for me."

"I can do whatever I want. You think about it and let me know."

* * * *

I don't need to think about his offer. I want to live with him. But that means I have to pay Conrad. While he sleeps soundly next to me, I send a wire transfer from my bank. This time, I send him enough to last him a year.

Then I send a text telling him to expect the wire in the morning and that there is no more where this has come from.

He writes back, "**That's a pity. Have a nice life**." I delete the conversation and block his number. I saw a quote once that read, "No man is rich enough to buy back his past." I don't remember who said it, but I hope like hell they were wrong.

Six Months Later

16

FALLING
Jules

"I can't believe I wore these all night," I groan and slip my feet out of the torture devices that masquerade as shoes. My poor toes flex after being confined for so long and sink into the soft rug that covers the floor under his bed.

"I love you in your sneakers, but I'd be lying if I said I wouldn't mind feeling the point of those in my ass while you scream my name tonight," Omar drawls from the bed behind me where he's spread out like a lion after a satisfying meal.

He had a meal all right: me. As soon as we climbed in after the event at Inner Temple tonight, he pulled me over to his side of the car, lowered the seat, and ate me until I was sobbing in ecstasy.

But it wasn't enough, and I can't wait to pick up where we left off. I don't think I'll ever get enough of him, and nothing makes me happier than when he makes it clear he feels the same way.

The last six months have been, unequivocally, the very best of my life, professionally and personally. I am in a place thirteen-year-old me couldn't even imagine.

And during a beautiful ceremony at the Temple Church this evening, I was awarded the coveted Pupil of the Year award.

I didn't have to scan the room to catch the eye of anyone as I walked to the stage to accept it. Tonight, Omar sat by my side, and when my name was called, he kissed me so long and hard that several wolf whistles accompanied the applause that rang through the room on my way to the stage.

He was on his feet when my speech was over and held my hand while I accepted personal congratulations from my peers and superiors.

"I want to show you something," he says, and I look over at the bed with a coy smile and wag my finger at him.

"I've gotta use the ladies', but get your *something* ready so I can hop on and make it worth the wait."

He chuckles, lifts his phone up, and taps the screen. "Not that *something,* my little nympho."

"You made me into what I am." I snicker and shimmy my hips. "And I can't wait to see it, but first I have to answer nature's call. Where's my phone?" I look around the bedroom and spot it on the bed next to Omar's black sock-clad foot.

I reach for it, but Omar makes a wild lunge from the bed, using his long arms to snatch the small clutch before me.

"What are you doing?" I stare at him, confused.

He pulls it out of the bag. "It's rude to use your phone in the bathroom." He glances at my screen and quirks his lip. "It's dead anyway." He rolls over and sticks it on the charger.

"Thank you, I guess. Be right back."

"If you're going to be in there long enough to need your phone, please for the love of everything holy, turn on the fan," he yells at me through the closed door.

"I've told you, I don't need the fan. Because my shit does not smell bad." I bite the inside of my cheek to stop myself from laughing out loud.

"Everybody's shit smells bad."

"Have you smelled *everyone's* shit? I know you haven't smelled mine, or we wouldn't be having this argument," I shout back.

"You were born to argue."

"And you were born to give me a reason to," I retort.

He just growls. I snicker quietly, but the smile on the face of the person staring back at me in the mirror while I wash my hands could be on a billboard that reads "a person in love."

I spot an *Architectural Digest* sitting at the top of a basket full of magazines. Omar's house is on the very front. And despite what he said, we've had several uninvited voyeurs coming by to take pictures. I'm so glad I said no to being included. It would make it so easy for Conrad to find me again. I banish the thought as quickly as it comes.

Nothing lasts forever, and I know this bliss won't be an exception to that rule. But I've stopped worrying about what's to come. I'm living in the moment, savoring every mouthwatering second.

I'm done and out in less than a minute and smirk when his

eyebrows shoot up. "I only had to pee, I told you." I shimmy out of my dress. "One sec and I'll come see the tile work that's got you so hot and bothered," I tease.

"Very funny." He tosses a small throw pillow at me. I shriek and duck just in time for it to sail over my head.

"I'm not being funny." I drape my dress onto the back of the chair of my vanity. "It's dead sexy that you're handy." I raise one arm and rest it on the door frame of the bathroom and put the other on my cocked hip. "I love watching you hammering more than anything," I drawl in a seductive voice.

His greedy gaze hasn't left me since I started to undress, but now he's put the phone down and undoes the front of his trousers.

"*You* in that lingerie is dead sexy."

"What, this old thing?" I run a hand over the front of my violet lace body suit.

He growls. "Come here, you. Let me show you how handy I am."

"Only if you promise to let me hold your screwdriver." I strut over to the bed and plop down next to him.

He slaps my ass and pulls me into his side. I drape a leg over his and rest my head on his chest. "I'm glad you've got jokes, and I can't wait for you to apologize for teasing me after you see this."

My phone starts to vibrate on the bedside table, as what sounds like an endless stream of notifications pop up. "What in the world?" I ask and reach over him for it.

He snags it and gives it to me.

"It's your IG notifications blowing up."

"Why would *that* be? I post twice a year, and my account is private."

"I tagged you in something tonight."

My heart stops. I close my eyes and groan. "What did you tag me in?"

"A video."

"Of what?" I ask with as much patience as I can muster.

"Part of your speech."

I prop myself up on one arm and look down at him in disbelief. He looks completely unperturbed. "Why?"

"Because I was fucking proud of you, and I wanted the whole world to know."

My stomach falls, and dread creeps up my spine in prickles of ice that chill me to the bone. "Omar, you have like twenty million followers.

I don't want to be in the public eye. We talked about this already. My job requires discretion. If you want back in the spotlight, I'm happy for you, but I don't want my face splashed across tabloids."

He flinches like I slapped him. "I didn't post a video of you with your ass spread out on my bed, Jules. Damn."

My eyes fill with tears. "Why would you do post anything of me at all? Without asking me first?"

He pulls me into his side, and I let him because I need the soothing his touch always brings. "Jules, *please*. Just watch it before you freak. Trust me." His voice is gruff, and his eyes are pleading. And that is enough. I do trust him. Like I've never trusted anyone in my life.

"Of course. Okay, let me see." He hands me his phone, open to a post with a video. I steel myself, open the link, and press play.

"I dedicate this award to every young person who's caught in a storm not of their making. Don't be afraid of the rain, let it nourish the parts of you left parched by your pursuit of constant sunshine. Don't run from the wind, lean into it. Spread your wings, and let it propel you. And have faith that if you work hard, when your opportunity comes—and it will come—you'll be ready to meet it.

"I believe in you. I am you. And this award belongs to all of us who defied the odds. Thank you, the Inner Temple, for this honor. I'll work every day to continue to be worthy of it."

I'd forgotten what I said when I got to the small podium. I didn't expect to win, and I hadn't prepared a speech.

I glance at Omar, press pause, and cup his face. There's an apology in my eyes and on the tip of my tongue. But he presses a hand to my lips to silence me.

"I love you, Beat. More than I thought possible. But keep watching, please." He presses play, and I tear my eyes from his face back to the screen. He cuts to a video of himself. I recognize the stone columns of the outside of the church. He must have done this while he waited for me to pose for official pictures.

His normally direct gaze drops to the phone, and his fingers fidget with the fringe of the bed's duvet. A flush spreads across his cheek, and I'm so endeared by the fact that he's nervous that I want to hurry up and watch the video so I can rip his clothes off and say a proper thank you.

He's sitting with his back against one of the columns outside the Temple Church. His dark gray tie is loose, and the top button of his crisp white shirt is open. He's smiling, and his breathtaking eyes are bright and intent. "Hey, people. It's been a minute, but I've been busy making up for lost time. The woman you saw in the previous video giving that incredible speech is the reason I'm in London. Not because I'm marrying one of the royal princesses or coaching a championship league team. Fuck whoever started *that* rumor. I'm here because *she* is. No one is more surprised than I am that I fell in love so fast and furious. But Jules is light, and color, and *so* much clarity. She's proof that change can happen in a split second. Because all it took to change my whole world view was meeting someone who understood me, heard me, saw me. And as if that's not enough, look how fucking *fine* my woman is. Actually don't look, cause I'm jealous as hell. Anyway, you keep asking when I'm coming home, and all I can say is that I'm already home. Not London. But *her*." He glances over his shoulder and actually *giggles* when he looks back at the screen. "Here she comes. She's going to want to kick my ass for this, but only until I get my hands on her." He winks at the camera, and the video ends.

I stare at him, speechless. My heart stutters and strives at the same time. I'm happier than I have any right to be.

"How mad are you?" he asks.

I shake my head, put the phone down, and swing my leg over his lap to straddle him.

"I'm the luckiest person in the world," I whisper through a throat clogged by love and want and a little bit of terror. He's amazing. I can't believe I found him and that he found me and we have this thing that's bigger than either of us imagined. "I thought…I'd always be alone."

His broad hand cradles my neck and draws me forward. "Not anymore. Never again. Not while I'm around."

There's a scream building in my chest that I can't release, and just when I think it's going to consume me, his lips cover mine. They are a lifeboat, and I'm not afraid of drowning anymore. I see the light, the way home. The barbed vines of despair that began their threatening creep up and over my heart cower in the face of his fierce claim of it as his own.

I lose myself in the moment and imagine that this could last forever. He doesn't know it yet, but these same lips that saved me from the drowned deep will be the instruments of our destruction.

Because not only will Conrad know how to find me and won't have to wait for luck to swing his way. Now, he knows I have more to lose than just my job.

And when he comes, not even my lionhearted lover will be able to save me.

17

FORGIVENESS
Jules

"This isn't working." Omar is naked but for his apron, on the phone, pacing in front of the stove. "Send me more resumes. But if the next batch is anything like these, we're going to have to hire an executive search firm."

I drop the post I collected on my way in and hop on a stool to admire his broad, muscular back and his delicious ass.

He pauses with his hand speared through his hair and his body bristled with annoyance as he listens intently. "It will take as long as it needs to take, Sam. I'm not rushing it or settling. I want the right person this time."

He turns toward me and holds his hand up as if to beg my patience and mouths, *I'm sorry.*

"It's fine," I whisper. He's been on the phone incessantly this week speaking with candidates his HR team has identified to fill his soon-to-be vacant CEO role. It's been a disaster from the start.

He kept insisting he was glad his father is stepping down. But then my man of action dragged his feet for a month before he finally approved the job posting. After another month of intensive searching, the first batch of candidates have all been disqualified. "Fine, that's your call to make. Just send me people who are actually viable. I'll call you on Monday." He hangs up and slips his phone into the front pocket of his jeans. "Sorry about that."

"It's fine. Is everything okay?"

"Yeah. I don't understand why this feels so hard. I'm glad he's leaving. But I don't want to replace him with someone who's not prepared to lead us in a similar manner. So far, not one of them has his breadth of experience."

"Maybe you should ask him to stay."

"Never." He scoffs and grabs a carton of eggs, a block of butter, and a small bag of shredded cheese from the fridge. "You don't know what they're like."

"I know you miss them. I know you need to forgive your dad."

"Jules, I can't. I just can't."

I move around the island to stand behind him, wrap my arms around his waist, and press a kiss to his muscular back. "You *won't* forgive him."

"He doesn't deserve it." He tenses in my hold but lays his hands over mine to hold me to him.

As if I'd ever willingly let go. "But *you* do, babe. And hiding in London isn't going to help you mend things."

He lets go and turns around to face me, his expression clouded by hurt and annoyance. "I'm not hiding."

"Okay, procrastinating then." He exhales harshly through his nose and turns back to his cutting board.

"I know you're angry with your father, but I promise that you will regret it forever if you don't find a way to mend that fence."

The knife lands on the counter with a loud clatter, and he turns to face me again. His hands are propped on the counter behind him, his eyes clouded by the unrest in his soul.

"I know. I *know*, Jules. He spent his whole life teaching me that when people showed you who they are, you should believe them. Well, he showed me that he's a liar."

I wince at the intractable anger in his voice. "Yes, *after* he raised you and loved you and supported you and sacrificed for you."

"But he acts like it's nothing. And he's waiting for *me* to apologize."

"And so you're going to do the same? Like for like? Is that who you are, my love?" I gentle my voice, taking all accusation out of it. I'm not moving a mountain, I'm stroking a bruised heart.

"I know it's hard, but everything worth having is hard." I step into his large body and offer mine as safe harbor. I wrap my arms around him, hooking my hands on his shoulders, and he sags against me.

God, I love him. Strong and vulnerable at the same time, he's got the kindest heart of almost anyone I've ever met. "Just think about it. That's all."

The muscles in his back bunch and flex. "If I didn't know better, I'd think you don't *want* me to stay."

"Don't be silly." I poke his back. "I just want you to be happy."

"Well, right now, being with you makes me happy."

My heart falls a little. I know he loves me and wants to be with me. I also think he's making that decision from a place of hurt and anger.

And he's right. I *don't* want him to stay. Since that video he posted last week went viral, waves have been forming on my horizon. Not minuscule ones that lap gently at the shores of my existence, taking small pieces of it every time. But ones large enough to wipe it all away. I've ignored the calls from an unknown number all week. But I'm not foolish enough to think that will stop him.

We've been on an inevitable course with the iceberg hiding below the tip of the truth he's unwittingly spoken. The anchor I dropped to hold us in place is showing its first sign of fatigue. Or at least the first I've allowed myself to acknowledge. I'm leaving on my first business trip tomorrow, and I'll be gone for three days. I hope the distance will give him some perspective and make it easier for him to imagine spending time apart while he goes to see his family.

"It's late." He dumps the entire cutting board into the sink. "I thought you were cooking dinner."

He frowns. "Nah. I'll go get a takeaway. You'll be gone for days, and I'd rather not spend the night cooking and cleaning up." He drops a quick, absent kiss on the corner of my mouth. "I'll be back." He unties his apron and strides out of the room.

18

FEAST OR FAMINE
Omar

I stood in line and only realized I'd forgotten my wallet at home when it was my turn to place an order. "You take Apple Pay here?"

"Look around, mate, what do you think?" The man sweating over his kebab stand scowls at me. I'd been in such a rush to get out of that conversation about my dad. She's right. I want him to stay. But I don't know how to ask.

"Sorry." I walk back up the high street and decide to just pick up food at the Effra. I have a running tab there. I place my food order and then step outside to call Layel.

"If feast or famine were a person, it would be you." My sister's exasperated relief is melodramatic, but I figure she's entitled to it. "Finally. My hail Marys have been answered."

"Well, here I am. You better start talking before an act of divine mercy cuts us off, too."

"That's not funny."

"I'm not laughing. I'm calling to see how likely you think it is that Dad won't resign if I ask."

"One hundred percent."

I groan. "Shit. Why hasn't he called me?"

She groans. "God, no wonder you two butt heads so much. You sound *just* like him."

"I'm nothing like him," I say, when in truth I'm afraid I'm everything like him. Being with Jules has shown me just how much my behavior mirrors his. He didn't forgive my mother, and I can't forgive him.

She grunts in disgust. "Ask him. And enough about our endless family drama. I want to talk about the real reason I've been trying to reach you. I saw your Instagram story. She sounds amazing."

"She is." I smile to myself.

"Oh my God, you just sighed." She sounds as shocked as I feel. "Who are you and what have you done with my brother?"

"Shut up. She's the only person I'm nice to."

"Well, congratulations. I wish I hadn't seen it online before you told me, though."

"It happened quickly, Lay."

"Well, I'm glad you're not alone, but I will fuck her up if she tries to keep you over there."

"I'll bring her home as soon as I can. I know you'll love her."

"Did you vet her?"

"Are you kidding?" I scoff.

"No. You're rich. Connected, powerful. You can't let just anyone in your life."

"God, don't start. Please."

"I just love you."

"And you want to make sure the only people who live off me are related by blood?"

"You are such an asshole."

I put my phone down on the bar and try to convince myself not to feel bad about what I said. It's true. That house she wants to put on the market was paid for by me. Her trips back and forth to Houston have all been on the expenses I've signed off on every month. She spends money without a single thought for where it comes from.

But until the shit with my mother, I'd never cared before. In fact, I've always felt lucky that I've been in a position to provide for my family. It's an honor, and thanks to my father I've done well enough that it's not a financial hardship.

Layel isn't a mooch. She's stayed home when I know she might not have if I'd been around. But my dad was alone, and she didn't want him to be. She had dreams she didn't chase to keep us as cohesive as possible. All while taking care of her kids.

I have a whole team of people to do the things I don't want or have the time to do. But I've never needed a personal assistant because Layel keeps my personal calendar, pays my personal bills, balances my personal accounts, and makes sure I'm at every family and corporate function. Money I can spare is the least I owe her. Jules is right— holding on to my anger is turning me into someone I'm not.

I pull out my phone and call her back.

She answers on the first ring. "I'm sorry. I didn't mean it. I love you and would kick anyone else's ass who talked to you like that."

"I know. And I love you, too. But this is what anger does when you hold on to it, O. Call Dad. Work this out so you can move on."

"I promise I will think about it. I'm sorry I've been such an asshole, and thank you for loving me anyway."

"I can't help it. And despite what you think, I understand how you feel."

Next, I call my father. My stomach is in knots while it rings, and then I relax when it goes to voicemail. I don't normally leave messages, but I do this time.

"Dad, it's me. I'm sorry for what I said. I wish you'd told me the truth about where she was. But I understand why you didn't. I also hope you know that whatever she and I might have become... I know I've only got one *parent*. I know there's no amount of money that would persuade you to leave my side. I love you. I'm sorry I haven't been there. I miss you. And I hope you'll consider staying. I need you. Okay. Sorry for the long message. I'm becoming more like you every day, I guess. Bye."

I stroll back in to wait for the food. "Omar, what's up?" Dominic greets as I walk in.

"Nothing, getting dinner and heading home."

"We miss having Jules upstairs. How's she doing?"

"Fine. Settling in." I snap my fingers as a thought occurs to me. "You know, I think I left a book in her flat. Can I go up and look or do you have a tenant in already?"

He frowns. "No, Jules is still on the lease. She didn't want to end it early, and it had six months on it."

"Oh, okay. I must have forgotten. I'll go check and be right back." I walk into the flat and flip the switch by the door. A small halogen lamp in the corner comes on. But as the room brightens up, I notice for the first time how small and dimly lit her flat is. Maybe it's because she's not here to brighten and expand it the way she does every space she enters. Like she has my heart. I can't wait for her to meet my family and friends.

When she comes back from this work trip, I'll ask her if she wants to come to Houston for Christmas. It's six weeks away now, so hopefully she'll be able to take a break. I grab a slice of Jodi's famous rum cake and head home.

19

GASLIGHT AND GHOSTS
Jules

As soon as Omar leaves, I go upstairs to run us a nice hot bath. The tub in his huge ensuite, which takes up half of the third floor, was delivered and installed last week. Tonight feels like the perfect time to christen it.

I turn on the shower and pull off my clothes while it heats up. My phone rings, and I run to grab it in case it's Omar. "Unknown number" flashes on my screen. Despite the warmth of the steam starting to rise from the tub, a shiver leaves gooseflesh all over my naked body.

Whoever it is is going to have to leave a message or send a text before I answer it. I hit the red x on my screen and hop into the shower to rinse off the day. The water pressure here is excellent—Omar complains it's a little forceful, but to me, it's like getting a massage. It only takes two minutes before the hot pummel of water starts to work its magic. My body loosens, but my mind is wound tight as a spring trap.

I really fucked up when I moved in with him. It made this heady fall inevitable. We aren't just physically attracted to each other, we *really* like each other. Reena, my chamber mate, and even Jodi warned me that living together was a bad idea. They said we hadn't known each other long enough and that we'd ruin what we were building by our households so soon. They were so wrong. It's been wonderful and easy, and we're solid as a rock.

But it was still stupid and selfish. I sit on the bench and hold my head in my hands while the water beats me down. I know this *has* to end, and I just wanted to enjoy it. And boy have I ever. I've been floating through time and space for the past six months. There are days I'm so happy, I wonder if it's possible to die of it.

But as those blocked number calls started to come with a greater frequency this week, I think the trepidation that replaced my happiness is much more likely to kill me. I'm not floating, I'm careening. There's a disquiet in my gut that grows more fractious every day. And today, it's so loud that not even the prospect of a wet, naked Omar can shake it loose.

The conversation about his family was hard. I didn't do it because I wanted to get him out of the way before Conrad makes landfall. I did it because despite what he was saying, it's clear the tension with his family is wearing on him. And the distance is a problem for the prospect of work. He has a crisis on his hands, and he's trying to handle it from here.

I turn off the taps of his hot steaming bath before I slather myself in his coconut lotion and pull on his dark gray, plush bathrobe. It's too long, and I sling the excess over my arm and carry it downstairs to wait for him.

Halfway down, the doorbell rings, and I laugh knowingly.

He forgot his keys. "Coming," I sing.

I untie the belt and let the robe fall open. On a stroke of inspiration, I put a hand on my bare hips. I check the mirror at the foot of the stairs and smile approvingly at the gratuitous display of my entirely naked left half before I fling the door open.

The welcome on my tongue, the laughter in my throat, the joy in my heart shrivel in breathtaking, perfect unison. My worst nightmare has shown up three months earlier than he should have. I clutch the robe closed and hastily retie it. But I don't take my eyes off Conrad Duncan, not even to blink away the tears pooling in them.

"Hello, Jewel, darling."

"How did you find me?" I ask even though I already know. That video. *Architectural Digest.*

His chuckle ruffles the hairs under his nose. "Just because you walk around with that nose of yours up in the air doesn't mean you're a god. You can't command me. Or get rid of me. Or ignore me. I've been calling you."

"Have you?"

He snickers. "As if you didn't know. Aren't you going to invite me in? I know your father taught you better manners than that."

My blood boils at him daring to speak my father's name. "As if you know a thing about what he taught me."

He nods repeatedly. "True. All I really know about you is what you did to him."

My heart races as anxiety and despair ratchet up to the same level as my anger. "You know I didn't do *anything* to him," I grit out.

"So you keep saying. Too bad the court didn't believe you, *Crown Jewel.*"

Hearing that name makes my heart hurt. It used to be the name of my father's pride and joy. And now it's the name of a criminal and a ghost.

"Shut up," I hiss.

He rocks back on his heels, and his smirk intensifies. "I don't blame you for changing it, by the way. It is *actually* the stupidest name I've ever heard."

I swallow the string of curses I want to hurl at him. He's trying to get under my skin. I'm not going to give him the satisfaction of knowing it's working. "What do you want?"

"Invite me in." His voice has lost all traces of amusement.

I hate him and myself for putting myself in a position he could exploit in the first place. He has the upper hand, and my heart is a runaway train, but there's not a chance in hell I'm letting him step foot into our home. "No. You have to leave. Now." I speak through barely moving lips.

"Either I come in, or I wait at the end of the street for your man to come back and tell him who he's got living under his roof."

Tears prick my eyes as I struggle with my choices.

"Stop wasting time, CJ. We know how this story ends. You give me what I ask for, and I go away for a while so you can keep your boring little life."

Tears sting my eyes, but I force myself to think. I can't let him in, but I can't let him blow my life up. "I'm not blowing you off. But this isn't the right time or place. Give me until tomorrow. Call me after 8 a.m., and I will answer, and we will talk."

"I don't have until tomorrow. I'm skint. I need a place to lay my head *tonight.*" He sticks his head in and swivels it from side to side. "You must have plenty of room here. I'm sure your man won't mind."

"I have a flat over a pub on Rattray Road. Go there and wait for me outside. I'll come down as soon as I can get away."

"Outside? Don't you have a spare?"

"There's one buried in the flowerpot right outside my door." I'm heartsick at the thought of him in my flat, but it's the lesser of two evils. "You can let yourself in."

"Who the fuck are you? And what the fuck are you doing at my house?" Omar's voice booms through the dark, and Conrad jumps and gives a small yelp.

"God, you scared the shit out of me, mate," he says, clutching his chest and laughing.

Omar steps into the light, past him and into the house, putting his body between us. "I'm not going to ask you again." He holds up his phone. "I'm five seconds from calling the police."

My heart jumps. If he calls the police, this is all over.

"Jules, tell him that you know me, dammit," Conrad shouts, and I enjoy the genuine panic in his voice for a second before I come to my senses.

I lay a hand on Omar's warm, solid shoulder. "Baby, it's okay. This is Conrad. We were in care together after my father died."

Omar turns to face me, his expression still thunderous, but the skepticism that should be there isn't. "And you invited him over? Tonight?"

"He texted to say he's in town. Turns out his Airbnb is two streets away, and he's only here for the night. I'm sorry, should have asked first." I'm ashamed of how easily this lie comes out of my mouth. Old habits die hard, I guess.

The tension in his face eases, and he drops a kiss on my mouth. "No, you shouldn't have. This is your home." He turns back to Conrad, his voice not as warm as it had been when he spoke to me.

"I'm sorry, Connor. I'm overprotective of my Jules. Nice to meet you. Where are you in town from?"

Conrad's eyes dart away, and the overly confident and intimidation demeanor he just displayed is nowhere to be seen. "Here, there, everywhere. Traveling around Europe. Just stopped in to refuel. It's too cold here."

"Well, that's too bad. We'd love to ask you to stay. I've been dying to meet someone who knew Jules when." He waggles his eyebrows at me with a mischievous grin that makes me want to cry.

He smiles at my man like they're old friends. I can see why Omar isn't suspicious. Conrad cleaned up nicely while away. His beard is trimmed and neat. He's tan and fit and looks like exactly what he says he is: a person who's traveling and only stopping to refuel. If I didn't know the dark that lay beneath that smile, I'd believe him. He turns his false smile on me. "Oh, that would be great. I'd love to stay for dinner."

"Yeah, and on a normal night, we'd love it. But we've got plans tonight. Next time you're in town, give us a heads up, okay?" Omar holds up his hands to show him the takeaway bags from The Effra.

"Yes, I can see I've interrupted something. So I'll just be on my way. Thanks for the kip, Jules."

"Goodnight, then," Omar responds.

"Night." He winks and turns on his booted heel and disappears like a ghoul into the night.

I contain the shudder of revulsion and try to return Omar's smile. He gives me a once-over. "Why'd you answer the door half naked?"

"I thought it was you, thought you'd forgotten something."

"I forgot my wallet, but they put it on my tab." He sets the food down and takes off his jacket.

I'd rib him for that normally. But right now, nothing feels normal. I take a step back, afraid that standing this close, he'll be able to smell the fear that's crashing against my heart like a typhoon overruns an entire coastline in a matter of seconds.

I inhale to catch my breath and keep the panic at bay. God, I think I'm going to throw up. "I opened the door and there he was." I press a finger to my temple to soothe my suddenly throbbing head.

"Woah, Beat. You feeling okay?" He's by my side in a matter of seconds, his arm around my waist, holding me steady. And I don't deserve it. I shrug out of his hold.

"I'm just tired. Do you mind if I go to bed?"

His eyebrows shoot up. "Right now? It's so early. I got dessert."

"I'm sorry. I'm knackered, and I have to be up really early to finish some work I didn't get through before court. Raincheck?"

"Of course." He tilts his head down for a beat, and when he looks up again, he's smiling. But I know he's only doing it for my sake.

"I'm sorry. I hate disappointing you."

"No, baby. Don't give it another thought." His expression softens, and he smiles, but the furrow between his eyes betrays his worry as he scans my face and thumbs the rise of my cheekbone. "You look wrung out. Go lie down. I'll see you in the morning. What time is the car coming?"

"Six a.m."

"Okay, wake me before you leave. I'll be up all night looking at candidates. I—" He stops short.

"You what?"

"I love you. Sleep tight. I'll see you in the morning." He drops a kiss on my lips and reaches for the bags of food.

I grab his hand, bring it to my lips, and press a lingering kiss to the back of it, having to fight my tears. "Thank you. I love you."

I wait until he disappears into the kitchen, just to make sure he's not coming back this way before I duck into the powder room underneath the stairs.

My queasiness is suddenly an acute nausea, and I barely make it to the toilet before I throw up. I want to lie down right there and close my eyes.

My heart…oh God, help me. I thought I had more time. I should have been more vigilant, I shouldn't have blocked his number. He has nothing to lose, and I know he'll make good on his threat if I don't cough up the cash. I've got much more than my career at stake now. I don't give it a second thought before I open the app for my brokerage account. I have enough here to last him at least a year. I won't waste it like I did the last six months.

I email my broker and text Conrad to let him know it will be a few days. Then I turn my phone to do not disturb before I drag myself to our bedroom and into the bathroom. I pull the stopper out of the tub and let the fragrant water drain away. While I brush my teeth, I close my eyes and try to steady my breathing.

Everything will be fine.

I just have to put up with him until he leaves again and disappears for another long stretch of time. Still, I don't look at myself in the mirror. I'm afraid I'll see a truth that not even my inner optimist can deny: Once this money is gone, I won't have anything to bargain with next time. And there will be a next time, for sure. Lying to Omar tonight made me physically sick. I know he deserves the truth, and I want him to hear it from me. As soon as I come back from this very important trip, I'm going to tell him about my conviction.

I'm not surprised by the rush of relief that follows my decision. However this ends, it will be a crushing weight lifted.

20

BROODING
Omar

I'm up brooding because Jules should have been home hours ago. She called me this morning—for the first time since she left on Monday morning, *without* waking me up—to tell me she was extending her trip for two days and wouldn't be home until Friday.

When my phone rings at 2 a.m., I answer it without checking the caller ID. "Finally."

"Sorry, I've been busy." It's my dad. I'm so relieved to hear from him that I forget how annoyed I've been that he hadn't called me back yet, either. "Hmmm, I thought you'd be sleeping," he muses.

"Does that mean you were hoping I wouldn't answer?"

"No. I'm just surprised you did. Seriously, this is the first chance I've had to call you back because I've dealing with your mother's estate probate and work, and Mimosa, and your sister. But I've been itching to talk to you. Thank you for apologizing. I'm sorry, too. For not being more honest with you about your mother."

"Thank you for saying that."

"I don't regret it, though. And I'd do it again. She didn't love anyone more than she loved alcohol. And I hate that she used your guilt to weasel her way back into your life."

"No she didn't—wait. What guilt?"

"Omar, I know you were driving that day."

I'm stunned. "You knew? Why did you kick her out then?"

"Because she was completely at fault. You were thirteen years old, having to drive yourself home because your mother was too selfish to not get drunk after soccer practice."

"How did you know?"

"She told me. She wanted to change her plea and tell the truth once she realized she was going to be charged with a felony DUI."

"She did?"

"Oh yeah. Until she found out she'd be responsible either way, but with a charge of felon child endangerment thrown in. She did the right thing. And so did I when I finally cut her loose."

I've misunderstood so much.

"I'm sorry. I should have said I knew, but I didn't want to tell you why back then."

"I thought I ruined your marriage."

"We did that all by ourselves, son. I should have made her leave before it got to that point. But it is not your fault."

"Thank you, Dad."

"That's my job. And I'm sorry."

"What was that?" I ask in mock surprise. "Two apologies in one day? Is the world ending?"

"Don't press your luck. Now tell me when you're bringing this woman home to meet me. I assume she's the reason you're still awake."

"In a way. She's out of town, though. But I promise we'll talk about it when she's back in a couple of days."

I promise my father I'll plan to come home soon and say my goodbyes.

Then I call Jules, but it goes straight to voicemail, and I wish I hadn't bothered.

* * * *

The chime of my doorbell wakes me up with a start, and I grunt and feel around the bed for my phone. I peer at the grainy image of the man at my doorstep. He rings again and then knocks loudly.

I climb out of my warm bed, hurry down to the front door, and yank it open.

"If you're a fucking reporter, you should just leave now." I bare my teeth at the lanky man.

He takes a huge step back, his eyes go wide, and his face pales. "I'm not a reporter." He clears his throat and attempts a smile.

I scowl and look him over. "So why are you ringing my doorbell at seven-thirty in the morning?"

"I have a special delivery for a Mr. Omar Solomon." He's wearing a bright blue uniform with...I lean in to read the small letters on the front breast pocket and groan.

"Oh shit. That's today?" I've been so annoyed I totally forgot Jules' early Christmas present was arriving this morning.

"Yes. If you could just sign here?"

"Fine. Sorry I growled at you." I sign the clipboard he thrusts at me. "Could we—"

He holds up a finger and dashes down the walk. "One moment, please," he calls before he disappears around the small wall that fronts my garden.

I sigh impatiently and lean against the door frame to wait. He reappears, carrying a large, gray carrying crate. "*This* is the twelve-week-old kitten you adopted six weeks ago." He holds it out to me. I just stare at it. I expected Jules to be back to take care of her. I don't know what to do with a cat. What if I hurt it?

"Sir, are you Mr. Solomon?" He leans back to look at the house number. "Or do I have the wrong address?"

"No, sir, you're in the right place. Can you bring her back tomorrow?"

His eyes widen slightly, and his smile falters for just a second. He pushes tiny round glasses up his nose. "Unfortunately, her spot at the kennel has already been assigned to a new animal."

"So is that a no?"

His nose twitches like he's going to sneeze, and sweat breaks out on his brow. "We *do* have a return policy. If you change your mind, you can call this number and arrange to have her re-homed." He pulls a business card out of his pocket and hands it to me.

I'm being ridiculous and giving this man a panic attack. "No, no. I won't change my mind. It's fine. I'll take her now."

He sags and wipes his forehead. "Excellent. She's just eaten, so you've got a few hours before you need to feed her again."

He lifts the crate and hands me a duffle bag that was slung over his shoulder. "There's enough food for today in the bag, and instruction for feeding and litter box management inside. There's also a litter box, litter, a bowl for water, and food. I hope it's love at first sight." And with a tip of his bright blue cap, he hurries down the walk again.

"I doubt it," I grumble.

There's a small mewl from the crate at my feet, and I stoop down to pick it up.

I shut the door with my foot and carry it into the kitchen, set it down on the counter, and open the little gate in the front.

As soon as I see the tiny midnight black kitten staring up at me, I know I'm a cat person. She's beautiful. I reach in and pull the tiny animal out of the carrier, struck by how light and small it is. There's a note inside, and I hold the kitten to my chest with one hand and pick up the bag with my other.

It purrs, and tiny claws prick my chest when I start up the stairs to the living room. As I sit on my couch, I place the warm ball of fur on my shoulder and recreate the painting on her iPad. I snap a picture and send it to Jules with no message.

Her message comes right away. "**OMG, I'll call you in five.**"

My phone rings less than two minutes later, and when I see her name on my screen, a knot I hadn't even known was there eases. "Hey, Beat."

"Hey, Break," she responds in her normal, sweet way. "Whose cat did you steal to take that picture?"

"She's yours. I adopted her before your trip was on the calendar, and they brought her to me today."

"What! Are you serious?"

I pull the phone away from my ear at her scream and laugh when it starts asking me to accept her video call. I accept the request for video and then put the phone down on the couch.

"Why am I looking at the ceiling?" she cries.

"Hold on a second." I position the cat so the heart on her belly is visible and turn the camera around so she's in full view. "Voilà!"

Her mouth falls open, and she slaps a hand across it to muffle her squeal.

There's childlike excitement on her face I've never seen before. "So you like her. She's yours."

"You are *joking*! She's mine?"

"Well, ours since I live here, too." I turn the phone over again. "Look at that little heart on her stomach."

"Ugh," she groans. "That's too much, my heart is going to explode. I can't wait to snuggle her. What are we going to name her?"

"I don't know. We'll think on it when you get home."

Her expression softens. "Thank you. I love you so much."

The tenderness in her eyes makes me feel like the luckiest man on the planet. "I love you, too. And I fucking miss you."

"Oh baby. I miss you, too. And I have good news. We got through the documents faster than we expected. I'm coming home tonight."

"Great. What time?"

"I'll text by noon to tell you the train time. But it'll be the evening."

"That's great. I'll make dinner."

"I can't *wait* to get home and eat your amazing dinner and smell you and sleep in our bed." She closes her eyes and smiles. "Just the thought of it makes me happy."

"Well, when you get home, I'll make you even happier."

"I'll call you by noon. I can't wait to talk."

"Me, too. Text me your train time."

I feel lighter than I have in days. We're all right. The distance I perceived was my imagination. I reach down and scoop the kitten up and take a good look at her. She blinks at me, and her tiny pink tongue darts out as if to taste the air. She makes a tiny little yowl that turns into a yawn. It's contagious, and I yawn, too.

"What am I going to call you?"

She looks at me and yawns again. And then she curls her tiny body around my hand.

My phone rings, and when I see Reece's name on the screen, I answer.

"How's my favorite asshole?" he says when I answer.

"Wondering why you called to ask that instead of texting."

"Because it's so much more fun to argue with you in real time."

"I mean, isn't it like 2 a.m. your time? Why are you awake?"

"I'm packing. I'll be in London tomorrow. I'm only there for the night, and it's last minute, but how about dinner? I want to meet the woman that's turned you into Lord Byron."

And the hits just keep coming.

"I'll book a table at Anabel's for 8 p.m. They gave me a free trial membership."

"So you're really thinking about staying?"

"For now, yes. But when Jules is done with all her training, I think she might be persuaded to move."

"Long game, then?"

"Something like that." I don't want to get into a conversation about what my plans are when it comes to Jules or my future here. Not before I have a chance to talk to her properly, and that hasn't presented itself in over a week. "What brings you here for the night?"

"I'm meeting Lucia in Cannes, she and her mother have been there for a week. The movie was just chosen as an official selection."

I clap at the mention of his wife, an acclaimed writer. "Lucia Vega Carras, international superstar. Give her my congrats."

"Will do. I'll be at our place."

"I thought you sold it."

"Changed my mind, but I'll tell you more at dinner."

"Cool. Anabel's is off Berkley Square. So you can walk over."

"Great. I'll text when I land."

I wink at my reflection in the mirror on my way up the stairs. "You lucky son of a bitch."

21

REVELATIONS
Omar

"**How do you feel about pasta primavera?**"
I text Jules on my way to the market.
She responds right away. "**The same way I feel about everything you cook. Yes. *Please*. That'll be nice with a glass of wine. I'm getting on the train. I'm pooped.**"

I stop at the cash point before I head into the bustling outdoor market Brixton is famous for. I'm almost to my regular green grocer's stall when someone taps on my shoulder. I turn around and come face to face with Jules' foster brother or whatever. "Connor?"

"Conrad," he declares with the same toothy grin he flashed the night I met him. But he looks like he may not have showered or even changed since then. Or maybe the afternoon sun is just making visible what I couldn't see in the semi dark. His eyes are bloodshot and smudged with dark shadows. "And I have never been so happy to see anyone in my life as I am to see you. Saw you and thought *I'm saved.*" He waves his hands in an odd double high-five.

"Saved? By *me?*"

"Yeah. I left my wallet at the flat and was about to walk all the way back but dreading it, like, cause I'm already gasping for a cuppa. But then I see you and figure I don't have to go all the way back there."

"I don't follow."

"You must have extra bob on you. If you could lend me a tenner that would be great."

I'm surprised by the brazen, entitled expectancy of the ask, but my mind is caught up on the first part of his sentence. "You have a flat around here? I thought it was an Airbnb and that you were passing through."

His eyes widen in surprise. "Didn't Jules tell ya? I'm crashing at hers while I'm here."

I'm too surprised to hide it. "Really?" *What the fuck?*

He grimaces but looks more amused than anything. "Ohhh, shit. Did I say something I shouldn't have?"

I shake my head and wave it off with a good-natured smile. "No. We didn't get to talk after you left, and she's been gone all week." I reach into my back pocket, pull out my money clip, and slip a twenty pound note out. "Here you go."

"Generous of you, mate." His eyes light up, and he shoves the money into his pocket. "I'll give this back in a few days."

My eyes narrow. "Consider it a gift. And since you're still here, why don't you come up to the house for dinner tonight? We're eating at seven."

"All right. Nice one." He holds his hand up for a high-five, and I hit it as hard as I can with a huge smile on my face. He yelps, shakes out his hand, and gives me a confused side eye.

"Sorry. I forget my own strength sometimes."

"No worries, mate. See you at seven, right?"

"Right." He mimes doffing his hat and turns to leave.

I put a hand on his shoulder to stop him. "One more thing."

He stiffens at the touch but has that same shit-eating grin on when he turns around. "Yeah?"

"How'd you find my house that night?"

"Oh." He relaxes a little. "It was 100 percent luck. I saw that video you tagged Jules in a few weeks ago. I reached out to her on IG, but she never replied."

"So how did you find my *house?*" I reiterate.

"That's where the luck comes in. I came off the train at King's Cross, stopped at the newsagent to buy a pack of Murray Mints, looked down, and what I do see but you on the cover of *Architectural Digest*. The article made the house easy to find. I've been thinking about Jules a lot. Really wanting to catch up after a long time. Thought it was worth a shot. So I rang the bell."

So she lied about that, too.

"Talk about luck," I say with a forced smile. "See you at seven."

I pull out my phone to text Jules, but I don't know what I want to say. I replay the last conversation we had the night before she left and connect dots that flew right over my head.

It wasn't a coincidence that the one hundred and eighty degree turn she took that night between me leaving and coming back was definitely to do with his appearance. But what she didn't tell me was that *he* was the cause or that she was letting him stay in her flat—a flat I'm now sure she led me to believe she'd vacated when she moved in with me. All of it sets off alarm bells in my head and makes my stomach churn. I look around the market and can't even remember why I came.

This can't be right. Jules has been lying to me? That's impossible. She tells me everything. *I* know her. And she certainly knows me. I've bared my entire soul to her. Why doesn't she trust me?

This week, when it took her three days to call me back, when she'd never taken more than three hours, I knew something was wrong. This morning, she sounded like her old self, but maybe she's just a really good actress.

No. No. She's real. There is no faking what's between us. She moved into my house and wanted to know what her half of the mortgage was. When I told her I didn't have a mortgage, she insisted on splitting the bills evenly. She still works two jobs, and she's never even hinted at wanting me to offer to support her financially. If I thought it was what she wanted, I'd be happy to. I love Jules, and I know she loves me.

So catching her red-handed in *two* lies is disorienting.

I'll get to the bottom of it tonight. But there's a part of me that's not sure I want to know.

22

VULTURES AND CANARIES
Jules

"I'm home!"

"In the kitchen," Omar calls out, and I crack the first smile I've managed in days just at the sound of his voice.

I toe my trainers off, roll my suitcase to the foot of the stairs, and take a quick peek at my face in the mirror. I look exactly how I feel: exhausted. But dinner with my man is going to be just what the doctor ordered.

I follow the heady aroma of garlic and olive oil and fresh baked bread to the kitchen. "I'm so sorry I'm late, and of course my battery was dead when I—"

My feet and heart stop dead in their tracks, and I blink hard to make sure I'm not just tired and seeing things. Because there's absolutely no way that Conrad should be sitting at the counter, resting his elbow on the same surface that Omar and I eat and fuck on.

Conrad picks up a tumbler of amber-colored liquid, leans back in his seat, and smiles. "You're right on time, Jewel. I was just about to tell a story you haven't heard before."

I try to pick my chin up off the floor before I turn to Omar with a "what the fuck is going on here" look on my face. "I didn't realize Conrad was joining us. I must have missed your text about that."

He's at the stove, head bent over the pot he's stirring. He doesn't look up, but the muscle in his jaw twitches.

"Omar?" I walk closer to him, my imagination running nearly as fast as my pulse. "Did you hear me?"

He nods but keeps his eyes on whatever he's stirring. "I ran into him at the market and figured since your fridge was empty, it was only hospitable of us to include him. I figured you wouldn't mind."

He lifts his head to cast me a sidelong glance. His eyes aren't furious, but he's pissed. "Conrad's correct. You're right on time. Dinner's ready. Let's eat."

I want to refuse, and as if he can tell, the irritation turns into a raised eyebrow, head-cocked challenge. I try to meet his stare, but then his eyes narrow, his chin quivers, and he lets me see that's not just pissed, he's hurt.

Shit.

This is a classic case of the student outpacing the teacher. *This* is an ambush. I'm sick to my stomach with regret, but it's too late for that. I've been caught.

I nod. "Okay, let me go wash up and I'll join you. Please don't wait for me to start."

"We wouldn't dream of starting without you," he says. I nod and give a tight smile that I know isn't fooling anyone and do my best not to run out of the room.

I text Omar as I hurry up the stairs. "**Come up, please. We need to talk**." I pace for a solid two minutes, staring at the phone, waiting for him to respond.

It takes a few more minutes for me to accept that either he didn't see my text or decided to ignore it. I just have to pray like hell that Conrad wants the payday I promised more than he wants to fuck up my life and hasn't said more than he should.

I didn't imagine I could hide him being here from Omar and was planning on telling him that Conrad was staying at my flat for a few days. I just wanted a night where I could forget he exists. I should have known better than to think I could keep my head buried in the sand without choking on it.

Omar set this up because he doesn't trust me to tell him the truth and wanted to catch me off guard so he could see it for himself.

Oh God. When I imagine how he felt finding out that Conrad was at my place, I hurt. Because his pain is mine, and I know in that moment, he must have felt sucker punched. For that, I deserve his ire, but I hope he'll give me a chance to explain myself. I gather my courage and head downstairs to face my reckoning.

* * * *

"I hate to break up this party, but I've got an early start." I stand and grab their plates without asking if they're done. Because after two hours of Conrad's verbal diarrhea and Omar pretending to laugh at his lewd jokes and the stories of his criminal exploits that he wears like a badge of honor, I'm past caring about keeping up appearances. I want him out of here so Omar and I can have this out.

"Oh shit, is that the time?" Conrad says. "How it flies when you're having fun."

"It does," Omar agrees. I turn quickly and walk to the sink. I've been fighting my tears all night, and I just can't anymore. But I don't want Conrad to see me cry.

He didn't spill any secrets about me. He talked about himself and the bloke he met in Spain that he couldn't wait to get back to. Every so often, he dropped an innuendo that only I would understand. But the sinister glances that accompanied them needed no translation, and Omar got tenser each time it happened.

"Conrad, I'll walk you out," I say without any pretense of warmth. I want him out of here so Omar and I can have it out. Whatever *it* may be.

He throws back the rest of his drink and sticks his hand out to Omar. "Mastermind, I'll be honest and say I hated your guts when you played for Chelsea. But I like you now."

"How funny. When I played for Chelsea I had no idea you existed. And now I hate your guts," Omar deadpans. Conrad looks confused but then laughs as if he's in on the joke. "Jules, he's a riot." He throws a hand over my shoulder, pulls me into a side hug, and jostles me.

"You've got yourself a good girl, here," he says to Omar. "She and I used to be birds of a feather."

"A canary and vulture may both have wings, but they aren't the same type of bird," Omar says with a smile that makes me feel afraid for Conrad and sorry for myself.

"I see you got yourself a smart one too, Jules."

"I'll walk you out now."

Omar stands. "I'm nowhere near as smart as she is. We'll both walk you out."

We walk in a strange single file to the door with Conrad in between us. I can feel Omar's eyes burning holes into the back of my head. I open the door and step aside so Conrad can pass. "Walk safely," I say when he's on the doorstep.

"Oh, I will. I promise. I'll see you soon, Jules." The bile in his voice is sugarcoated, but just as bitter as he tips his imaginary hat at me.

"I can explain," I say, my back still to the silent tower of furious man behind me.

"I hope so. But first, I gotta piss. I've been holding it for hours because I wasn't leaving him alone with you for a minute. I'll meet you upstairs in the sitting room."

23

EVERYTHING AND NOTHING
Omar

I throw my head back and let out a sigh of deep, if fleeting satisfaction. My fucking bladder nearly burst during dinner. But my mind gave up the ghost as soon as Jules walked into the kitchen and looked like she'd swallowed a roach.

Everything about this week makes sense now. And whatever it is that's going on with them, Jules isn't a willing participant. But she'd rather lie to me than tell me the truth.

I don't even know where to begin. She's sitting on the couch, staring at the door with a pinched expression and her hand pressed to her stomach as if it's the source of her pain. "Are you okay?"

Her gaze drops to the floor, and she nods. "I'm sorry you found out he was here before I could tell you. But I *was* going to tell you."

"When?" My response is clipped, but my tone says everything else. She closes her eyes and sighs.

"When I got back. I wanted to tell you face to face." She looks so earnest and regretful.

I cock my head. "You told me you'd given up the flat."

She blinks. "No, I didn't."

"Then why did I think it?"

"I don't know. But you absolutely assumed it."

"And you didn't bother to correct me."

"Because we've never talked about it. Not once." She stabs her finger into the cushion.

I look up and think hard again. I don't remember the conversation.

"Fine. But forgive me for not giving you the benefit of the doubt.

Because you absolutely lied about Conrad."

Her face contorts as if she's in pain, and I hate that I put that expression there.

This tension isn't us, but *we* can't be us when this man is casting a shadow over our home. We've always picked our battles, but we've never pulled our punches, and I'm not starting now. "Who is he? *Really.*"

She stiffens and pulls her head back to gaze up at me with molasses brown eyes, the flecks of amber in them glinting in the sunlight. But instead of the joy she normally looks at the world with, they're full of worry. "He's my foster brother."

"You haven't ever mentioned him once since we met."

"I haven't been in touch with him in years, Omar. He's not part of my daily life—honestly, I didn't even know if he was still alive."

"Then why the hell is he living in your goddamn house? He's a criminal, for God's sake."

Her eyes narrow. "He committed a crime. He is not a *criminal.*"

"What's the fucking difference, Jules? And from the sound of it, he's committed a lot more than one crime. He's made a whole career out of it."

She crosses her arms over her chest and scowls at me. "You don't know that."

"Do you know different? I can't afford to have my name attached to people like him. And neither can you."

"People like him? *I'm* people like him." She raises her voice in an uncharacteristic display of temper that makes me take a whole step back.

Her expression hardens, and the hairs on the back of my neck stand up at the void of emotion in her eyes. "I just clean up better. And if you can't afford to have your name attached to him, then you can't afford to have your name attached to me."

"What in the world are you saying?"

"I'm *saying* you of all people should know that no one is as bad as the worst thing they've ever done. And that not everything is black and white."

"What has he got on you?"

Her face crumples, and I see the writing on the wall.

In a split second, I've gone from the man who conquered the mountain to hanging off the edge of it by my fingertips. I've got to decide whether I should climb my way back up or let go.

24

CONVICTED
Jules

I wasn't ready for this. Omar comes to stand in front of me, and I can't bring myself to look at him.

"When you decide to start telling the truth, let me know. And until then, I think we need to take a pause." His cold voice is like a hammer hitting my heart.

"You're breaking up with me?" I croak.

He looks away. "I need to think." His voice is monosyllabic, his expression unreadable.

"Omar, I'm sorry," I say and take his hand.

But he pulls away. "Me, too. I thought we had everything." His voice is rough, and he doesn't meet my eye.

"We do." I walk up to him and grab his forearms.

He shakes me loose. "Until you started lying to me and letting that man get between us."

"Conrad is just—" There is a break in my voice while that look in his eye breaks my heart.

"Don't say his name," he snaps, his voice low. "I fucking *resent* him. He knows things about you that you've hidden from me. And the way he looks at you honestly terrifies me. Because whatever his hold is on you, it's strong enough that you're afraid of that *fucking* weasel instead of kicking him in the balls and telling him who the fuck you are."

"I'm so sorry—" is all I can manage to say. It's all I feel.

"For what, Jules? What have you done? Did you sleep with him?"

He raises his voice, but the raw hurt in his eyes is what gets my attention. I'm not going to drag this out.

I take a deep breath. "No. I've never slept with him. It's not like that between us and never has been. I know I've been unfair to you. But I love you so much." A sob breaks my voice. "Please don't walk away. Please give me a chance to explain."

He flinches like I slapped him. "Walk away? From *you?* Jules...*Nothing* could make me voluntarily leave you. But lying to me about this man feels like you pushing me away."

I shake my head and let him go. "He's not the problem, Omar. He's just a symptom of it."

He curses under his breath, his jaw clenched so tightly the muscles are jumping under his skin. "I'm not sure what's going on with you and that ...*whatever* he is. But if you don't stop talking in riddles and start telling me the truth, I'm not sure how much longer I'll even care."

There's no tenderness in his gaze, no smile threatening to tug up the corners of his frown. There's no light in his eyes, no *me* in them. I'm terrified, but he already knows something is wrong, and the longer I keep denying, the less he's going to trust me.

If I could, I would throw myself at his feet and beg him to let me have tonight and promise to tell him in the morning. But that would only delay the inevitable.

Conrad was right about one thing. I thought I had the power of a god and tried to erase my past. His appearance here has brought me crashing down to earth. He didn't intend to, but he's given me a clarity and certainty that I've needed.

This is no way to live. What good is my new identity if I have to lie to the man I love?

"Can you give me a minute? I just need to get something out of my suitcase, please. I will explain."

I walk on legs made of lead and grab the file I went to Birmingham to get yesterday. It's my complete file from my lawyers, and I added all of the newspaper clippings and photos I'd kept from the year the girl I'd been died.

I'm no stranger to loss. I have lost more than I've ever had—and I may be about to lose him too. I can live with that. But I can't let him think anything else was a lie. This time we've had together has allowed me to be the truest me I've *ever* been.

I hand the file over to him with trembling hands. "Read this and then we can talk." He takes it but just stares at it.

"What is this?"

"Everything I haven't told you."

He looks at me warily and flips it open.

I close my eyes.

Omar Solomon has been the biggest surprise of my life. I didn't know it was possible to love someone so much. To have complete faith in their word. To hate falling asleep without them beside me.

I have to trust that he loves me enough to forgive me. He may not forgive me, but at least he'll know everything. I can stop pretending that what I've been doing is something more noble than lying. And if this spells the end for us, I'll find a way to make peace with it. But my heart will be broken forever without him.

I shake off that voice in my head. I know beyond the shadow of all doubt that he cares about me. And what he cares about, he'll never abandon.

He *has* to forgive me. I can't even contemplate anything else.

I sit next to him silently while he reads my history and pray like hell I'm right.

25

SHATTERED
Omar

I flip through the newspaper clippings slowly. I read every word, some of them more than once and inspect every photograph closely. As Jules sits quietly next to me in the warm kitchen, I'm colder than I've ever been. This is death by a dozen heartbreaks. Everything I know about her past is a lie.

The girl in the photos is her—a younger version but her. Her real name, Crown Jewel Hayford, is as absurd as the myth of lies she's told me since the first day we met. The only thing that was true is that her father died when she was thirteen.

She left out the part where she was convicted of his murder after being seen on CCTV buying the gasoline that soaked her father's workshop and the flat above it where they lived. There were witnesses who testified to hearing them argue, hearing her scream that she wished he was dead. And despite her insistence that there had been someone else in the shop that night, neither forensics nor witness statements confirmed it. She shocked everyone on her first day of trial by pleading guilty.

I can't bring myself to look at her.

I'm afraid to. This can't be real.

I want to be dreaming and wake up to find that I was hit by a truck on my way to her house that night. That Conrad never came here and she was just Jules Quist.

I dig my nails into my palms, and my chest tightens at the sting. I'm *not* dreaming, and the woman I love is not at all who she said she was.

"Omar…" Her voice is the same, and my heart responds the way it has since the first time I heard it—it lifts a little. But now, there's also quiver of unease in my stomach where the truth has settled. "So this is what you've been keeping from me?"

"Yes."

"And this is what Conrad is holding over you?"

"Yes."

"How does he know?"

She sighs and focuses her eyes again, and the bleakness in them twists my heart. "He worked for my father. When I was charged, everyone in town turned against me. Except him. He was my sole character witness. He told them I would never hurt my dad. I was so grateful even though I was still remanded."

"So what happened to turn him into your enemy?"

"I don't know. I literally bumped into him at King's Cross Station one night a few years after I moved to London. He was busking for money and homeless. I brought him home with me, let him stay. Tried to encourage him to get a proper job. Made the mistake of telling him how much money I'd managed to save from mine."

"He wanted it?"

She nods. "He started by asking me for help. Money for a debt. He needed a car. But one day he asked me to lend him more than half of what I had left to invest in some business deal. Of course, I said no. Told him I'd had enough and he needed to sort himself out. And that's when my pet snake turned on me."

"What did he do?" I demand, so angry I wish I'd kicked him out this morning.

"Threatened to write a letter to the college I attended to tell them what I'd failed to disclose if I didn't. All I have is my future, Omar. I just want to build a life and make sure youth offenders have good representation in court. So I gave him what he asked for. Got on with my life. Last year, he found me again. I gave him half of my savings, and he fucked off to Ibiza."

"The calls from Spain?"

"Yup. I blocked his number. I'm not listed. He doesn't know where I live. I figured as long as he couldn't reach me I'd be fine. And he wouldn't ever give up the dirt he had on me because then he'd have to find someone else to sponge off."

She presses her lips together and then releases them with a long exhalation. "But then there was the IG video and the *Architectural Digest*'s cover. He found me in no time. Except now, I have a real golden goose."

"Shit." I close my eyes. "Fuck *that*. Go to the police."

"I paid him."

"Why?"

"I omitted my conviction when I applied to the Bar. If I out him, I out myself. I lose my job. I can make more money, but if he reports me, I'll be disbarred, and it would have all been for nothing. I sold some of my investments. I have half a million pounds in my account waiting to be transferred."

I grab her by the shoulders. "Are you out of your mind?"

"No. He can report me to the Bar. I could lose my job."

I rewind to the first bomb she dropped. "You *lied* on your application?"

She closes her eyes. "I only decided to read law because I wanted to find a way to clear my name, and I knew that the best way to beat the system was to be part of it. My plan was, once I qualified as a barrister, I'd be able to access court records and hunt for the evidence the police and my expensive-ass lawyer missed. But then I became a barrister and met Reena and Dominic and Jodi and…you." Her eyes soften, and she swallows audibly, and I'm torn. I want to comfort her, but I can't.

"I decided I didn't want to dredge it all up again. I've made a name for *myself*. I love my job. It's all I have. I can't risk it for anything."

"Good to know I count as nothing."

Her head snaps up, her eyes blazing. "Omar, be fair. This was supposed to be a temporary, enjoyable interlude that would end when you went back to America. I hoped I'd never have to tell you. That we'd get to walk away with nothing but fond memories."

"Wow, I wish you'd told me that before I fell in love with you."

"I did tell you that. You didn't listen."

"Oh, so this is my fault?"

"No, but it's not my fault that I'm alone in this world and can't rely on anyone but myself."

"You could have relied on me."

"Not if you'd known this."

"Well, I'd much rather know your shit than live on your lies. They are fucking poison. The truth is terrible sometimes, but it's necessary.

And I just can't understand what I've done to make you think I wouldn't show you the same compassion you showed me."

Her swallow is audible and wet, and her voice quavers with an anguish that's as palpable as my own. "When it started, I didn't expect *us*." She waves a hand between us. "And this isn't the kind of thing I tell people on a first date. Not because I want to deceive you but because it's been used against me. I didn't know I would love you and that you would love me, too."

"Fine. But when you did, you kept on lying. You should have told me."

She purses her lips and eyes me with skeptical eyes. "So if I'd said, 'I was convicted of killing my father when I was thirteen. I didn't do it, I couldn't have because I loved him more than I loved to breathe, but I pled guilty because my lawyers told me to and I was a scared thirteen-year-old girl with not a soul in the world to hold my hand. I served my time, but I can't live my life as I choose because of a crime I didn't commit. So I changed my name and started a new life. And I wanted the temporary pleasure you're offering.'" Her voice breaks. "If I'd said all of that, would you have brought my iPad back to my place, or danced with me and made love to me?"

"We'll never know because you didn't give us a chance to find out."

She closes her eyes and blows out a harsh breath. "You haven't spoken to your father for the better part of a year. I knew." She opens her eyes again and the bleakness in them is nearly unbearable. "You were supposed to leave. You said so."

I laugh to keep from bellowing. "Sorry I ruined your plans."

"That's not what I meant. I'm just telling you what my rationale was."

"There's no rationale for misleading me like this. Were you never going to tell me?"

She shakes her head. "I didn't kill my father. I wanted something in my life to not be tarnished by that." She sounds so tired.

"Then why aren't you trying to clear your name?"

"I just wanted a clean slate. I'm so sorry, sorrier than I can say that I dragged you into this. But nothing has to change. If you can see past the name and see it's me—the same woman you've always loved—can't we please go on, just as we are?"

"What, with you paying a blackmailer and practicing law illegally? No. We can't do that. At least not together."

She starts to sob, and my soul rejects the sound. I swore I'd never make her cry anything other happy tears. I'm breaking my word and breaking her heart. I hate seeing her hurting, but I can't comfort her.

"I have to go."

"Please don't go," she whispers, and I shake my head. I can't stay here and listen to her cry.

"I have to. I can't think here." I grab my wallet.

"Where are you going?" She stands right in front of me.

"I don't know." I walk to my office and grab my laptop, my iPad, my passport, and my Kindle. While I gather, I plan what I'm doing next.

I'll buy a ticket at the airport and fly straight to LA and then drive to my house in Calabasas. I can be alone there and think.

I can't look at her. Because then I'll want to stay, and I can't. I walk back out to the foyer where she's still sitting on the stairs, sniffling loudly. "When will you be back?" she calls after me when I turn for the door.

"I don't know. I don't know anything."

26

RUNNING IN CIRCLES
Omar

I planned on going to the airport. But then I remembered Reece was coming tomorrow and that I have a key to his place that he gave me to use in case of emergencies.

If this doesn't qualify as an emergency, I don't know what would.

I send him a text to let him know I'm there and turn my phone off.

I don't want to talk to anyone. About anything.

I don't think I've ever been this conflicted about or angry with anyone as I am with Jules right now. I don't believe for a second that she killed her father. I can't imagine her—alone, so young, facing an impossible future after losing so much. I just don't understand why she didn't tell me. But the lie, the fact that she was going to let me go and make a fond memory.

I lie down on the couch, vacillating from wishing I'd never met her, to wishing she'd trusted me, to understanding why she didn't. But when sleep finally claims me, all I know for certain is that my heart is completely broken.

* * * *

The smell of coffee wakes me up. I glance at my watch and groan. It's a few minutes past noon. The clink of plates from the kitchen brings me fully awake. "What the hell?" I rush down the stairs two at a time until I see Reece sitting at the kitchen table. "What are you doing here?"

"Last I checked this is my place," he says and looks me up and down. "You look like hell."

"I thought you were coming tomorrow."

"It *is* tomorrow." He raises an eyebrow.

I realize for the first time that the light in the room is from the windows he's drawn the blinds up on and not the overhead lights I used last night. "Shit." I run a hand through my hair and look around the room. I should be at home.

"If *you've* lost track of the days, then whatever's got you here must be a crisis."

I scowl at him. "I'm not having a crisis."

He studies me with a dubious frown. "Last time you had this much hair on your face was after Chelsea let you go."

I curl my lip at his insinuation and brush the crumbs off my T-shirt. "I'm fine. Just being a bum. Is that a crime?"

"What happened with your lady?"

"How'd you know?"

"Because you told the whole world that she'd made a believer out of you. Then you text that you need a place to crash, when you have a whole house less than thirty minutes away."

"We had a fight, and I just need to think, Reece," I grumble and turn to walk back up the stairs and head for the nest I've made on the couch.

He puts a forceful hand on my shoulder. "Nope. Don't sit down. You need to shower, shave, and eat. You go do the first two, I'll order breakfast, and we can eat while we talk."

I hate being told what to do, but after being stuck in this holding pattern of inaction, I'm grateful for the kick in the pants.

I can feel his eyes on me as I leave the kitchen, and I can only imagine what he's thinking.

I'm thinking about Jules. I'm afraid to turn on my phone. What if she hasn't called?

I try not to let that worry me as I shower.

But it's like trying not to breathe.

I keep replaying the scene when I left. I'm ashamed that I left her crying like that, but I didn't know what else to do.

The door's buzzer sounds, and I finish getting dressed and go join Reece in the kitchen. He's on the phone, listening more than he's speaking. I grab a steaming cup of coffee and two croissants and take advantage of his preoccupation to eat. When the flaky warm pastry hits my tongue, I groan. I haven't eaten in…I don't know how long.

Reece puts his phone down and grabs a cup of coffee. "So what sank the *Love Boat*?"

"It's not funny."

"Sorry, just trying to add a little levity."

"She's been lying to me about something. I found out."

"I see," he drawls. "What did she lie about?"

"I trust you with my life. But it's not my story to tell."

"No need to explain. I'm glad to hear it, actually. It means as mad as you are, you're not ready to turn your back on her."

"You know me. By now, I'd be done. I don't want to be done with her. She's genuinely sorry. I love her, so fucking much. I just don't know how to live with the truth."

"Okay, so we have to fix this. Can you give me an idea of the severity of her lie? Like on a scale of 'these aren't my natural breasts' to 'I'm married.' Where would you say it falls?"

I choose my words carefully, telling him as much as I can without saying too much.

"She has a criminal record. She never said a word about it, made up a whole story about her background. I only found out because someone from her past showed up and started blackmailing her. She still tried to hide it all."

"Woah, shit. I see." Reece's expression is grim. I can't imagine what he'd think if I told him the whole thing.

"She pled guilty, but only because her lawyer advised her to."

"Do you believe her?"

"Yes."

"And she's the one?"

"Yes. If she's not the one, then there isn't a 'one' out there for me. She's perfect. A little messy, a little less than punctual, but fuck, Reece. Yes. I was sure, so sure. And then I wasn't. And she was crying. I didn't know what to do."

"So you ran."

"I didn't run."

"You always run when you don't want to deal with something."

"No, I don't."

"From LA to London, from London back to LA. From LA to Houston. From Houston to London. Now, you're thinking of going back to LA." He ticks off all my moves on his fingers. "Face it, you're a runner."

I open my mouth to argue and then shut it. Maybe he has a point. "I just needed to think."

"When was that?"

"Ten hours ago."

"And you haven't spoken? You shouldn't let the sun go down with you and your woman not on the same page."

"You're not helping."

"But did leaving make things better?"

I run my fingers through my hair and growl in frustration. At myself.

"No."

"And can you understand why she didn't tell you? Not excusing it, but asking if you can see how she could love you, live with you, but keep that secret."

"No, actually I can't. If she'd told me sooner—"

Reece's short, sharp chuckle stops me mid-sentence and seems to take him by surprise, too. His eyes widen, and he runs a hand over his grin while he subdues it into a thoughtful frown.

I raise an eyebrow in surprised annoyance. "What the fuck is funny?"

He clears his throat. "I'm sorry, I had a random, unimportant thought. Go ahead, finish your sentence. Please." He waves his hand a few times, gesturing like he's giving me the right of way. "If she'd told you sooner—" he prompts.

I rewind back to where I'd stopped talking but can't remember how I was going to finish that sentence. *Would* I have responded differently?

"I don't know," I answer finally.

"I have a theory. And I want you to hear me out and think about it before you respond." He raises both of his eyebrows. "Deal?"

"Fine. Just say it."

"Does she know about the situation with your dad?"

I nod. "Yes."

"So... she knows you haven't spoken to your own *father* in months. Can you imagine why she might be afraid to tell you?"

"It's *my* fault she deceived me?"

He holds a hand up in protest. "All I'm saying is if she didn't tell you, maybe it's because she knew she couldn't. She's human, Omar.

We're terrified of losing the things and people we love."

"Are you telling me you'd be okay with your wife keeping her past from you?"

"I've accepted that you can only know as much about someone as they want you to know."

"Bullshit."

"That's life. You never finish getting to know someone. It's the gamble we take when we let our guards down."

"I'm not a gambler."

"Then you need to leave this woman alone. Because if you tell her you love her and ask her to share your life, then you don't get to pick and choose which parts of her to keep. You've got to accept all of her or nothing."

I eye Reece while I weigh his words. He's given up a lot. His job as head of his family's film studio, his home in Los Angeles to move to Baja where they've made a home until she can live here permanently again.

"Do you have any regrets? About Lucia?"

He doesn't even look up to reply. "Not a single one. She's my world. No one comes with a lifetime warranty. They are going to break, fuck up. And it's up to you how you move forward. I know you're mad. But if you even *think* you might be able to forgive her, then you need to talk, figure it out. Or not. But it's not fair to go dark."

"I know." Yes, she owes me an apology, but I owe her one, too. I really hurt her.

I turn my phone on. There are dozens of texts but none from her.

I check my voicemail and breathe a sigh of relief. There's a voicemail from this morning.

"I KNOW YOU'RE ANGRY. I'M SO SORRY. WHAT I SHOULD HAVE SAID YESTERDAY IS THAT I'D DO ANYTHING TO KEEP YOU. BECAUSE THAT'S WHAT I MEANT. I HAVE SOME ERRANDS TO RUN, BUT I'LL BE BACK IN A COUPLE OF HOURS. UNLESS YOU DON'T WANT ME TO COME BACK. AND EVEN THEN, I'LL NEVER STOP HOPING THAT YOU'LL FORGIVE ME. YOU STOLE MY HEART, BUT I WOULD HAVE GIVEN IT TO YOU GLADLY. THIS HAS BEEN THE HAPPIEST YEAR OF MY LIFE, AND SO MUCH OF THAT IS BECAUSE OF YOU. SEE YOU LATER, I HOPE."

I listen to it twice before I check the time. She left this ninety minutes ago. She's got to be on her way back. I could get there in twenty minutes if I'm lucky.

"I have to go."

"I figured. So I guess dinner's off tonight?"

I'm about to agree but take a page out of Jules' book and shake my head. "No, it's on. But come to the house."

"Okay, Mr. Optimistic."

"Thank you, man. She's rubbed off on me."

He nods and looks up from his phone with a smirk on his face. "You're really in love. Holy *shit*."

"I know, man...I hope I didn't damage the bridge I've spent the last nine months building beyond repair."

God, I've been a complete hypocrite. It took me twenty years to tell my father the truth about what happened that day.

And Reece is right. It's not fair to ask her to be honest with me and then push her away because the truth wasn't what I wanted to hear. She's not the only one who broke faith. My stomach knots. I just hope she can forgive me.

27

FOR THE LOVE OF HIM
Jules

I open my eyes to a pitch-dark room, groggy and thirsty. I turn over, instinctively looking for the warm body I've gotten used to waking up next to and gasp. The cool, undisturbed space where Omar's big warm body should be brings me fully awake.

I draw my knees up to my chest and rest my cheek on one of them. I don't need to turn on the lights or call out to know he really left. I sat on the stairs for hours, not taking my eyes off the door, waiting for him to come back. Hoping against hope that he'd return.

There's a small meow and the click of delicate claws on the hardwood. I fumble for the switch on the bedside table lamp. The light is bright enough that I can make out the silhouette of her arched back and her long curved tail right before she leaps onto the bed. She eyes me, head cocked to one side with an unblinking sapphire stare.

I don't blame her for being skeptical of me.

After all, I'd forgotten all about her until a loud, distressed yowl from the dining room shook me out of my stupor. She was pacing back and forth inside a crate big enough to hold a tiger, and when I opened the door to let her out, she darted out and disappeared.

This is progress. I found her under the bed last night and when I reached a hand toward her and tried to coax her out, she hissed and backed away. I tried again, but only half-heartedly, and gave up when she batted a paw at my hand.

Numb and exhausted, I shut the door to make sure she couldn't sneak away again and lay down, cocooning myself in the white down comforter. I only planned to close my eyes for a few minutes. But a glance at my wrist confirms what I suspect—it's almost nine o'clock in the morning. I grab my phone to check for notifications. He hasn't called or messaged. He didn't come home.

My heart sinks. What am I going to do?

The cat meows, and I push my worry aside for a minute. She must be starving and probably pissed all over the floor while I slept. I reach a hand toward her but stop mid motion. My father had a scratch on the back of his hand that he said was courtesy of a cat he picked up without permission

I put my hand out a few inches, palm open. "Hello darling, I'm Jules." She meows softly. Her nose twitches, and she takes a step toward me. She's several feet away. But after last night, this feels like progress.

I move until my hand is close enough to touch the top of her head, but I don't. "I promise I'm not a shitty mum. You caught me on a bad day."

She nudges my fingers with the cool, smooth tip of her nose.

"That's it, sweetie. Come on." I pull my hand back, keeping it just out of reach, and she meows in protest. But she takes one tentative, delicate half-step toward me.

I keep drawing my hand back every time she takes a step toward it.

"You can trust me," I praise her.

She comes slowly, her eyes moving between my hand and my face all the way until her front paws are touching the tips of my toes.

I reach around her slowly, and her head follows the movement of my arm. She stiffens when I curl a hand under her soft belly but relaxes as my other hand curls to support her legs and bottom. I'm surprised by how light she is. I didn't realize she'd be so small at nearly three months old.

"Come on, let's go find you something to eat." Happy to have something to focus on besides my sorry state of affairs, I say the command words to turn on the lights downstairs and make my way to the kitchen in search of food and water.

She curls up in my arms, content to be carried down the stairs. I set her down once we're in the kitchen, and she prances around the island. I follow her, and sure enough, there are two bowls and a small bag of food with feeding instructions on a large label.

While the cat eats, I walk through the house I've started to think of as home and marvel at how normal everything looks still. Our shoes are piled by the front door. The post that was delivered while I was licking my wounds in bed is scattered on the black and white herringbone tiled entryway floor. The spare keys are in the small bowl by the door, and the faint scent of neroli is in the air.

This is home, lived in, loved in. Safe.

But the silence and darkness that have replaced the light, music, laughter, moans of pleasure, and deep sighs of contentment say different.

The bright ache where only flutters of happiness used to be says different. But sleep has done wonders. I leave him a voicemail to tell him what a few hours' hindsight has taught me.

I was trying to have my cake and eat it too, and my dad taught me there is no way to take without giving. Whether you realize it or not.

I thought I was ready to live without Omar until I got a taste of what that would mean. Losing my law license is nothing compared to losing the possibility of a future he's a part of.

I've apologized and made promises. Now I need to show him that I mean what I say.

28

ROYALE MESS
Omar

It's pissing down rain and colder than it should be when I leave Reece's. I have an umbrella, but I don't open it on my way to the Tube. This rain is a reminder that constant sunshine creates deserts. And that rain doesn't just erode and melt and sweep things away. It also nourishes and revives. The love that's taken root in my heart has soaked up the rain that started falling last night, and even though I spent it away from her, it's stronger today.

On the train ride home, I try calling Jules every time I get a signal but only get her voicemail.

By the time I get home, I'm soaked and frustrated. The house is dark and quiet when I burst through the front door. "Jules?" The only thing I hear in response is the echo of my voice as it travels through the empty house.

The kitten winds her body through my legs, her little tail curling around my ankle. I scratch her ears, and she purrs and arches her delicate back in pleasure. "Oh, I'm the biggest shit. I forgot all about you when I stormed off and left."

I check my watch. Maybe Jules had to go into work. Or whatever errand she had to run took longer than she expected.

I walk through the house and don't see a single thing that belongs to her. Not even the bottle of lotion she keeps by the sink in the kitchen. I panic all the way up the stairs and sigh a relieved sigh when the faint smell of my soap lingers in the air and I see her side of the bed is unmade. She slept here and left this morning, then. When I get back downstairs, I find the file she gave me last night sitting exactly where I'd left it.

It's not lost on me that someone did to her what I did to my mother. I know my father believes she paid her due, but he wasn't there. She may have been the reason I was behind the wheel, but that doesn't change the fact that I hit the cyclist. No one should live with the burden of sins they didn't commit. I couldn't do right by my mom, but I'll do right by Jules.

I send her a text and then get to work on the other thing weighing heavily on my mind. Her case. I take pictures of all the pertinent files and email them to the only lawyer I know well enough to trust: Remington Wilde.

Then I close my eyes, just to rest them until Jules comes home.

My phone's ring wakes me up with a start. I lunge for it, hoping it's Jules. But I'm not disappointed when *Remi W* flashes on my screen.

"Remi, what do you think?" I ask in lieu of hello.

"The evidence against her is circumstantial, but compelling. I see why she was convicted. She had a good lawyer, but he had no real vested interest in the outcome—he got paid whether she won or lost."

"Please let there be a 'but' in there somewhere," I groan.

"*But* it's too neat of a package. The evidence is everything they would need to get a conviction. And there's no such thing as a slam dunk when there's no direct evidence of her having set that fire. There's something amiss. I don't see a request for the production of all the Crown's evidence. Maybe it's just not here, but your best bet is to get your hands on the Crown's file."

"What am I looking for if I can get it?"

"I would want to know why she couldn't wake him up. Was a toxicology done? I'd want to know more about the people who gave the statements that attested to the argument where she threatened him. They're not going to give it to you or anyone you send on your behalf. Especially if they repressed or manufactured evidence."

"So what can I do?"

"I can't tell you that, friend. I'm still an officer of the court. But what I know is that you'll need someone who knows their way around networks and servers. And who's got a good, a *really* good nose. Luckily for you, I know just the person."

"Oh thank fuck."

"Yeah, well, no promises, but if there's more, she'll find it. I'm texting you her number. Call her and tell her I sent you."

"Thank you, I owe you."

"Yeah, you do. When are you coming back to Houston so you can pay all your debts?"

"As soon as I pay the most outstanding one." I check the time. It's been three hours since I texted Jules. I call her again—voicemail again.

I call her office. There's no answer.

I call The Effra. Dominic tells me she hasn't been by.

Remi's text comes, and I decide to focus on what I can actually control. Jules will be back, and I want to have more than apologies and forgiveness to offer when she gets here.

* * * *

Whoever said a burden shared is a burden halved has never met Dina Lu, the investigator that Remi connected me with. She took my burden and obliterated it in a matter of hours. It's just past noon when her email comes through. I skim over her introduction and recitation of the task Remi gave her to get to the crux of the message.

"**This file is full of red flags. First and most glaring is that there was no tox screen done. The witnesses who gave statements stating they heard her arguing with her father both had criminal records that were sealed after her trial. I found them, and they're attached. The most interesting thing I found is the repeated mention of the name Royale and a reference to emails and transactions. I started with the emails because they're much easier to hack. And in her father's email, less than a week before he died, is an email to an N. Royale in which he threatens to expose a lie if they didn't meet his demand for an increase. I didn't know what the increase referred to. But his bank records just came through. That's why this took me so long—they had been archived after all this time. But it was very worth the wait. I found a regular monthly deposit into his account of ten thousand pounds for the ten years of records I was able to get. The money came from an offshore account registered to a shell company that appears to have been created solely to launder this money. The shell company is defunct now, but it was registered to an LLC that's registered to a subsidiary of Royal Fragrance, D/B/A Monarch International.**

None of this was presented as evidence or given to her defense team. Or if it was given to her defense team, they didn't do anything with it. Maybe it's my general mistrust of criminal prosecutors, but if I was to hazard a guess, I'd start with the former."

My heart slams against my chest at that last sentence. Monarch is the company that Noah Royale is the head of. I do a quick calculation and relax a little because in 2008, he would have been in high school. A quick search tells me he went to high school in Houston, nowhere near the UK. It only takes a quick search on their company website to see the smoking gun. The only other N. Royale is his mother, Nora. I can't fathom the connection, but there has to be one.

I read the rest of her email. "I've spoken with a friend who has some contacts at the Met. Best thing would be for you to have a conversation with her, record it, and hope she sings like a bird. Let me know where this trail with the Royales leads. I'll send more information as I find it. But I hope this gives you a good start. I hate that she was screwed by a system that should have protected her. Second chances are rare and priceless—but she's more than earned hers."

I spare a few minutes to write back with my thanks and to ask for an invoice. But I'm coming out of my skin with impatience. Nearly six hours have gone by since I got home, and Jules isn't back and hasn't returned my message.

I call her again. It goes straight to voicemail. So I send an email to her at work, forwarding everything Dina sent.

I'm putting my phone away when it buzzes again with a reply email. I smile at how quickly she responded, but it fades when I open the email and see why. It reads,

"The email address you're sending to doesn't exist. If you believe you've received this email in error, please contact us as helpdesk@15QBW.co.uk."

I check the email address I used, reading each letter to make sure I didn't leave one out. But I didn't. My nerves prickle with a sense of foreboding. Where the hell is she?

29

FALLING SWORDS
Jules

"Who said no man is rich enough to buy back his past?"

"What?" My officemate in chambers, Alex, lifts his head at my musings.

"I think it was Oscar Wilde, right?"

"Maybe. But take it with a grain of salt. He's a pessimist." He stands and gathers his papers and sticks them in his briefcase. "What's on your schedule today?"

I close my eyes and release a weary sigh. "Nothing but paperwork. Are you going to the RCJ?"

"I wish. I've got a client in Surbiton."

"Have a good one."

"Same to you. All right, I'm off." He grabs his raincoat from the hook behind our door and walks out.

"Yes, that's right, it was Oscar Wilde," I say aloud to the empty room. Pessimist or not, he was right. I glance out the window of our lower-level office. The rain is relentless, and it's so cold. I can't remember the last time it was this cold in September. Maybe I should wait until it's a little warmer. Or when it's not raining. I really should start carrying an umbrella.

I pop the black elastic on my wrist and stop my runaway thoughts in their tracks. My mind, if I allow it to, will wander to places it doesn't have time for, and I'll talk myself out of doing what must be done.

Must.

Falling on my sword will hurt, but it will also cut Conrad off at the knees. I know it's the right thing. I spent the morning in my office getting my affairs in order. I have clients that I needed to make sure wouldn't be harmed by my removal from their case.

I thought I knew what loss was—after all, I'd lost everything once before. But there's a difference between the loss of things and people you didn't choose—that life just gave you—and the collapse of every manifestation of your hopes and desires. It turned me into the very thing I'd been trying my hardest not to become—a victim, afraid. I've been looking over my shoulder again, waiting for the other shoe to drop.

When I chose to read law, I didn't just do it because I hoped to have the tools to correct the record one day. There are some days when I'm not sure I deserve to. I didn't set that fire, but I've lived with the guilt of surviving when he didn't.

My heart was shattered when I lost him, and nothing will ever fix that. But I can try to set the record straight.

It won't change the fact that I lied on my Bar application. That I didn't do it for ill doesn't matter. There's no amount of righteousness to justify stealing a place at Inner Temple. And as long as I try to hold on to my ill-gotten gains, Conrad will be able to hold on to *me*.

I take a deep breath and call Mr. Bone, our head of chambers, and ask for a meeting.

He's in, available, and invites me to come see him now.

I gather all of my possessions with me and leave my files in order so the person who replaces me can pick up where I left off.

I take long, confident strides toward my certain execution. I'm not going to walk out of there whole. And I know it. But I'm going to find a way to survive it. I stop in front of a tall solid wood door with a lattice pattern carved in it that resembles a medieval portcullis. And how appropriate. This is the passageway to a kingdom I have no right to enter.

I knock on the door and walk in to find Mr. Bone, the man who gave me the chance of a lifetime, sitting behind his huge desk smiling at me warmly.

"Juliana, come in, please." I smile at his use of my full name. It gives the appearance of a formality between us that couldn't be further from the truth. I'll miss this and him.

"Thank you."

My legs start to tremble, and I sit in one of the dark burgundy tufted chairs across from him.

"Now you said you had something to discuss. But first, I want to tell you that we're going to offer you a tenancy. I can imagine you've had queries from other chambers since your award, but Fifteen Queen's Bench Walk is a place you can build your career and flourish."

His kindness, his assumption of what brought me here, all of it is a painful reminder of what I'll be leaving behind.

"I know. There's nowhere else I'd rather be than here, Mr. Bone."

His smile deepens, and the lines around his eyes and mouth remind me that this man is an institution. No matter what happens after this, without his favor, no one will work with me.

"I have come to tell you something I should have from the start."

His smile disappears, and his shrewd, hazel eyes narrow. "I'm listening." He sits back in his chair, hands folded on his crossed legs, and waits.

"My name, the name I was given at birth, is Crown Jewel Hayford. I changed it to Juliana Quist when I started at the LSE."

He throws his head back and starts to laugh. "Oh, my dear, is that all? I can understand why you would do that. Whatever were your parents thinking?"

"My father named me. I never knew my mother. But I didn't change it because it's absurd. I changed it to hide the fact that I had a conviction, one that led to a custodial sentence and a period of time on parole."

His laughter dies, his expression hardens, and his mouth thins to a white, harsh slash in his face.

"I was thirteen when I was convicted. I did not commit the crime I was accused of. But the evidence, while circumstantial, was compelling enough for the Crown to find me guilty. I wanted a new beginning. I wanted a chance to live a life that I knew, with that conviction attached to my name, would never be mine." I drop my eyes to my lap, no longer able to meet his stony stare.

"I know it was wrong. I knew it when I did it. But I hoped I could overcome that by being the best barrister I was capable of being. Of working for a population of people who reminded me of myself. But I see now how impossible that is."

"What brought you to that conclusion after such a long time of being committed to your deception?"

His voice holds no censure, but each word is a lash on my back.

"Someone I knew and trusted began blackmailing me. He threatened to come to you and reveal my identity. He came to my home and threatened my relationship."

"You mean… Mr. Solomon didn't know either?"

The surprise in his voice is so painful to hear. Of course, he expected Omar to know. He's my partner. And he should have.

I look down at my hands clasped in my lap. "I'm deeply ashamed of the trust I have betrayed, and I'm not here to ask for forgiveness or even understanding."

I hand him the envelope. "I've written my resignation letter to save you the trouble of sacking me."

"If only it were that simple," he says in a voice steeped in regret, and my head snaps up. His eyes are full of compassion, and it only makes my heart ache deeper. "You haven't committed a crime, thank goodness. But this job isn't all you're going to lose."

My heart lodges in my throat as I listen to what I have to look forward to. "You'll be struck off. There will be a hearing, but in a case like this, it will merely be a formality."

I nod. I knew this, and yet hearing him say that the only thing I've ever achieved in my life will be taken away kills my composure, and a tear gets loose before I can stop it. I brush it away. The last thing I want is to act like I'm the aggrieved party.

He hands me a tissue. "Your saving grace will be that as a pupil, you've been under the supervision of a barrister who has been the representative of record in all of your cases. If you'd waited to come forward after you'd been given this tenancy, you would have had clients whose cases would be called into question. You'd face civil and criminal penalties far more severe than those you'll face now."

"Criminal?"

"Honestly, I've never encountered this before, so I can't say if this will go beyond the tribunal that will hear your case and decide on whether you may remain an officer of the court."

"I'm so sorry." It's not close to sufficient, but it's all I've got.

"Oh yes, I know. You must be. You are such a brilliant, doggedly hard-working young jurist, and I do believe you would have had an extraordinary career."

"Thank you," I hiccup through a sob.

"I will represent you before the tribunal."

My head snaps up. "You will? Why?"

"Because I believe in you and want to give you the best chance possible. I'm not one to blow my own trumpets, but no one can give you that more than me."

I'm so grateful and so unworthy. "Oh, thank you so much. I don't even know how to begin."

He pats my shoulder. "I'm sorry it's come to this. I will liaise with the tribunal and call you when I have a date for your hearing. I'd say within the month. They'll want it done for Winter Holidays. So perhaps you can spend the time getting some much-needed rest. And then, I want you to come back here and work as a clerk to keep a roof over your head until you know what you're going to do next. How does that sound?"

"Oh, Mr. Bone" is all I can manage.

"Hugo, please." He stands, arms extended. "Come here, you."

I stand, walk over to his side of the desk, and accept the hug. The warmth of the contact undoes me completely, and I cry enough tears to soak the front of his crisp white shirt.

He holds me the whole time and pats my back soothingly until I'm done.

"If our profession has shown us anything, it's that good people get caught in bad situations all the time. Most of our clients aren't walking around looking for trouble when they find it. We know what desperation drives people to. You had the courage to come in here to face the consequences when you could have just disappeared."

"Thank you. I'm so grateful for your compassion."

"You've done the correct thing." He pats my shoulder. I'm so grateful that he can still see the good in me I'm nearly dizzy with it.

But I walk out of his office and leave behind the job I love. And the knowledge that I may also lose the man who has become my home in this same long, long arc of comeuppance sobers me.

I walk and walk and walk until I find myself in the only place I know I'll be safe. When I arrive at the house on Brixton Hill, light beams out from the stained glass window at the top floor, and the doubt that had started to slow my steps as I got closer to him is gone. That's my sign. He's home. I don't know if he wants to see me.

I have no right to ask anything of him. No right to him at all.

I'm afraid if I ask to come in, he'll say no. I use the key he gave me to let myself in but go no further than the foyer. I hear him coming and hold my breath.

30

HOME
Omar

The alarm beeps to indicate that the front door has been opened. "Jules?" I run down the stairs and find her standing there, staring up at me—soaked to the bone and shivering and so beautiful that I lose my breath.

"Where have you been?"

"Walking." She shudders. "I'm so cold. Can I come home, please?" Her voice trembles, and each word is punctuated by a sharp inhale.

"Beat, come here." I grab her and tug her into my arms. She wraps her sodden body around me like a vise, so tight it hurts my ribcage, and lets out a wail so keening and cacophonous that I know it's been building for a long, long time.

"I'm so sorry, Omar. For everything. I love you. I understand if you can't forgive me, but please know that what I feel for you is real. I painted myself into a corner. But I've done what's right. I'm so, so sorry." She goes on apologizing for perceived wrongs and grievances, and I don't interrupt until she's said it all.

Only when her tears and her words run dry do I speak. "I know you're sorry. I forgive you. *I'm* sorry I left like that. And this is your home. I am your home. Everything is going to be okay. I promise."

31

HOPE
Jules

"You *know* her?" I ask after Omar shows me the bank records, the email, the evidence that my father threatened a very rich and powerful person in the days before his death. Evidence that never saw the light of day at my trial.

I waited until I'd changed and dried off before I let myself sit down and look through it all. I climbed into the shower and cried with relief that Omar's arms were still open to me and that he hadn't just forgiven me, he was trying to help me.

This is the first piece of new evidence I've come across in nearly fifteen years. I can't believe Omar has a connection to these people.

"I know her son."

"Do you like him?"

"He's someone I admire tremendously. He comes from a family that owns one of the largest manufacturers of fragrances—their scents are used in everything from high-end perfume to air fresheners and cleaning products. I invested in a project with her son, Noah, in 2019. Silent investor, but yes. He lives in Las Vegas, but the company's headquarters are in Houston."

"Where you were living?"

"Yes, where I have a home. His parents live in my neighborhood—but in the towers. She's notoriously reclusive."

"Who runs the company?"

"His father does. But Noah has a commercial development business, and that's who I invested with. The project I invested in—a stadium—was complete before I left, and my investment is being returned with the interest on the schedule we agreed upon."

"Do you have any pictures of her? Maybe I've seen her before around the shop or something."

"No, there are hundreds of photographs of her husband, Noah, his sister and youngest brother, but she's never photographed with them, at least not in public."

"Is she British?"

"Not as far as I can tell. The company biography says she's a Houston native."

"So, what, my father was blackmailing her? For what?"

"I don't know, but we can find out."

"How? I doubt she'll tell us on the phone."

"I can't imagine it either. And we need to catch them unaware. If his wife made regular visits to the UK, then he'll know it. They've got another project—a multi-use structure in Rivers Wilde, the enclave where I life. They're raising capital for it. I'm going to email him and express an interest in it. I'll ask for a meeting in Houston, they're really big on making deals that feel like they're being done with a handshake. Every meeting we had was at their home—over breakfast or lunch."

"Are you interested in the project and going back to Houston? You said wild horses couldn't drag you back there."

"They can't. But my love for you can."

I'm panting again. Breathless with gratitude for this man who loves me. But afraid that he's hoping for something that won't manifest.

"What if we can't get what we need? I've got my tribunal hearing in a month."

"What tribunal?" He looks startled, and I realize I haven't told him what brought me here in the first place.

"I resigned today. It was good of them to let me instead of giving me the sack I deserve."

"Is that why your email bounced back?"

I nod miserably.

"Wait, did that motherfucker *out* you?" He shoots to his feet like he's about to run out of the house and go find him.

I put a hand on his arm. "No, no. I went in myself and told Mr. Bone everything. You were right. It was wrong. And as long as I was living that lie, he'd always have a hold on me."

He runs a hand over his face. "What did Mr. Bone say?"

"He was kind, but his hands were tied. He had to let me resign, and the tribunal, despite giving the appearance of being an opportunity to plead my case, is a mere formality. I have a month. But he's offered to let me clerk there while I figure out what's next." The offer that made me so happy earlier leaves a bitter taste in my mouth. "I'm grateful, but being a clerk in the same place I used to be a barrister might be too hard."

He winces and blows out a harsh breath. "Beat, I'm so sorry. Shit."

"Me, too. I came here because I couldn't imagine being anywhere else. I wasn't sure if you'd have me, and I don't want you to feel like that you owe me anything."

His eyebrows shoot up in surprise. "Come on, you think we found this love, this friendship, this home in each other just to walk away from it when things are hard?"

My chin trembles, and I squeeze my eyes shut. My immense relief makes me dizzy. I drop my face into my hands and shake my head at how close I came to losing my biggest blessing. This experience has scared me straight.

"Jules, are you okay?"

I nod and lift my head to look him in the eye. And as soon as I do, my racing heart slows, and a smile I didn't think I'd find again tugs at both sides of my mouth until it hurts.

The tension that furrowed his brow and tightened his jaw eases, and he smiles. It's weary, but it's true.

"I'm sorry I hurt you. I'm sorry I lied to you. It won't happen again. Your trust is priceless, and I hope I can earn it back."

He jerks his chin back and shakes his head. "I trust you, Jules."

I draw in a huge breath and press my lips together to stop them from trembling. I blink to clear my tear-blurred vision, and he wipes the small stream of tears off each cheek with his thumb. "I was angry and terrified." He picks up my hand and laces our fingers together. "I know you're sorry. I forgive you for it. I *believe* you."

I close my eyes again and cover my mouth with my free hand to muffle my sob. I didn't realize I needed to know he did until he said it. "Thank you."

"You're welcome, my heart. And I think you deserve some good to come your way without you having to bleed for it. So whatever I can do to ease your path, I will."

"Thank you."

"You're welcome. And thank you for coming home. Thank you for looking after Beat."

I close one eye and look at him sideways. "Looking after *myself?*"

"The cat. That's what I named her."

"Oh my God, you didn't."

He grins. "I absolutely did. After her mama, my heartbeat."

My head falls back on a carefree laugh. I cup his face and lean forward to kiss him, quickly. I can't believe I'm touching him. "Oh my God, you...where did you come from?"

"It doesn't matter where either of us came from. All that matters is where we're going, together." He straightens suddenly, drops my hand, and sits back and picks up the notebook that's been between us on the couch. His expression is all business now. "Let's get business out of the way so we can make up for lost time." He frowns. "Wait, is Conrad still in your place?"

I can't wait to never have to hear or say his name again. I nod grimly. "The money from the shares I sold will hit my account tomorrow. That's what he's waiting for."

"We'll sort him out. But first, important things. Do you have a passport?"

"Yes. I can travel as a visitor to the United States, but with my conviction, I'll never be able to live there permanently."

"We're going to get that conviction overturned. We have several solid leads. We'll get over that mountain, baby. And until we do, we'll be in London. We love it here."

"Do we?" I ask, skeptical of his enthusiasm.

"Yes. We do." But I get the feeling I'm not the only person he's trying to convince.

"Okay."

He nods once and closes his notebook. "Now I'm going to email Noah, get our tickets booked, and let my sister know I'm coming. Then I've got an errand to run."

"Are you driving?" I ask.

"Yeah. Why?"

"Can I come with you? I have something I need to do."

32

GTFO
Omar

"Oi, what the hell are you doing here?" Conrad jumps up from the couch where he's lounging, watching television like he doesn't have a care in the world.

"It's moving day," I announce in a cheery voice, a grin that's as friendly as a shark's on my face as I hold the door open. "Get the fuck out."

"Hell, no. I'm not going anywhere. Jules and I have an arrangement. She wouldn't be happy you coming round here like this."

"I know all about your arrangement."

His head bobs like a chicken's, and he grows pale. "She told you?"

"Yes. She did."

"And you don't care that you're living with a killer."

"Not at all. In fact, I sleep safer at night knowing she's there. No one's fucking with her, right?"

His eyes bulge. "You can't be serious. I can't believe it."

"The only thing you need to believe is that last night was the last time you'll ever sleep in this flat again. Like I said, it's moving day. Get your shit and get out."

He crosses his stick-like arms over his nearly cavernous chest. "Not until you cough up some money. You're a fucking billionaire, what's a million pounds to you?"

I laugh without any humor. "I'm not a billionaire. But if I was, I still wouldn't give you a penny. You clearly don't know the value of money or what it means to work hard for it. But you're about to find out. Get the fuck out."

He shakes his head. "I'll tell everyone. Her job. I'll go to the papers. I'll make you sorry."

I roll my eyes. "You can leave on your own, or I'll call the police and have them escort you out."

He sneers at me. "What, afraid you'll break a fingernail?"

"No. Just not stupid." If I lay a finger on him, he'll go to the police. Sue me for battery. I'm not taking the bait. "If you leave now, I'll let you put on your shoes and take whatever you can carry with you. If I have to call the police, we'll sit here together while we wait for them, and I won't let you touch anything in this apartment. Besides the crime of blackmail, I'm sure you're in violation of your parole terms. So when they get here, they will certainly arrest you, and you'll be carried out in just what you've got on now."

He glances down at his pasty bare chest, boxer shorts, and bare feet.

"Either way you're leaving. What will it be? I don't have all fucking day."

He grabs his T-shirt and slips it on. He stomps around the living room until he finds his shoes in the rubble of garbage he's managed to compile in just a week. He glares at me while he stoops and hops around to put them on. "I'm going straight to *The Sun*. They'll pay what you wouldn't. Then I'm going to her job, and I'll tell them what she's done."

"And I don't see why *The Sun* would be interested in a story about a woman who was a youth offender and turned her life around. But go ahead. Shout it from the mountaintops, we do not care. But I'll tell you what: You aren't getting so much as bus fare from either of us, ever again. Hurry the fuck up," I snap when he starts glancing around.

"I need my travel card."

"Hear that?" I ask, and he looks at me and actually cranes his neck in my direction.

"I don't hear anything."

"That's exactly how much I care about what you need. Buy a new bus pass."

He turns pained eyes on me. "I'm skint, man. I had debts to pay with that money she gave me. I don't have anything."

"Sell that nice new phone or those stupid shoes you're wearing. I do not care how you do it, or where you go next. Just that you're gone."

"Jules wouldn't—"

I move so my face is close enough for him to see the truth of what I'm about to say in my eyes. "Don't you ever utter her name again. Don't even think about her. Forget she exists and be lucky that I care more about her than I do about giving you what you deserve. And if you ever, ever come near her again, you won't see me coming, but I will. And I'll make you wish you'd never heard the name Juliana Quist. You have five seconds to decide what happens next."

I pull out my phone, dial 999, and start counting.

"Asshole," he shouts as he grabs his phone and a backpack off the couch and darts out the door.

"Damn right I am."

33

THE BOYFRIEND EXPERIENCE
Jules

Conrad runs past me so fast I don't think he realizes I'm there. Omar asked me to wait outside, but I couldn't help it. The doors are as thin as the walls, and I heard every delicious word he said.

He comes out a few seconds behind Conrad and stops short. His brows snap together, and he frowns. "I thought you were waiting outside."

"I still am, technically."

He shakes his head, but he's smiling again. "All's well that ends well. Come on. Let's go home." He grabs my hand and leads us down the stairs to the street level entrance.

"You were extra growly in there."

He laughs. "Is growly a word?" He opens my car door and taps my ass before he runs to his side.

"It's a word. And it was hot. Like foreplay hot."

"Really?" He casts me a sideways glance as he pulls out of the spot and back onto the road.

"*Really*," I say and spread my legs on the seat. "See for yourself."

He keeps his eyes on the road, but that dimple is winking at me as his fingers dance up until they reach the apex of my thighs. He cups me there and presses down. The bolt of pleasure is delicious, but I want more.

"Wait." I brush his hand away with a saucy smile and hook my thumbs in my waistband. "If we're doing this, in this sexy car, then I want the full experience." I lift my hips off the seat and tug my leggings and panties down until I can spread my thighs.

He glances sideways at me and lets out a whistle. "Are you trying to make my heart stop? Putting a fucking banquet in front of me when I can't eat it."

When he stops at the next red light, he glances out of the window. "But I'll certainly take a sample." He covers my pussy with the flat of his palm, pressing it into my clit. His fingers slide between my lips, and he presses two fingers into me. "God, you're so fucking wet."

He pulls away when the light turns green and keeps his eyes on the road but keeps his fingers inside me. "Keep your hand on the gear shift and move it when I say."

I do as he asks, moving the gears until he gets to fourth. "Okay, we should be good until I have to stop again."

His fingers don't miss a beat. "You are a really good driver. This is peak level multitasking." My giggle turns into a gasping moan when he curves his finger inside me.

"It helps to have an excellent copilot, but for what I want to do to you, it's not going to be good enough."

"And what is it you want to do?" I ask through labored breaths.

"Let me show you." He pulls his hands from my body and makes a sharp turn a few streets after Clapham Junction, pulling over into the first empty parking spot we find. It's a residential street, quiet but not deserted. "Oh my God, we can't park here. Someone will walk by," I say even as my hips rock up in search of his hand and the pleasure of its caress.

He grins. "My windows are completely tinted. They would have to come right up close and peer in to see anything." He pulls up the parking break. "Now, where were we?" Before I can answer, he leans over, takes my nipple into his mouth, and sucks hard.

"That feels so good." I slide my hand into his thick hair.

He releases my breast and lifts his head and gazes at me with half closed, lust-glazed eyes. "I know it does." He licks three of his fingers at once and then his hand is back where I need it.

I moan and roll my body, trying to take him deeper.

He groans and adds another finger. "Oh baby, you're so wet, I want to put my dick inside you. I need to start taking condoms with me when I leave."

"Your fingers aren't a bad substitute." When he lowers his head to my breast, I tug it back up. "I need your mouth on mine. Kiss me," I pant.

"Whatever you need." He kisses me, wet and hard, pumping his fingers deeper and rubbing my clit.

His fingers move faster, and my hips keep pace. I close my eyes, my breaths coming faster and harder until the only sound in the car are my moans and whimpers, the wicked, wet slide of his fingers in and out of my body.

He breaks the kiss. "How are you feeling?"

Every inch of my body is tense and focused on the tight, coiling pressure building inside of me. "I'm so close, so close, don't stop, please."

He drops his head to my breast and flicks the nipple before he pulls it back into his hot mouth and sucks. It takes less than a minute to get me there, and then pleasure and him and us are all I know. "Oh my God, Omar. Yes. That's so, so good." My toes curl so tightly it hurts, and my fingernails dig into the soft leather of the seat as my body rides the seemingly endless wave of my blistering orgasm.

He draws his fingers out of me and sucks them into his mouth, closes his eyes, and groans. "You taste so good. I can't wait to get home and spread you out on our bed."

"For the rest of the day," I add and pull my shirt down. I fish my panties off his floorboard but don't bother putting them back on before I slide my leggings up.

"So was that everything you expected from the experience of being fingered in your boyfriend's car?"

I turn my head on a languorous sigh, satisfaction pulling my kiss-bruised lips up at the corners. "Everything and more."

He grins, puts the car into gear, and pulls out of the spot we parked in.

We wind our way back out to Brixton Lane, turn right up the hill, and go home.

One Week Later
Rivers Wilde
Houston, TX

34

FULL
Jules

"Are you hungry?" Omar asks.

"Famished. Is there somewhere we can stop before we get to the house?"

"Of course. We'd be spoiled for choice, actually. But for something quick, we'll go to Sweet and Lo's—you'll love it. When we've got time, I'll take you down to The Market."

"Are we almost there?"

"Minutes away."

My heart skips a beat. I'm about to meet his family, and I'm more than a little nervous.

We landed in Houston this morning and spent hours getting through immigration and claiming our luggage. From the awful smell of petrol that permeates the air around the airport to the endless stream of billboards and electrical wires that run along the freeways, my first impression of Houston is that of a soulless sprawl of commercial developments and concrete.

He pulls off the next exit and makes an almost immediate right turn.

The landscape transforms from the seemingly endless stretch of highway we've been on for nearly an hour to something out of a dream.

The road appears to be the main artery of the subdivision. It's bisected by a grassy, tree-lined knoll that seems to double as a walking path.

From a multicolored structure that says "welcome" in at least a dozen languages to the wide, smoothly paved streets lined with glass-front shops to the strip of green tree-lined mall that divides one side of street from the other, it says, "This is a place where we live *together*."

When Omar promised that this place was going to make me feel at home instantly, I thought he was exaggerating. But he wasn't.

Even from the car, the enclave of Rivers Wilde is nothing short of welcoming.

We approach a roundabout with a huge fountain in the center, and he takes the first exit. Ahead of us, the street seems to stretch on for miles, the uniformity of the storefronts disrupted by their individual logos, but the care in planning shows in every detail. Hyacinth blooms from bushes in between each shop, and a string of fairy lights runs from tree to tree in the center median.

He pulls into a parking spot. "We're here."

"Here" is a charming café that is straight out of one of the many American television shows that depict small town life as charming, eclectic, and warm.

"The Mastermind is back!" a dark-skinned man whose broad, toothy smile reminds me of my Dominic shouts when we walk in.

The same bright yellow signage that graces the glass-front window of the shop floats in suspension from the high ceiling above his head. "Sweet and Lo's."

"Lotanna, my man," Omar greets the grinning man who steps around the counter and rushes toward us, arms outstretched.

"Sweet was going to send a search party looking for you soon." They share a warm hug. Then Lotanna turns his beaming smile on me. "And then we saw your video. You naughty boy. How could you go find your wife and not call us immediately?"

I giggle at his calling Omar a naughty boy. He doesn't look a day older than him. "I'm Jules."

"Well, what a perfect name. You certainly are a jewel." He holds his hand out for a shake, and I return his bright smile even though I'm a little bummed he didn't hug me, too. "Thank you. So nice to meet you." I take his hand.

"The pleasure is all mine." He lifts my hand and bows a little to press a kiss to the back of it. Heat rushes up my neck at the compliment, and I glance at a grinning Omar. He mouths, *I told you so.*

Lotanna straightens. "Now I have to make sure we restock our PG tips for you, but until then, you have to try Sweet's special blend." He waves us toward a table. "Sit, let me bring you something."

Omar shakes his head. "No, Lo, we're not staying. We just landed and are exhausted."

The other man nods with a knowing expression. "And your sister is waiting. I know. She came in earlier to buy scones for your British jewel." He smiles at me. "I hope you like scones. She insisted all British people do."

"I like them just fine."

"Well, you wait until you taste them. They are very unique and made by our very own Regan Rivers."

"Oh, like the same name that's on the subdivision?" I ask, intrigued that this isn't some large corporate development, but a family run one.

"Yes, she's actually a Wilde—they founded this place we call home, but she married Mr. Rivers, and now I guess she's both."

"You, this man!" a loud feminine voice booms from behind us and I jump and glance over my shoulder.

A tall, statuesque woman with skin like polished mahogany and wide sparkling eyes that betray her disapproving frown approaches us. "This isn't happy hour." She comes to stand next to Lo and bumps his hip with hers. He turns to face her and narrows his eyes at her, but his smile is all tenderness. He taps a finger on the tip of her nose. "It's always happy hour when you're here." He leans down to kiss her. "And don't shout at me in front of Omar's wife."

"What?" She turns her head sharply toward us, her eyes wide as she looks between Omar and me. "You got married and you didn't even bring her to meet me first?" she scolds Omar with a wag of her finger. She looks at me and then clasps her hands in front of her chin and grins from ear to ear. "Oh, you dey too fine." She reaches over to nudge Omar's shoulder with a playful smile. "I see why you dey hide 'em," she says with a sly smile.

"Why, thank you. But he hasn't been hiding me," I respond with a smile as wide as hers. "It's been years since I heard anyone speak pidgin."

"Dear Lord," Sweet gasps and presses a hand to her chest. "She understands pidgin. Omar, I approve of your wife." She pulls me into a warm hug. She smells like garlic and lemons, and by the time she lets me go, I'm looser and lighter. And pretty sure she's my new favorite person.

"I'm not *actually* his wife," I correct, but this time with a laugh.

"Trust me, you are. If *he* has brought you home, then that's what you are," she beams at me. "It's very nice to meet you. I'm Sweet... in name and spirit."

"Until you insult Nigerian jollof." Omar winks at her.

"*That* is a hill she will die on," Lo chimes in.

"Stop telling tales about me." She smacks his arm and then tugs it to pull him into a hug. "We're so happy to have you back. The place wasn't the same without your scowl or your ability to clear a room with one look," she says, patting his back and smiling with her eyes closed.

I can't believe Omar has never mentioned these people or this place. Out of sight is out of mind for him, I guess. But I can't imagine, even if this is my only encounter with them, that I'll ever forget it.

"Is this place yours?" I ask, looking around the large, beautifully decorated café. It's relatively uncrowded at ten in the morning, but it's got the capacity for a large number of people.

"You're lucky you came before the lunch rush starts. Otherwise, I would have had to wave at you from the kitchen."

"I'm glad, too. It's nice to be back."

"I hope you're staying for as long as you were gone." She looks expectantly between the two of us.

I reach for Omar's hand and lace our fingers together. "I hope so, too."

"Let me give you some of the kolaches we have left over from breakfast. And your honeycomb latte. Do you want two or does your lady only drink tea?"

He grins at her and turns his gaze to me. "Coffee or tea?"

I hate to live up to the stereotype, but my nerves are already dancing around like crazy, so I ask for one of the sparkling fruit spritzers I spied on their menu.

"A woman after my own heart." Sweet smiles and disappears. The door chimes, and Lo's attention turns to the customers that just walked in. "Okay, let me go and do my work. But come back tomorrow for breakfast, and we'll talk. I want to hear all about the lady who harpooned you."

"Wow, they're lovely," I whisper as we stand aside and wait for Sweet to come back with whatever it was she said she was bringing. I've forgotten already, but I haven't forgotten the excitement on her face as she mentioned it.

"Yeah, everyone here is...in their own way." His smile is so fond and endearing.

"Why haven't you ever mentioned them?"

"Honestly, since I met you, this place fell into my rearview. Working on the house in London, living there I started to think of it as home. But yeah, this place is great."

The affection in his voice squeezes my heart. "How did you find it?"

"A friend of a friend recommended it. I moved in right before my first semester and never left. And *that* was my study spot most days." He turns us and then points to a table in the corner, partially obscured by a huge glass display case where mouthwatering sandwiches and pastries are laid out and calling my name.

"I'm going to need a new wardrobe if we stay here long. Good Lord, but no one can beat you Yanks when it comes to portion size."

"That's the first time you've called me that."

"I guess…it's the first time I've thought of you that way."

"Mr. Solomon?" We turn to find a young woman, dark-haired and remarkably pretty, whose nametag reads Bianca holding a white pastry bag and a drink carrier. "Sweet asked me to bring this out and told me to say she was sorry, but she had to get something into the oven."

"Thank you." I take them out of her hands, and her eyes widen.

"Are you English?" Her voice has an awe in it that I don't understand.

"I am," I answer.

She beams and claps her hands together. "Oh my gosh, I love your accent. I love London. I've only been once but—" She claps a hand over her mouth. "I'm sorry. I talk too much, and you're taking this to go. Uh, Sweet put some of the garlic knots in there, but frozen so you need to heat your oven to 350 and pop them in for ten minutes," she recites.

"Okay, thank you."

"Gosh, I could listen to you talk…"

"Bianca, there are customers waiting," Lo chides from behind the register, and her freckled cheeks flush.

"Bye for now. Nice to see you, Mr. Solomon. I'll tell my dad you're back."

"Who's her father?" I ask as we walk back out to the street where we parked and stroll to the car hand in hand.

"Remington Wilde."

"Oh. The lawyer we spoke with. Oh my goodness, Wilde. Like the neighborhood."

"Yes, his grandfather and father founded this place."

"And that's his daughter? It's totally a family affair, huh?" I ask, excited and feeling a sense of longing that I wish I didn't. "So is this like the high street?" I settle the food on my lap and buckle the safety belt.

"Yeah, I guess you'd call it that. The rest of the neighborhood shoots off from the roundabout at the top of the street."

"Okay, and that's where your house is?"

"Yes, I'll show you as we drive. And later we can walk back down. It's nice at night, too."

"Okay," I say, expelling a deep breath as my nerves start again.

"Don't be nervous. They'll love you." He reads my mind and squeezes my hand before he pulls out of the parking spot and joins the light flow of traffic.

He drives like he does everything else: confidently and deliberately, but fast. The high street rushes past outside in a blur, but I make out a huge salon, a yoga studio, a greeting card shop, and a bookstore and make note of all of them.

"Wow, you don't have to leave for anything, do you?"

"That's the whole point," he agrees as we approach the roundabout he mentioned. And it's like stepping into an entirely different landscape than the high street. A seemingly endless stream of cars make their way around, and in the center is a huge brass horse with a crown on its head and a huge R and W on its chest.

"That way to the office park and the market, which is actually a huge food hall and market." He points to the right as we pass the first offshoot. "That way to the high-rise community." He points down a long street that appears to be another, more modern take on the high street. "There is where the schools, the management office, and the post office are." He points down another long tree-lined lane. "And this is The Oaks," he says as we turn onto a street flanked by bronze gates.

"This is the place you live if you want quiet mornings and evenings and space enough so your neighbors can't hear you screaming when you come."

"Yes, I'm sure that's exactly what they had in mind when they built it." I give him an indulgent smirk before I turn my attention to the window. The houses that line this street are detached brick, two-story villa-like homes with large, beautifully manicured lawns and trees with large glossy green leaves and fat, lush cream-colored flowers hanging from them. Two women walk hand in hand behind three young children on bicycles with bright helmets and huge smiles.

A South Asian man stands in his driveway watering a flowerbed, and a woman with dark hair is kneeling down in the grass next to him, digging. Similar scenes greet me as we turn and meander deeper into the subdivision. The houses change, depending on the street, some small bungalows, some huge mini mansions, but there's a cohesiveness in the sense they all give of being home, and refuge.

"We're here," Omar says, and we turn into a drive that makes a half circle in front of a huge white brick house with black shutters and large windows on its façade. The front is lined with hedgerows, and the black lacquered front door is lined with bright pink flowers I don't recognize. "This is so beautiful," I sigh and unbuckle my seatbelt. "How could you bear to leave it?" I ask, genuinely amazed that he could.

"I guess I knew something better was waiting for me."

"Aww, my love. Thank you." I lean over the center console, and he meets me halfway. It was meant to be a light, quick kiss, but it's the first time our lips have touched since we arrived, and my hunger for him is ignited. We linger on each other's mouths, and every time one of us pulls away, the other pulls them back. The slam of the front door comes just as his tongue darts out to probe my mouth, and he groans.

"Later," I whisper and take a deep breath before I face his family.

A small woman with long, dark hair and a glowing honey brown complexion a shade or two darker than Omar's is rushing toward us. She's waving a tea towel in the air and sporting a grin that I'd know anywhere—it's the same as Omar's from her fuller top lip and dimples to the way her nose crinkles at the same time. "Show time," he says before he opens the car door.

"What does that mean?" I ask, but he's out and grabbing his sister into a hug before I even finish my sentence.

I open my door and climb out. I hope he's right. We didn't talk about how we'd answer questions about my past. Despite what the record states, the fact that the people who know me best believe me has given me a sense of freedom from the stigma and shame I've walked around with.

But I'm not sure now what I'll say if they ask about my parents.

"Layel—this is my heart. I call her Beat, but you can call her Jules."

"Jules." Layel cries my name like it's a declaration and throws her arms around me. She's several inches shorter than me, and I bend a little to hug her back. "Oh my God. My brother is in love, fucking finally. I'm so happy to meet you. You have to show me your ways because there's no one he has ever called his love with that look in his eyes before."

She lets me go but grabs hold of my hand. "Mar, my baby, you're all grown up," she says with pride on her face.

He runs a tender hand over her head. "Had to happen sometime."

They exchange a smile and then she claps her hands together as if to commence a race. "Let's get inside. Do you need help with your luggage?"

Omar shakes his head and heads to the back of the car. "No, I've got it. But you can take this." He hands her the bag from Sweet and Lo's.

She slaps him with the tea towel. "You didn't. I've been cooking all morning."

He scowls. "I'll tell you what… I haven't missed how deft you are with that towel."

"Well, if you weren't so naughty, I wouldn't need to be," she shoots back without any apology.

She drapes an arm around my waist. "I've always wanted a sister," she says softly. And in a louder voice, "I hope you don't get tired of his bad attitude and dump him."

"You must be talking about yourself. No one has ever dumped me."

"Only 'cause you didn't give them the chance," she says. She looks at me, grins, and winks. "Come on in. I'll heat up whatever Sweet sent over since you're hungry. Dad is coming over to eat, but he won't be here for another hour."

"I can wait," I say and let her lead me inside. I was hungry when we arrived, but right now, I feel incredibly full.

35

PRODIGAL
Omar

"The prodigal son returns," my dad says and raises his glass of water in the air.

"What's a prodigal?" Hannah asks from beside me.

"Someone who leaves their family for too long," her mother answers.

"Oh yeah. Then that's totally you, Uncle Omar."

"And with a welcome like this, do you wonder why?" I tease. But their welcome has been more than warm. Layel's house is right next door to mine, and she's run back and forth between the two houses to get things she needed to make lunch.

I asked why we didn't just eat at hers, and she said she wanted my first night in my house to feel like home. It's as sparsely decorated as the house in London was when I first moved in, but since we've been here I've been making a note of all the things it needs. Jules is at the top of it.

"We're glad to see you, son." My father's eyes are warm and soft, and I raise my glass to mimic his gesture.

"I'm glad to see you, too." I am. I was nervous about what it would be like to be back here in the place that somehow became our family hub. I didn't need to be.

My dad had nothing but a warm hug for me and Jules, too.

The kids have inundated her with questions about London and clothes and weather and music. She's great with them. I don't know why that surprises me, but it does. I'm not sure what kind of family she wants, or if she wants one at all. I love the idea of a mini Jules running around, but I'd be happy for it to just be us, too.

"So Juliana—"

"Jules, please," she corrects with a smile, and I don't know how I missed the pronunciation she uses that makes it sound like Jewels. Oh my girl, she's so clever.

"Jules," my father repeats with an equally warm smile, but his eyes are shrewd and assessing, and I know he's about to give her a good once-over. "Omar tells us you're a lawyer."

She swallows hard. Her eyes dart to me across the table, and in them I see a plea for help. I just give her a reassuring smile. Whatever she wants to tell them is fine. The truth is always scarier in our heads than out loud anyway.

"I'm training to be one," she starts, her eyes still on mine for a second before she looks back at my dad.

"I see. So you're in law school?"

"No, I finished. But once that's done we have to do a vocational training that gives us practical experience. It's called a pupilage. I'm not quite done with mine."

"Oh," Layel sighs, a pout on her face. "So you have to go back to finish."

Jules puts her glass down and folds her hands in her lap. "I do have to go back, yes, but Omar doesn't."

It's my turn to frown. "No, I don't. But I will."

We eye each other in a silent war of wills. We haven't talked about this at all, and I certainly don't want to talk about it in front of them.

Layel clears her throat, and Jules snaps her eyes shut for a second. When she opens them again, they're clear. "I'm sorry. I'm tired and hungry, don't mind me," she says with a bright smile that convinces everyone at the table but me that she's telling the truth. "But really, this place is amazing."

"You just wait until summer and you're sweltering. You won't think so then," my dad says.

"So how did you two meet?"

"Officially at a party—"

"Where I turned her down for a dance and then broke her nose."

Hannah gasps. "What?"

"You make it sound awful," Jules chides. "He did turn me down when I asked him to dance. But he more than made up for it later." She smiles at me, and I know she's remembering our first time. Heat blooms on the back of my neck, and blood rushes to my dick. She knows what she's doing, and I'll get her back later.

"What about your nose?"

"I walked up behind him and surprised him. He head butted me. It wasn't a serious break. I didn't need surgery or anything. He took me to the hospital and waited while they bandaged me up. And took me home after. But I'd had a crush on him for so long and I finally had my chance, so I left my iPad in his car so he'd have to come back over."

"Ah, a Chelsea fan, are you?" my father asks knowingly.

"I don't know a thing about football. I bartend at the pub in his neighborhood. He came in every week, but we'd never spoken. I didn't work up the nerve until the night we ended up at a mutual friend's party."

I cover her hand with mine. "And once I got an up-close taste of perfection, I knew I'd never have enough."

"Oh, Omar..." She turns the hand under mine over and links our fingers, and we share a smile. I wish I could bottle this feeling—the contentment in her eyes matches what I feel down to my soul. I hope like hell this lead we're chasing pans out. But if this doesn't, if it takes forever, I'll try forever, because she deserves to live in the same sunshine she shines on all of us.

I shake my head and pull her to me, and her warm body comforts and calms me as she nestles into my chest, burrowing her nose into the space between my pecs where my heart beats for her and the rest of the people I love. I cup the back of her head and press a kiss to the top of it.

"So why'd you say no when she asked you to dance?"

"Because I'm a shit dancer, and when I realized it was her, my nerves got the best of me."

"You? Nervous around a girl?"

"A woman," I correct my sister and wink at Jules. "And yes. I knew she was way out of my league."

"But...you dated the Kardashians," Hannah chimes in next to me.

"I didn't date any damn Kardashians. Jesus," I growl.

Jules snickers. "I don't know why he keeps denying it. Everyone saw him, right?"

She and the girls laugh.

My dad just looks confused. "You dated a Kardashian? When?"

"Never," I groan. "You little shit," I whisper to Hannah and get a huge grin in return.

"No one saw anything. You're supposed to be on my side," I say to Jules.

"I am. But you're so much fun to tease."

I narrow my eyes at her, and she only smiles wider. "I thought you were tired." As if on cue, she yawns. Her eye widen as if she surprised herself, and she stretches. "It must be this amazing meal. I've never had Tex Mex before, but I think it's my new favorite food."

"Well, you're in the right place. It's basically our state's official cuisine. And Rivers Wilde finally has a Tex Mex restaurant. They have music every third Saturday. We'll go."

"If I'm still here, I'd love that." She meets my eye for just second, and I see the worry in them even though she's smiling. "Do you mind if I go shower and have a lie down?" She stands and picks up her plate before she reaches for my dad's.

I put a hand on her arm to stop her. "Don't worry about that, you go get some rest."

She shakes her head. "Layel made this beautiful meal, the least I can do is load the dishwasher."

"Not at all," my father says gently but firmly and looks at Layel. "Why don't you make sure Jules has everything she needs upstairs? Omar and I will clean the kitchen."

My sister's jaw drops, and she gapes at my father. "*You* are going to clean? Like with your own hands?"

I laugh at the incredulity on her face, but my stomach churns. She's right, he's not a modern man in the sense that he believes whatever else a woman does, the kitchen is her domain and not a place men belong. So I know this means he's really desperate to talk to me alone, and I can only imagine what he's got to say.

* * * *

"What is she hiding?" my father asks just as I'm drying the last of the pans. When we came in here, I was sure he was going to grill me about Jules. Instead, he asked about the house in London and seemed proud of the fact that I'd done all of the work I could myself. We talked about my wanting to invest in the Royales' new project and that I had a meeting with him tomorrow. He caught me up on what he'd been working on and his health, and I thought I'd only imagined the question in his eyes when he looked at her. Layel and Hannah stuck their heads in the kitchen to say Jules was settled and in the shower and that they were heading home so she could take Hannah to her tennis lessons.

I sigh and drop the dish towel. "She's not hiding anything, Dad."

"Okay, so what isn't she saying?" he presses.

My head hurts, and I'm tired, but I want to get this over with. I'm not ashamed of her, but I don't want to tell him anything she wouldn't say herself. "She's probably not going to be offered a tenancy at her chambers when she finishes her pupilage."

"Why not?"

"Because I lied on my application, and when I told them, they fired me."

We whip around in unison. "Beat, I didn't hear you come down. I thought you were sleeping."

"My shower refreshed me, and if I sleep now, I'll be up all night." She smiles like she didn't walk in on us talking about her, and I wave her over.

"Jules, I'm sorry. I just—"

"You love your son. It's okay. I'm glad Omar has a family like this." She tucks herself into my side and looks up at me. "I love him, too. And I don't want you to have any doubts about who I am."

"You don't have to say anything you don't want to."

"It's okay. This is your family. I hope they'll be mine one day, too." She pats my chest as if she can feel my heart thundering. This is the first time she's spoken about our future in a concrete way, and I nod.

"I hope so, too."

"My father died in a fire that I was accused and convicted of setting. I was thirteen and pled guilty to avoid the trial and to reduce my sentence. But I didn't set that fire. I loved my father very, very much. He was all I had in the whole world, and we came because we're trying to find new evidence to have my case reopened."

I keep my eyes trained on my father while she speaks and am braced for any sign of disdain. He can think what he wants, but I'm not going to let anyone treat her badly.

"I see" is all he says, his expression neutral until he looks back up at me with tears in his eyes.

I have never, not once in my 37 years of life, seen this man come close to crying. "Dad, are you okay?"

He wipes his eyes and takes a deep breath to compose himself. "I'm very proud of you, son. So proud of you. You know better and have done better than me already."

I glance at Jules, and concern is etched on her face. "So you're not upset?"

"That you're in love with a wonderful woman who has overcome unfathomable circumstances? No. I'm not. I'm happier than I've been in a long time."

He walks over to Jules and extends his arms. "Come, daughter. Give me a hug."

My two worlds collide and lock into place next to each other, and there's a crack of thunder and rain starts.

"Damn it," my father says. "I left my radio outside on my porch. I have to go. I'll be back later with Mimosa. She sends her love." He dashes out of the house.

"Does he live in Rivers Wilde, too?"

"Yes, but in the Ivy with the cool kids."

"That story gets easier to tell every time. I can't believe he responded like that."

"We've all come a long way. You okay?" I ask her, searching her face for signs of strain.

"Almost."

"What do you need, baby?" I ask, and her smile turns sharp and sensual.

"You between my thighs."

I lift her into my arms. "Your wish, my command."

She wraps her arms around my neck while I carry her up the stairs. "I'm so happy right now."

"Me, too."

I'm glad we built this day into our trip. She needed this moment of feel good. I just hope we'll still be feeling this way when the sun sets tomorrow.

36

BATTLE ROYALE
Omar

"So is this place like Rivers Wilde?" Jules asks as we turn down Rivers Oaks Blvd from San Felipe.

"Not even close. This isn't an everybody's welcome kind of community."

"The houses are so big." She gawks at the mansions on both sides of the street. "How can *one* family live in such a big house?"

"Very easily."

"Can't imagine." She yawns and stretches.

"Are you tired?"

"A little. I think it's that huge breakfast because I slept so well."

"Me, too." I forgot how comfortable my bed in this house is. "Okay, this is theirs." I nod at a driveway right after the stop sign. We turn into a long, circular driveway.

"Shit, who is that?" Jules mutters and points at a baldheaded, bearded man in all black standing at the front. I instinctively pump my brakes and slow down.

The plan was that we'd ring the bell, and while whoever answered it went to inform Mr. Royale I was here, Jules would sneak up the stairs to Mrs. Royale's private suite of rooms.

As we get closer, I realize who the man standing at the front door of the enormous house looking like a fucking assassin in his all-black garb, black Ray-Ban Wayfarers, a completely bald head, and full beard is.

"That's Noah."

"Wow, he's…really *big.*" Jules' voice is full of awe.

I scowl at her. "Put your tongue back in your mouth. He's married."

"I remember, and I was just saying…"

"Yeah, I know what you were saying."

"You know that clean shaven jaw of yours is my catnip." She runs her hand along it.

"And now I also know you get thirsty when you see a big man with a beard."

She glares at me. "I am *not* thirsty. And why are you teasing me when you should be panicking?"

"Panicking about what?"

She looks at me like I just told her I'm an alien. "What?"

"Omar! He wasn't supposed to be outside. How am I going to get into the house with him standing there?" Her voice pitches higher on that last sentence.

I put a hand on her leg. "Don't worry. Whatever is happening right now, we're not leaving here without what we came for. He and I are scheduled to go see this structure and meet with his dad. If he tries to change things up, I'll insist that I won't do anything until we drive over. We'll leave. You just wait for your chance. There's also a back entrance. We'll make it happen."

She draws in a big breath and lets it out. "Okay. Trust the plan. Got it."

We roll to a stop right in front of the man we're discussing, and he bends down to peer into the window and wave. I hold up my hand to let him know we need a minute.

I take Jules' hand and squeeze it.

She squeezes mine back. "Let's go." The brave smile on her face makes me fall in love with her all over again.

I lean over and kiss her quickly. "It's show time."

When I open the door, Noah walks around the car to my side.

I don't blame Jules. Noah Royale cuts an impressive figure. He's tall, a few inches taller than my six foot two, and built like a tank. His bald head glints in the sun, but there's not a drop of sweat on him, like even it knows better than to annoy him.

I stick out my hand in greeting. "Nice of you to roll out the red carpet and meet us yourself."

He rolls his eyes and pulls me into a bear hug that takes me by surprise but that I return. "It's really fucking nice to see you. It's been too long," he says and pats my back before he lets me go.

"This is my girlfriend, Jules. She's dropping me off before she heads into town to shop." I don't know why I'm giving him the details, but it doesn't matter because he's not looking at me anyway.

"Nice to meet you," she says and then adds, "I'm a hugger, too." He laughs but wraps her in his arms and lifts her off her feet. When he sets her down, I nudge her. She grins at me, and I scowl. Noah takes off his sunglasses and leans forward, peering at her. "Do I know you?" He runs his eyes over her from head to toe. Not in a lascivious way but like he's trying to recall where he's seen her before.

She stiffens slightly and shakes her head. "Not unless you've spent a lot of time in southwest London."

Noah's eyebrows pop over his sunglasses, and his brow furrows. Then, the huge, sly grin I remember splits his beard. "Holy *shit*. You're English?"

"I am."

Noah slaps me on the arm. "I'm glad your time there was so fruitful." He glances back at the house. "It's a shame my mother's locked up in her bedroom. She was a real anglophile. She would have loved meeting you."

That sets off my radar—him calling her an anglophile firms up a real connection to the UK.

"Has she been before?" Jules asks in a matter-of-fact way.

"A lifetime ago," he says and then slips his sunglasses back on. "Down to business. There's been a slight change in plan. My dad's held up by a call so he's still in his office. I'll drive us over, and he'll meet us there."

I nod. "That works."

"I swear I know you," he says to Jules.

"I have one of those faces," she says with a smile but turns so she's standing in front of me with her back to him. She gives me a wide-eyed "What the fuck?" look but says, "Have a good lunch, my love. I'll see you later." She lifts up on her toes, kissing my cheek.

"Later. Drive safely."

She climbs back in the Dodge Charger we rented, and I'm distracted by how fucking hot she looks behind the wheel of that car. I watch her drive away.

"I bet you could listen to her talk all day, huh?"

"I could," I agree. "So which way to your car?"

I turn to face him. His eyes are on the retreating tail lights of Jules' car, and only when she turns out of the driveway does he turn to look at me. "The car is being brought around now. It'll be just a minute."

"No problem, no rush." I'm sure Jules is idling around waiting for us to leave before she comes back.

"So you got money to burn or you just a sucker for my projects?"

"Neither. I like the sound of it, want to hear more and hope we'll find a common ground."

A black Corvette swings from around the back of the house and stops right in front of us. A young man dressed in all white hops out. "Mr. Royale, she's got a full tank and fresh detail." I feel bad misleading him, but Jules needs answers.

"Thanks, Bola." He gives the man an impatient but civil smile and climbs in.

I fold myself into the cramped interior of the car. "Hit that button, the seat will push back."

I do and am relieved when my legs have room to extend. "Nice wheels."

"I agree. My wife hated it."

"Hated? Like past tense?"

"Yep. She left me three months ago."

"Oh man. I hadn't heard that. I'm sorry."

"Well, I didn't advertise it, and she seems to have gone to ground. I don't even know where the fuck she is," he grumbles in his deep gravelly voice.

"Is that why you're moving?"

"Yeah. I can't stand being in this city without her. Everything reminds me of her, and it's making me crazy."

"I'm sorry. And shocked. You guys were attached at the hip."

"Yeah, that's what I thought. It shocked the shit out of me when she served me with divorce papers out of the fucking blue."

"Wow. You were blindsided?"

"Yes. And she was resolute. I got on my knees and begged her. She left anyway. Once I get this project off the ground, I will too."

"Are you sure you're going to be able to manage it from afar?"

"I'll try. But I promise if it's not working, I'll man up and come back. This project is personal, this was my stomping ground in high school. I can't believe it's sitting abandoned. This part of Southwest Houston needs a new, upscale, and versatile retail center. Sharpstown is an ideal location, and the structure's bones are sound."

"I can't wait to see it."

37

SMOKING GUN
Jules

Despite that hiccup at the beginning, Omar's plan worked incredibly well. I circled the block once to give him and Noah time to leave and just pulled back up to the house. I park my car in the back where it appears the house staff parks and hope no one notices one odd car out of the dozen sitting there.

Houston's River Oaks neighborhood, where the Royales live, is masterplanned, just like Rivers Wilde but with an entirely different vision. This is not a place where everyone is welcome. The mansions that line River Oaks Blvd are modern renditions of the sprawling estates England is famous for. The Royales' home is right off the main street and the biggest home I've ever been inside of.

The family clearly has a lot of faith in their neighbors and the distance of the house from the street, because the front door is unlocked. I walk right in and book it up the stairs and am already on the landing when I hear a man's voice call for someone. Dina's intel said she was cloistered in a suite at the end of the hall. I hurry toward the door, my heart racing, my skin slick with sweat, and the recorder on my phone on.

I knock lightly on the door, and a woman calls, "Come on in, Trixi."

I don't know who Trixi is, but I'm not going to walk away now. Not when I am so close to something I hadn't imagined possible. I step into the dark, cavernous room. All the curtains are drawn, and but for a small light on the side of the bed, it might as well be evening.

"You're very early today, but I'm glad of it. This book Silas bought me is a—Who are you?" Her almost lazy drawl turns into a sharp, urgent bark. She sits up and reaches over on her bedside.

"Please don't call anyone. I'm not here to hurt you. My name is Crown Jewel Hayford, and I think you knew my father."

Her hand freezes, hovering over the phone beside the bed. "What did you say?"

I repeat myself, and she deflates, falling back on the bed. "How did you find me? I thought…you were in prison." Her voice loses all of its energy.

My heart stutters. "You… How do you know who I am?" I'm shocked.

"I knew your father. I've seen your picture."

"Can I please turn on a light so I can see?"

"Nora?" a man's voice calls from outside the door.

"Get in there," she hisses and points at a door to the left of her bed.

"Why?"

"If he finds you here, he'll call the police. Go, hurry," she orders, her reed thin arm pointing toward the door.

I do as I'm told. As soon as I shut the door, she calls, "Come on in, Silas."

I press my ear to the door. "I'm running late to meet Noah and a potential investor. I wanted to make sure you had everything you need."

"I'm fine, honey. Thank you."

"Are you sure, sweetheart? You look a little pale."

"I'm tired. I was drifting off when you knocked."

"Well, you rest now, my dear. Want me to pick you up something from Ousie's?"

"That would be wonderful. Thank you."

"You're welcome. I love you. I'll see you later."

"Tell Noah hi for me," she calls.

I wait until I hear the door close before I walk back out. She's out of bed drawing the curtains open, and light floods the room. It's decorated in a sea of white and gold. But I don't look around at the details. I watch the woman who might have had my father killed for any sign of recognition. She's olive-skinned and dark-haired. Even dressed in her loose-fitting pajamas, I can see that she's as slight as a bird.

"Sit," she orders, pointing to one of the chairs by the window.

"Did you have my father killed?" I ask the only thing I care to know.

"What?" She gasps and sits down in one of the chairs herself, crossing her legs and leaning back as if she'd been pushed. "I thought you killed him. What in the world are you talking about?"

"You...you were sending him money and then he wrote, threatening you for more, and then he was dead."

She shakes her head in disbelief. "Is that what you think? That's why you're here?" She could be lying, but the shock in her voice sounds genuine. And she knows who I am. "Why else would I be here? I don't know you from Adam."

"Sit down, please, Jewel. Please," she adds in a softly pleading voice when I hesitate. I'm too devastated to argue. I can't believe this isn't the smoking gun I hoped for.

"What was going on between you and my father?"

"We had an affair. A long time ago. And when it was over, I came back to my husband and never saw him or set foot in England again."

"What were you paying him for?" I shake my head in despair. "Who are you?"

She watches me with her eyes narrowed and her chest heaving. "I'm sorry you found me. You weren't meant to. But he wasn't supposed to die, either."

"What do you mean? Who are you?"

"I loved your father, Jewel. And I'm so sorry for what happened to him. It broke my heart when he died and even more so because it was at your hand."

"I didn't do it. And if you loved him, why have I never heard of you?"

"Because I paid him not to tell you."

"Why?"

She stares down at her hands for a full minute, and I have to restrain myself from grabbing her by the collar and shaking her until she tells me.

She lifts her head and looks me dead in the eye. "Because I am your mother."

My slack jaw falls down to my chest, and the hair on the back of my neck stands up. "My mother died giving birth to me."

"That's what he told you."

"He wouldn't lie to me."

"He did, but only because I asked him to. And provided for you. And my husband and children don't know you exist. And I never want them to."

The words are a punch to my gut. "Why?" I hear myself ask.

And she answers me. By the time she's done, I'm sorry I asked.

My ears are ringing, my pulse is out of control, and I'm lightheaded.

"I'm sorry I bothered you," I mutter, and without looking at her, I stand.

I hear her call my name, but I don't look back.

I put one foot in front of the other, retracing my steps until I'm back in my car. I make it all the way down the drive and onto the main street before I completely unravel.

I pull over, my head on my steering board, trying to catch my breath. I replay what she said, fighting my tears with everything I have. She's not worth them.

I'm not sure how long I've been sitting here when the scream of close-by sirens makes my head snap up. I flinch and lift my hands to shield my eyes from the flashing lights of three police cruisers that have completely surrounded my car. I go from numb to reeling in the space of one heartbeat. Oh my God. She called the police? I keep my hands on the steering wheel and use my phone's voice command to call Omar and let him know I'm in trouble.

38

CHAOS
Omar

"This is great." I am sincerely impressed with the scope and size of the abandoned shopping mall he's walking me through.

"I think so, too. Let's get back to the office, and we can talk numbers if you're ready to move forward."

I nod. "What about your dad?"

"He said he had to stop at the house. Probably to check on my mom."

Alarm bells ring in my head. I pull my phone out to text Jules. **"Leave now."**

He takes his sunglasses off and wipes his eyes like he's tired, oblivious to my panic. "She's got agoraphobia. It's a damn shame because she used to be...man, larger than life. She traveled all over the world and was the head of the division that sourced our fragrances in the nineties. When I was a kid, I had nannies and barely saw her. And then, when I was old enough to not need her anymore, she suddenly was locked in her room and couldn't leave the house."

"When was that?"

"I don't know. I was maybe eighteen. So like 2011. I can't believe it's been that long."

"Listen, do you mind if we postpone the meeting till—"

A loud ring interrupts me, and he pulls his phone out of a holster in his jacket, and for a second, I think it's a gun.

I try to call Jules while he's talking, but his conversation draws my attention and raises my panic. "What? Who? Shit. Fuck. Okay, I'm on my way back."

"What is it?"

"There was an intruder. Someone broke into my mother's room."

The surge of panic makes my head spin. What the hell? "Is your mother okay?"

"I dunno. My dad said he got there just as they were running out. They got away, but he's called the police, and they're looking for them."

Thank fuck she got away.

"Can I drop you somewhere? I've got to get back to the house and see what the hell is going on."

I wave off the offer. "Don't worry about me. I'll catch an Uber. Or call Jules. I'll be fine. You go ahead."

I call Jules like a madman for a solid two minutes. Then I order an Uber to take me back to my house, and in the five minutes it takes for him to arrive, I call her at least fifty times. Her phone goes straight to voicemail.

"Jules, I swear to God, if you don't call me back, and you're fine when I see you, I'm going to fucking spank you. I swear. And not in the way you like." I leave a voicemail and try to think.

My phone rings, and it's her. "Beat, what the hell—"

"Omar, I messed up." She's whispering, but her panic is palpable.

Mine even more so. "What happened? Where are you? I'll come get you."

"I don't know where. I'm in our car, and the police just got here. There's three of them, and I don't think—"

"Please step out of the vehicle," an angry male voice booms from behind her.

"Break...oh my God. Listen. She's my fucking *mother*. I love you so much. I'm so sorry."

Then the line goes dead.

* * * *

"Mr. Royale isn't pressing charges." A cool as a cucumber looking Remington Wilde walks out of the door marked No Entry.

"They better not be, motherfuckers. I swear to God, Remi—"

"Listen, if you're going to live here, you should know that I'm not a criminal lawyer. I came down because you're a friend, but I'm going to give you someone else's number—"

"We don't need a criminal lawyer. She didn't break into anything, and if they so much as think of saying she did again, I don't care what it means or what it costs, I will make sure they don't have another truly happy day in their lives again."

Remi sighs, hands on his hips, and shakes his head. "Again, I'll send you the number for my friend who practices criminal law."

"Whatever. Can I see her?"

"Yes. She's being processed, but you can go back and sit with her in a minute."

"Thank you, Remi. I'm sorry to pull you away from work."

"It's all right. You guys come to dinner on Friday at our place. Tyson and Dina will be there, and she's itching to meet Jules."

"We'll do our best."

He pats my shoulder. "I'm sorry this didn't pan out. We can talk about that more on Friday. Go get your girl. She's holding up, but she looks like she's about to shatter."

Fuck. My gut clenches. She's been back there for hours now.

He knocks on the door and waves up at a small camera at the top of it, and with a buzz, it unlocks.

I walk down a too brightly lit hallway and past the first door and stop when I see Jules sitting at a table through the window next to it. She's curled her body into itself, her hands are tucked between her knees, and her head is bent. It kills me to see my Beat so flat and out of tune.

I open the door slowly.

She looks up then, and her eyes are exactly what Remi described. Shattered.

"She's my mother. She thought I killed him. And she left me to face it on my own. She didn't want me to ever find her."

I'm so angry I don't know what to do with myself. But I push it aside and focus on her. "Baby, I'm so sorry." I move to stand in front of her chair and drop to my haunches so she doesn't have to look up at me.

She shakes her head. "I didn't do anything to her. I have the whole thing recorded and as soon as they give me my phone, I can prove it. I just... I can't believe she called the police."

"She didn't. Her husband did."

Her face creases with confusion. "What? How? He wasn't in the house when I left."

"I don't know. His statement says he chased you out."

"He's lying. When I get my phone back, I can prove it. I forgot to stop recording until I pulled my phone out to call you after the police showed up. But...why would he make that up?"

"I don't know Jules. I don't understand any of this." I've never felt more helpless in my life. "We'll get to the bottom of it. But first, tell me what happened in her room. She said she's your mother? How is that possible?"

She shrugs. "I don't know, but I believe her."

"But...Noah is my age. His sister Rachel, from what I remember, is ten years younger than him. Which would make her two years younger than you. So I get that she wouldn't have a clue. But if his mother had a baby when he was eight years old, he'd absolutely remember."

"Can you hold me. Please? I'm so cold," she asks. Her voice is a hollow version of its normally animated cadence. I'm livid. But I'll focus on that later.

I sit in the chair next to hers and pat my knee. "Of course, come on."

She climbs onto my lap, curls up cross-legged, rests her head on my shoulder, and tells me how Nora Royale ended up in love with a candlemaker from the West Midlands. "She used to travel throughout the potteries for the company business. They met, and she said it was an instant attraction and that she fell head over heels. She left her family for a year and stayed with him. She said her husband doesn't know, and she hopes he never has to. She said he'd been so good to her and didn't deserve the pain it would cause."

"I can't believe this." This is mind-blowing.

"She said it was an escape from a life she felt trapped in. Her oldest child had been shipped off to boarding school. She had a career she loved, but her husband worked all the time, and she was lonely."

"She left him?"

She nods. "She said when she got pregnant several months into their relationship was when she started having regrets about leaving her husband. She said..." Her voice trembles, and I wish I could throttle this woman. "She said she got very depressed after I was born and didn't *bond* with me. Couldn't *look* at me. She missed her son and husband so desperately and wanted to leave. Her husband agreed to let her come home, but she couldn't tell him about me, so she signed away her parental rights. My father was angry and begged her to stay. For my sake. She couldn't. But she agreed to look after him and me for as long as he needed. She set up the shell corporation and used it to send him money every month. They never spoke again. She knew nothing of me until a couple of months after he died when she said *something* made her type his name in her browser's search bar. The first result of the search was an article about his death."

"And the daughter who'd been arrested for killing him," I add with disgust.

"Yes. She was torn by her guilt and regret. She became depressed, anxious, terrified of going anywhere lest she wreak havoc on someone else's life. She used to leave her room. Now she only does so at holidays. She said her husband had been through enough. That her children had suffered enough."

"What about your suffering? I'm so fucking sorry she hurt you."

She sighs heavily. "I can't cry, Omar. Not for her. But for my father…and how much she hurt him. And how he hid it from me so I wouldn't know she didn't want me. I think back now, to all the times he talked about her and how he made me believe she died giving birth to me. And now I realize he was telling the truth."

"Oh, Jules. I'm so sorry." I feel ten different things at once, anger most of all, but I'm saving it for the people who did this to her.

"I'm not. My dad was such a *great* parent. He learned how to do my hair. He took me bra shopping and bought my maxi pads and taught me how to cook, and fish, and make candles, and how to love and forgive and survive. I didn't miss a thing. I didn't need her then, and I don't need her now."

I know she means it, but the hurt in her voice is unmistakable. "No you don't."

"The worst part of this, honestly, is that we're back to square one. We came all this way, and we don't have anything to take back with us. Nothing that will get them to reopen my case."

"So this is…"

"Salt in the wound. I wasn't looking for my mother. But knowing I had one like her who is such a coward does make it sting even more."

"We'll never stop looking. There's more to go on."

"They may be dead ends." Her lack of optimism kills me.

"They won't be. Someone set your father's shop on fire with you inside. You weren't meant to survive either. We'll go back to England, and we'll keep looking."

"But what about your life here? You have family and friends and a community of people that love and care about you. You have that beautiful house and your sister and her family, and your dad. He needs you. I don't want to take that from you."

"Jules, all you've ever taken from me are sadness, loneliness, and confusion. I know you love it here, so do I. But I won't live anywhere that you're not. We have the house in Brixton—we did that together. We can be happy there. Your candlemaking shop awaits."

She sighs. "I want to change my name back. My father gave it to me. Even though he called me Jewel. But he said I was the jewel in his crown, and I changed it because I wanted to start over and I—oh God." She swallows audibly. "I haven't been to see him. They wouldn't let me go to his funeral. And then, when I got out, I couldn't bear to go there after I'd admitted to taking his life. But I miss him so much, Omar."

"I know. I know. I'm sorry. But you are not alone. And you won't be again. We'll face everything together."

I'm a man of my word, I keep my promises, and these I'll keep to her, too.

39

LUCKY PEOPLE
Jules

"This is bullshit." I toss the police report onto the dining room table.

Omar picks it up and scans it. "So she wasn't screaming for help?"

I scoff. "Not even close. In fact, the only time she looked really afraid was when she heard someone coming and asked me to duck into the closet, and I waited there until he was gone. It *was* Mr. Royale. But he never saw me."

"And I thought he was at the office."

"I think he has an office in the house. But if he was there, I didn't see a hint of him."

"I can't believe he told them he chased you out of the house. Why the hell would he want you to be arrested?"

I replay the exchange in my head. "When I was in the closet, I heard him say he was going to meet Noah and that he'd pick up lunch from a place called Louise's or something. When I walked out of the house less than ten minutes later, no one shouted after me. There wasn't a car in the driveway when I left again."

"How did he know you were there?"

"I don't know, but I'd bet money he's got hidden cameras in her room." In my practice, I've met men who are polite, respected, successful, and coddle their wives, but only to control them. I don't think she could leave even if she wanted to. I yawn and roll my neck to try and loosen the tension. "I know you want to listen to the recording on my phone, but I'm exhausted and don't really want to hear it all again."

"I understand. Come on, we'll get back to this in the morning." He drapes an arm over my shoulder. "You okay?"

"No." I lift my head up and look up at him. He smiles down, and the wear and tear of a long day have left shadows under his eyes. "Scratch that. Today sucked. It hurt. But at the end of it, I'm standing here, holding your hand. So, I'm more than okay...I think I might just be the luckiest person I know."

* * * *

"Hi, baby, do you miss us?" Omar coos at Beat through the FaceTime call with Dominic, who's keeping her for us while we are away.

"She misses *me*. She's used to you being gone," I tease.

"No way. That's my girl, isn't she? We bonded, didn't we, Be?" He nuzzles the phone like it's the cat's face.

"Okay, that's enough. If Jodi sees me over here talking on the phone with this cat in front of my face, she'll never let me hear the end of it. And all she does is lie in the window like she's trying to get a tan and eat. She won't even play with me."

"That's what cats do, Dom. And they don't play with random humans."

"Well, you two have spoiled this cat. I'm giving you one more week and then I'm calling one of those boarding places."

"We'll be back in less than a week. Thank you for watching her."

As soon as the call disconnects, I pull the phone out of Omar's hand and toss it to the cushions along the window seat. Dom called just as Omar was getting out of the shower. He's completely dry now, but he's still got his towel wrapped around his waist. He grabs the bottle of Jergens by the bed and starts to slather it all over himself. And while he does, I kneel between his spread thighs and tug his towel out of the way. I hold my hand out for him to pump some of the lotion into it.

His dick is already semi hard when I wrap a lubricated hand around it and open my mouth over the crown.

"Oh, Jules. Your mouth. I could live there," he groans and runs his palm over the curve of my head and down to the center of my back.

I circle the broad head with my tongue and then suck just the tip the way I know he likes. I wrap my hand around the shaft, and he covers it with his. I suck and stroke until I taste his salty pre-cum. I get to my feet. "I want to ride you until I come."

"Okay."

"I mean it. Don't get impatient and flip me over," I warn.

"I won't. I promise." He makes the sign of the cross over his heart.

I let my robe fall to the ground and straddle his thighs, drape my arms over each shoulder, and gaze into his eyes. "I love you."

His eyes blaze with so much tenderness, and he kisses me hard and deep while his fingers stroke my pussy. "My girl. Always ready," he whispers against my mouth.

"Always," I repeat and grip his steel-hard, velvet soft dick again and glide down, slowly but as easily as rain melts sugar, until he's seated inside me to the hilt. He grips my ass and spreads my cheeks, and I start to move my hips, up and down, rolling and grinding and fucking my man until I find the right rhythm.

"My baby. I can't get enough of you, love you so fucking much." His voice is strained, but those words do something to me that feels too good to actually be good for me. But I don't even care. I close my eyes and let my body take over.

The first spasm of my climax makes my eyes snap open. "Oh, yeah. I'm coming, baby."

He lowers his head and laps at the tips of my nipples. "I love that so much," I sob at the intensity of the pleasure.

"I know you do." He does it again and again and again until I'm teetering on the edge of my climax.

"I'm coming." I clutch at his shoulders and scramble for purchase as my climax flings me up and up and over so hard that my body quakes in his lap, my thighs trembling from exhaustion.

He kisses me, drives himself deeper, and rubs my clit at the same time. "My woman. My girl. My Beat. Mine," he says between hard thrusts into me, and I am frantic, so close, so happy.

"Omar, Om—Ahhhh." My voice breaks as my body rides the crest of my orgasm.

He wraps one arm around my waist, pulls me down flush against his chest, and holds me there. He buries his face in my neck and starts to pump his hips frantically until he arches his neck, pressing his head into the pillow, his face caught in a harsh, beautiful grimace when he roars my name and empties himself inside of me.

I collapse on top of him and catch my breath. He's still breathing hard and has his eyes closed when I lift my head. "You're mine," I say softly.

His eyes snap open, and he nods, his lips tipping up slightly in a smile. "Completely yours." He cups the back of my head and pulls me down for a quick, hard kiss.

We lie there, me draped over him, slick with sweat, well-loved and okay because we have each other.

40

PUZZLE PIECES
Omar

When Jules falls asleep, I slip out of bed. I get dressed and leave the house, not bothering to check the time. I don't care if I wake the whole neighborhood up, but I'm going to let the Royales know they fucked with the wrong person today. And I don't care who hears. Jules may want to be discreet, but I don't.

The motion-detecting lights come on when I pull up to the front door of their oversized house. I hop out with the car still running and decide to forgo the doorbell in lieu of incessant banging.

The door flies open, and Noah stands there in nothing but his Iron Man briefs.

"What the fuck are you doing here, Solomon? You want to get arrested too?"

"Try it and I'll make sure your mother's name is in every tabloid I can find."

His eyes narrow. "Your girlfriend broke into this house and terrified my mother."

"Did your mother say she was terrified?" I ask.

He opens his mouth and then slams it shut. "I haven't talked to her. But my father said she was screaming for help and when he got to her room, he saw your girlfriend running out. He chased her, but he's an old man, and he was worried about my mother."

"He's lying. She wasn't screaming, and he didn't chase her. When she left, *she* was the one in tears. And your father wasn't anywhere in sight."

"Why should I believe you?"

"Well, I have a recording she took of the entire encounter on her phone. But you have cameras all over this property. They'll answer that for you. Have you looked at them yet?"

He narrows his eyes at me, but some of the fire and brimstone is gone from his expression. "No. I haven't. But I will, right now. Come in."

He turns and stomps off, leaving the door wide open. I follow him through the house down a wide corridor that runs the length of it. It's eerily dark and quiet. And no one else has come to see what the noise is about. He throws a door open so hard it cracks against the wall behind it. Light from inside illuminates the hallway, and I step into a room with wall-to-wall screens.

The portly man who is sitting in the chair in front of them is sound asleep. "Is he dead?"

"No, he's deaf." Noah puts a hand on the man's shoulder, and he wakes up with a start but is fully alert right away. He starts to sign furiously and then relaxes when Noah responds.

"Where's the footage from this afternoon?" Noah speaks and signs at the same time. The man frowns and then signs something in response.

"When?" Noah asks, and the alarm in his voice puts me on alert.

"What's going on?" I demand when he lets out a string of curses.

"One second," he says and then speaks with the man once again. "Come on. We need to talk."

I follow him for a few steps and stop. "Let's talk here. Tell me what he said."

He runs a hand over head and closes his eyes. "My dad called and asked him to erase all the video recordings from today right after he called the police."

"I knew it. He's hiding something. But why?"

Noah's head snaps up. "What the fuck did she want? Your woman? Is she a journalist or some shit?" His voice is angry, but not at all as forceful as it had been when he answered the door.

"No. We came here looking for answers about her father's death. Your mother knew him, and we thought she could shed some light on his final days."

He frowns and cocks his head. "My mother knew *her* father?"

"That's an understatement. Yes, she spent a year plus in England with him when you were a kid."

"I think I'd remember if my mom lived in England for a whole fucking year."

"Do you remember? You were maybe eight or nine when she was there."

"No, she spent a year taking care of her mother in Mexico when I was kid."

I laugh without any humor. "Double-check that story, too, maybe."

"I don't know what is going on, but if you can give me a few days, I'll find out."

"We'll be here for another week. You know how to reach me."

41

CHAMPIONS
Jules

The week flew by in lazy days spent reading and swimming and eating. I've soaked up every second of it, and the only thing I've missed about London is our cat.

"I'm so sad you're leaving," Kal, Remi's wife, shouts in my ear to be heard over the woman at the karaoke machine on the stage at the front of the restaurant where we're having dinner.

As much as I love the vibe of this place, it's the people who have really made me fall for it. "Me too. I love it here. I hope I'll be back."

She squeezes my hand and pats it reassuringly. "You will be. That man of yours will make sure of it."

I smile and nod, but I don't know how. We've spent a lot of time with them and Tyson and his wife this week. And we made fast friends. This is the existence I used to dream of. Friends, a community, love, home. It's even sweeter than I thought it would be.

"Hey, I'll be right back," Omar says from my other side where he, Remi, his younger brother Tyson, and his wife Dina are having a spirited argument about basketball. He presses a kiss to my cheek, and I reach out to grab his hand. "Where are you going?"

"Be right back," he responds and drops a kiss on my nose.

I have butterflies in my stomach because this man who's as faithful as the sunrise loves me so much that I could swim in it. But every day we've spent here with his family and friends, in that amazing house that feels like home, I've grown more and more guilty that he's coming with me.

I'll do everything I know how to make sure he never regrets it.

"This song is dedicated to my heartbeat. My Crown Jewel." I whip around to look at the stage and scream in surprise to see him standing there holding the microphone. But as soon as our eyes find each other, my heart skips a beat, and when it starts again, we're alone. On that same sea where he first kissed me and where we made ourselves.

"You're a winner because what they tried to break is blooming. I love you, Beat. Nothing can dim your light. Pity the fool who tries."

I blow him a kiss, and he catches it in his palm and flicks his fingers at the crowd like he's spraying water from them. "Sharing the love. You've just been blessed. Now fucking clap for me or I'll be annoyed."

The jazzy piano intro plays, but I don't realize what song he's singing until the guitar strums a few chords in. And I'm crying before he gets to the second line of "We are the Champions" by Queen. I laugh in delight, and the tears pooling in my eyes spill down my cheeks now, but they are the happiest tears I've ever cried.

He's really not a dancer or a singer, but it's the most beautiful thing I've ever seen. He sings to me and nobody else, and I'm mesmerized and humbled because every word could have been from my heart.

He knows it completely and always gives it exactly what it needs.

And I *needed* this reminder. This song. The lows of my life don't define me. Nothing anyone else says or does changes the truth. He sings the chorus, and I sing with him. Him and me, we are the fucking kings of the world. We can do anything when we do it together. He is my ride or die. Nothing will break us—it might bend us a bit, but we will never break.

* * * *

It's after midnight when we pull into Omar's driveway and park next to a black Ferrari with Noah Royale perched on the side of it. Sunglasses and all.

"What is *he* doing here?"

"I don't know."

"Are you investing in his project?"

"I don't think so."

"No, don't say that because of me," I beg. I don't want him turning himself inside out on my behalf anymore. He has a whole life outside of me, and I've already taken too much.

"It's not because of you. It's because I won't have anything to do with the family led by people who fuck with lives and think nothing of it. But I like him."

"You do?"

"Yes, he's honest. And passionate. He's a good guy."

"I'm sorry if this messes up your friendship." I remember how fondly he spoke of him before we got here.

"You have nothing to be sorry for. Come on, you go on in, and I'll deal with him."

"Solomon, we need to talk," Noah says as soon as we climb down.

"I'll be right in, Jules," he says and squeezes my hand.

I'm too tired to argue, but I can't take my eyes off Noah. If Nora Royale *is* my mother, then he's my brother. When she said her husband and children couldn't know, I thought about him. I wasn't looking for her, or *them* in the first place. But now… I have a brother. Someone who shares half my DNA. I wish I could get to know him.

"You *look* like her," he says. Even behind his dark glasses, I can feel the intensity of his stare.

"Did she tell you?" I ask.

"Yes. That's why I'm here. You were right to come. But you were barking up the wrong tree. Can I come in? I need to talk to both of you."

Epilogue

Jules

It's like time stood still in Stow-on-the-Wold when we pull onto the road that rings its lake. It's a blustery August morning, fitting as these windy days were my father's favorite. He didn't mind that it cooled his wax down too fast and always left a window open. Wind, he said, carries scent and stories and can tell you what's coming your way before you see or hear it. I roll the window down a crack and lift my nose to catch it.

"What do you smell?" Omar asks.

"Bread, laundry detergent."

"No brimstone?"

"I'm still nervous," I admit as we round the small lake toward the cemetery where my father was laid to rest.

"Me, too. You think he would have liked me?"

I quirk an eyebrow. "Does it matter?" I laugh.

"Very much." He sounds solemn. "I can't imagine what I'd do if my family didn't accept you. In our culture, marriage isn't just two people coming together, it's two families becoming one. And so yeah, I'd like to think that wherever he is, he approves of me."

Lord have mercy, this man and his words. "Oh, Omar, he'd call you a break, too. You act like I'm special, but so are you. You're the best person I know. The best friend I've ever had. You're my home."

"I love it when you sing my praises. Don't stop."

"Oh, stop. I'm trying to be serious."

"So am I. It's nice as hell to know someone thinks I'm amazing because when we get back to Houston, I need to figure out what I'm going to do with the rest of my life."

I groan and drop my head into my hands. "And you've been doing so well." I asked him to stop talking about Houston like it was a definite thing. We've been meeting with the private investigator, and the most promising thing we've discovered is that two of the people who testified to hearing me argue with my father left the village soon after, and when we traced them, they were living higher on the hog than pensioners from The Potteries should be. But that in itself wasn't enough to make the Crown Prosecutor even give us an appointment.

Especially since the tribunal went as expected, and I've been officially disbarred from the Courts of England and Wales. I've thrown myself into making candles, and my Etsy store is doing well—I earn more there than I did as a pupil, and now I only go to the Effra as a punter. But I love what I did, and if I can get this conviction overturned then I can reapply.

But all of that is a pipe dream, and I need to manage my expectations.

"I was going to wait until we got home to tell you."

"Tell me what?"

He continues like he didn't hear me. "Because I didn't want to overshadow this visit."

"Omar," I screech and nudge his elbow.

He keeps his eyes on the road, his expression set on neutral, but he's fighting a smile. "But I think I should tell you now because I think you'll want him to know, too."

"If you don't start talking—"

"I got an email from Noah Royale this morning. He and his mother are flying to London tomorrow."

My excitement fizzles. "And?" I didn't want to talk about them either. I was still sore from her rejection and in general didn't want anything to do with them other than to forget them.

"He said he'd talked to his parents like we asked and even recorded it so he could listen to everything again to make sure he hadn't missed anything."

"And?" I repeat with exasperation.

"And…he sent me the recording. And I want you to hear the end of it."

"Okay."

"You ready?"

"Very." I grip my hands in my lap and try to be calm and not scream at him to hurry.

He chuckles and then hits the play button on the dash of his car.

"Of course I knew. Do you think I'm an idiot?" a man's voice shouts.

I hit pause. "Who is *that?*" I gasp.

"Silas Royale," he responds.

"That is *not* Silas Royale. I heard him through the door. His voice is as gentle as a lamb. He's not capable of—"

"Stop talking and listen. You're ruining the mood," he snaps and presses play.

"Nick, what are you saying?" Nora's voice cuts in, sharp and distressed.

"I'm saying you still loved him. You think I didn't know that you were siphoning off my money to pay for your love child? I found your diary. And I found the transactions and decided to pull that thorn in my side out once and for all."

"What does that even mean?" Mrs. Royale cries, and this time, her voice quavers.

"It means I hired some kid who was up for the job and paid him to get rid of both of them. I don't know how she survived. But then it didn't matter because everyone thought she did it."

"You let a child go to jail for murder?"

"What, should I have gone instead?"

"Yes!" she shrieks.

"Mama, calm down." Noah's gravelly voice comes on tape for the first time.

"No. I have lived with you and you knew and didn't say anything?"

"Why would I?"

"When he died, so did you. And you never once asked about your own daughter. You didn't hire her a lawyer or finally confess to me so you could go be by her side. I didn't think you cared."

"Oh my God," Noah's voice again.

"Nick, you can't be serious."

"I am. And what are you going to do? Walk out of here and go tell the police? Noah's my son and he wouldn't betray me."

The recording cuts off.

I sit back in the seat. "He did it? It was *him?*"

"Yes."

"And they're coming here to attest to that?"

"Yes."

"But why? He's her husband."

"And you're her child. I haven't spoken to her but Noah has said she's incredibly remorseful. She wants to do the right thing. The least she can do is tell the truth so we can get your case reopened."

The sob that wrenches free from the depths of my soul where all my hope was buried is so loud that it scares me. I throw my head back and scream. I scream until my throat is raw and then I laugh. I've never been so happy I don't think ever.

"Yeah. I had the same reaction, but in my head cause I wanted to surprise you."

I launch myself across the console and grab his neck. The car swerves, and he puts one arm around me and tightens his grip on the steering wheel with the other. "I'm going to be free, Omar." I say it, and I can't believe I'm saying it.

"Yes, you are. And you can tell your dad that he can rest easy because you're fine now."

I nod and shake my head in wonder, letting him go and falling back in my seat, my body sprawled, my eyes staring at nothing on the ceiling.

"Thank you."

"You're the one who broke into the house."

"But you're the one who broke the chains around my heart so I could. I'd given up."

"Only for a minute. You were going to get back to it. You just needed a break."

I chuckle. "I see what you did there."

"Yeah. Now let's go and see your dad."

I wait while he walks around to get my door and take the hand he offers to help me out. And we walk hand in hand to go and tell my dad the news.

"You know, I understand why they call you The Mastermind. You play the long game."

He bends his head to kiss me. "Yeah, but for you, I'm playing the forever game."

"And you're winning."

The End

Also from Dylan Allen and 1001 Dark Nights, discover The Daredevil.

Sign up for the 1001 Dark Nights Newsletter
and be entered to win a Tiffany Key necklace.

There's a contest every month!

Go to www.1001DarkNights.com to subscribe.

**As a bonus, all subscribers can download
FIVE FREE exclusive books!**

Discover 1001 Dark Nights Collection Nine

DRAGON UNBOUND by Donna Grant
A Dragon Kings Novella

NOTHING BUT INK by Carrie Ann Ryan
A Montgomery Ink: Fort Collins Novella

THE MASTERMIND by Dylan Allen
A Rivers Wilde Novella

JUST ONE WISH by Carly Phillips
A Kingston Family Novella

BEHIND CLOSED DOORS by Skye Warren
A Rochester Novella

GOSSAMER IN THE DARKNESS by Kristen Ashley
A Fantasyland Novella

THE CLOSE-UP by Kennedy Ryan
A Hollywood Renaissance Novella

DELIGHTED by Lexi Blake
A Masters and Mercenaries Novella

THE GRAVESIDE BAR AND GRILL by Darynda Jones
A Charley Davidson Novella

THE ANTI-FAN AND THE IDOL by Rachel Van Dyken
A My Summer In Seoul Novella

A VAMPIRE'S KISS by Rebecca Zanetti
A Dark Protectors/Rebels Novella

CHARMED BY YOU by J. Kenner
A Stark Security Novella

HIDE AND SEEK by Laura Kaye
A Blasphemy Novella

DESCEND TO DARKNESS by Heather Graham
A Krewe of Hunters Novella

BOND OF PASSION by Larissa Ione
A Demonica Novella

JUST WHAT I NEEDED by Kylie Scott
A Stage Dive Novella

Also from Blue Box Press

THE BAIT by C.W. Gortner and M.J. Rose

THE FASHION ORPHANS by Randy Susan Meyers and M.J. Rose

TAKING THE LEAP by Kristen Ashley
A River Rain Novel

SAPPHIRE SUNSET by Christopher Rice writing C. Travis Rice
A Sapphire Cove Novel

THE WAR OF TWO QUEENS by Jennifer L. Armentrout
A Blood and Ash Novel

THE MURDERS AT FLEAT HOUSE BY Lucinda Riley

THE HEIST by C.W. Gortner and M.J. Rose

Discover More Dylan Allen

The Daredevil: A Rivers Wilde Novella
By Dylan Allen

"I dare you to let me watch..."

It was the wickedest of propositions, made by the most devilish of men.

It doesn't matter that Tyson Wilde has got a killer smile, wears a suit like it's his job, and oozes spine-tingling sex appeal. I should say no.

Because beneath the surface of that cool, disinterested exterior, lies passion hot enough to burn. I danced too close to it once and have the scars to prove it.

So, on *any* other night, in any other city, and if he'd been even a *fraction* less mouthwatering, I *would* have been able to resist.

But it's my birthday, we're in Paris, and it's *him*.

I can't say no.

I don't want to say no.

And this time, no matter how right we feel together, I won't let myself forget that when this weekend is over, we will be, too.

We're only *pretending* to be lovers to land a deal.

Success will mean a promotion—one I want more than anything.

At least, that's what I thought.

Falling in love was a danger neither Tyson or I saw coming.

And it will cost one of us *everything*.

* * * *

I've been telling myself what I told Tyson that night—leaving each other alone is for the best. Since then, I've distracted myself by helping my dad with a passion project and holding my best friend's hand through some of the darkest days of her life.

And my new job on the competitive intelligence team at Wilde kept me busy.

I was born with an uncanny ability to read people. It made my teachers, friends, even my parents uncomfortable at times. I'm not a mind reader, so I could never say why, but I could sense when someone liked me or didn't. Whether they were lying or not. And I was never wrong. As an adult, I make a living hunting down the truth and protecting people from liars. My mother used to call me a human lie detector.

Human lie detector my *ass*. I didn't see the liar in the mirror until the lie blew up in my face.

Two weeks ago, I sat watching my best friend, Beth, being serenaded by the love of her life, and realized that despite the crushing disappointment of my failed marriage, I wanted a moment like that, too. My fairy tale didn't have a white knight who whisked in to take me away, but a man who was strong enough to handle me.

And who was secure enough to tell the whole world that I was the most important person in his life. Not on a stage in front of the whole world like what happened to Beth—I mean, that would be mortifying—but in ways that say I matter. I needed that.

And as that realization sank in, all I could think about was Tyson and the kiss that made me burn for more.

I wanted to finish crying on his shoulder and talk to him about his dad, tell him about my mom. I wanted to give him a soft place to land, too.

I got back from that visit with Beth, determined to find Tyson and tell him all of that. But like the hero in every Greek tragedy I read in high school, by the time I realized my fatal flaw, it was too little, too late.

That same day, I saw the announcement about his posting to Paris. His going away party was tonight, and even as visions of disastrous scenarios that all ended with a very public rejection swam in my head, I said I'd be there. I wanted at least to say goodbye. And maybe, if I hadn't blown it, get a chance to say much more.

I'm riddled with doubt for most of the ride over. What am I even going to say? What if he's not home? Or not alone? I shake that thought loose. I spent ten years in a marriage that lasted nine years too long. I'm done putting my happiness on hold. If he rejects me, I won't kill me. But wondering if he was the one I let get away, just might.

About Dylan Allen

Wall Street Journal and USA Today Bestselling Author, Dylan Allen writes compelling, dramatic, emotional romances with exceptional, diverse characters you'll root for and never forget

A self-proclaimed happily ever junkie, she loves creating stories where her characters find a love worth fighting for. When she isn't writing or reading, eating, or cooking, Dylan indulges her wanderlust by planning her next globe-trotting adventure.

Dylan was born in Accra, Ghana (West Africa) but was raised in Houston, Texas. Dylan is a proud graduate of Tufts University, Howard University School of Law and the London School of Economics and Political Science. After twenty years of adventure and wild oat sowing, Dylan, her amazing husband and two incredible children returned to Houston where they now make their home.

* * * *

I love to hear from readers! email me at:
Dylan@dylanallenbooks.com
Are you on Facebook? Join my private reader group, Dylan's Day Dreamers. It's where I spend most of my time online and it's a lot of fun!

Discover 1001 Dark Nights

TRICKED by Rebecca Zanetti ~ DIRTY WICKED by Shayla Black ~ THE ONLY ONE by Lauren Blakely ~ SWEET SURRENDER by Liliana Hart

COLLECTION FOUR
ROCK CHICK REAWAKENING by Kristen Ashley ~ ADORING INK by Carrie Ann Ryan ~ SWEET RIVALRY by K. Bromberg ~ SHADE'S LADY by Joanna Wylde ~ RAZR by Larissa Ione ~ ARRANGED by Lexi Blake ~ TANGLED by Rebecca Zanetti ~ HOLD ME by J. Kenner ~ SOMEHOW, SOME WAY by Jennifer Probst ~ TOO CLOSE TO CALL by Tessa Bailey ~ HUNTED by Elisabeth Naughton ~ EYES ON YOU by Laura Kaye ~ BLADE by Alexandra Ivy/Laura Wright ~ DRAGON BURN by Donna Grant ~ TRIPPED OUT by Lorelei James ~ STUD FINDER by Lauren Blakely ~ MIDNIGHT UNLEASHED by Lara Adrian ~ HALLOW BE THE HAUNT by Heather Graham ~ DIRTY FILTHY FIX by Laurelin Paige ~ THE BED MATE by Kendall Ryan ~ NIGHT GAMES by CD Reiss ~ NO RESERVATIONS by Kristen Proby ~ DAWN OF SURRENDER by Liliana Hart

COLLECTION FIVE
BLAZE ERUPTING by Rebecca Zanetti ~ ROUGH RIDE by Kristen Ashley ~ HAWKYN by Larissa Ione ~ RIDE DIRTY by Laura Kaye ~ ROME'S CHANCE by Joanna Wylde ~ THE MARRIAGE ARRANGEMENT by Jennifer Probst ~ SURRENDER by Elisabeth Naughton ~ INKED NIGHTS by Carrie Ann Ryan ~ ENVY by Rachel Van Dyken ~ PROTECTED by Lexi Blake ~ THE PRINCE by Jennifer L. Armentrout ~ PLEASE ME by J. Kenner ~ WOUND TIGHT by Lorelei James ~ STRONG by Kylie Scott ~ DRAGON NIGHT by Donna Grant ~ TEMPTING BROOKE by Kristen Proby ~ HAUNTED BE THE HOLIDAYS by Heather Graham ~ CONTROL by K. Bromberg ~ HUNKY HEARTBREAKER by Kendall Ryan ~ THE DARKEST CAPTIVE by Gena Showalter

COLLECTION SIX
DRAGON CLAIMED by Donna Grant ~ ASHES TO INK by Carrie Ann Ryan ~ ENSNARED by Elisabeth Naughton ~ EVERMORE by Corinne Michaels ~ VENGEANCE by Rebecca Zanetti ~ ELI'S TRIUMPH by Joanna Wylde ~ CIPHER by Larissa Ione ~

RESCUING MACIE by Susan Stoker ~ ENCHANTED by Lexi Blake ~ TAKE THE BRIDE by Carly Phillips ~ INDULGE ME by J. Kenner ~ THE KING by Jennifer L. Armentrout ~ QUIET MAN by Kristen Ashley ~ ABANDON by Rachel Van Dyken ~ THE OPEN DOOR by Laurelin Paige ~ CLOSER by Kylie Scott ~ SOMETHING JUST LIKE THIS by Jennifer Probst ~ BLOOD NIGHT by Heather Graham ~ TWIST OF FATE by Jill Shalvis ~ MORE THAN PLEASURE YOU by Shayla Black ~ WONDER WITH ME by Kristen Proby ~ THE DARKEST ASSASSIN by Gena Showalter

COLLECTION SEVEN
THE BISHOP by Skye Warren ~ TAKEN WITH YOU by Carrie Ann Ryan ~ DRAGON LOST by Donna Grant ~ SEXY LOVE by Carly Phillips ~ PROVOKE by Rachel Van Dyken ~ RAFE by Sawyer Bennett ~ THE NAUGHTY PRINCESS by Claire Contreras ~ THE GRAVEYARD SHIFT by Darynda Jones ~ CHARMED by Lexi Blake ~ SACRIFICE OF DARKNESS by Alexandra Ivy ~ THE QUEEN by Jen Armentrout ~ BEGIN AGAIN by Jennifer Probst ~ VIXEN by Rebecca Zanetti ~ SLASH by Laurelin Paige ~ THE DEAD HEAT OF SUMMER by Heather Graham ~ WILD FIRE by Kristen Ashley ~ MORE THAN PROTECT YOU by Shayla Black ~ LOVE SONG by Kylie Scott ~ CHERISH ME by J. Kenner ~ SHINE WITH ME by Kristen Proby

COLLECTION EIGHT
DRAGON REVEALED by Donna Grant ~ CAPTURED IN INK by Carrie Ann Ryan ~ SECURING JANE by Susan Stoker ~ WILD WIND by Kristen Ashley ~ DARE TO TEASE by Carly Phillips ~ VAMPIRE by Rebecca Zanetti ~ MAFIA KING by Rachel Van Dyken ~ THE GRAVEDIGGER'S SON by Darynda Jones ~ FINALE by Skye Warren ~ MEMORIES OF YOU by J. Kenner ~ SLAYED BY DARKNESS by Alexandra Ivy ~ TREASURED by Lexi Blake ~ THE DAREDEVIL by Dylan Allen ~ BOND OF DESTINY by Larissa Ione ~ MORE THAN POSSESS YOU by Shayla Black ~ HAUNTED HOUSE by Heather Graham ~ MAN FOR ME by Laurelin Paige ~ THE RHYTHM METHOD by Kylie Scott ~ JONAH BENNETT by Tijan ~ CHANGE WITH ME by Kristen Proby ~ THE DARKEST DESTINY by Gena Showalter

On Behalf of 1001 Dark Nights,

Liz Berry, M.J. Rose, and Jillian Stein would like to thank ~

Steve Berry
Doug Scofield
Benjamin Stein
Kim Guidroz
Social Butterfly PR
Ashley Wells
Asha Hossain
Chris Graham
Chelle Olson
Kasi Alexander
Jessica Saunders
Dylan Stockton
Kate Boggs
Richard Blake
and Simon Lipskar

Made in the USA
Las Vegas, NV
01 February 2022

42557652R00146